On impulse,  open the front c "Hi," she said, s̲_ ̲ ; trying to appear extra friendly. She dian t wan̲ t̲o̲ ̲_ ̲ e̲ them, but her curiosity had gotten the better of her and she had to know. "I'm Maddy. We just moved in. Do you guys live in the neighborhood?"

The boys looked around at one another. Nobody spoke. Maddy knew she was being stupid. She shouldn't have come out. She wasn't sure what she was trying to accomplish besides looking like a crazy adult. She felt like one too. "I was just curious what you were talking about. I happened to see you pointing at my house."

The tallest boy's eyes went wide. He looked ready to jump back on his bike and pedal away, but the youngest boy bravely took a small step closer to her and hollered, "They say that someone was murdered in your house. Is it true?"

She tried not to react, but her mouth definitely dropped open. "Murdered?" Maddy shook her head. "Uh, no. I don't think so."

The little boy turned back toward the older ones and puffed out his chest. "See! I told you!"

She watched them as they got back on their bikes and pedaled away with lightning speed without another word or even a quick glance back.

The Mortician's Wife

by

Jody Wenner

This is a work of fiction. Names, characters, places, and incidents are either the product of the author's imagination or are used fictitiously, and any resemblance to actual persons living or dead, business establishments, events, or locales, is entirely coincidental.

The Mortician's Wife

Cover Art by *Debbie Taylor*

The Wild Rose Press, Inc.
PO Box 708
Adams Basin, NY 14410-0708
Visit us at www.thewildrosepress.com

Publishing History
First Edition, 2023
Trade Paperback ISBN 978-1-5092-4962-6
Digital ISBN 978-1-5092-4963-3

Published in the United States of America

Dedication

To Scott and Olivia for living (with me), laughing (at me), and loving (me).

Chapter One

1912

Beatrice Westmoreland sat down with pen and ink by candlelight to compose a death announcement. Spring rains rattled the windowpanes as she considered her words carefully. A dampened chill recently snuffed out by the crackling of a fire in the cast-iron box in her sitting chambers allowed the room to radiate with a comfortable warmth, but Bea's pen weighed heavily between her fingers.

She fretted over each and every word as it pertained to the deceased. Her new responsibility was not one she took lightly. She did not know Harriet Gold in her living form but wanted to do right by her spirit. She attempted to channel the late woman, asking Harriet how she wished to be remembered. Beatrice was met with silence, but it was a soothing quiet that helped her mind sort the words to place on the parchment before her.

The mortician, under usual circumstances, might be the one to traditionally write up the obituary, but Charles had been glad to let his wife take over the role. He was more inclined to keep the calculations within his ledger in pristine order, as words came harder for him. His only reluctance in handing over the task was that he would have preferred a more straight-forward approach to the announcements than what his wife took. He had instructed Beatrice to stick with the facts, as he was a man of sound logic and reason, but Bea would not be swayed on this particular point.

Thus, Charles did not assist Beatrice in her mission to acquire information regarding the dead, but a family was often inclined to get things off their chests when meeting with the mortician to make the final funeral arrangements, if for no other reason than gaining their own sense of peace. The relations of Harriet Gold were no different than most, except perhaps her husband who sat properly stoic for the duration of the call in the sitting room adjacent to the parlor. The room offered a soothing environment of pale décor, aromatic florals, a roaring fire to combat the spring chill, and gas sconces that glowed on either side of the grand marble mantelpiece. Charles had built the funeral home with all of these details and more in mind. Comfort was important to a bereaving family during this difficult time.

While the town folk seemed to be warming to the mortician's role as a man in possession of medical insight, and thereby looked upon with some amount of reverence as opposed to that of an undertaker, some were still slow to accept these new rituals over the previously preferred custom of keeping the departed at home in view should one wake. This was where Charles had his work cut out for him, but Harriet beamed in quiet amazement from afar as she watched him softly convince the old farmer that his parlor was a more favorable locale for the unpleasant event, and thus the business was thriving.

Mr. Gold had simply grunted in response to any

questions Charles posed during their talk. "Would you prefer a home viewing? Or might you consider having something here in our front parlor? This would free you from sorting out arrangements to not delay your spring plantings. We would take care of everything, right down to the dressing, hair, and shoes. The florals will be freshly placed, and the chairs will be set for when the minister is called upon to say departing words. My lovely wife will play somber musical compositions on the baby grand throughout the service, and, of course, we will handle the casket and burial as well."

Even a man of the old ways, such as Nathan Gold, was inclined to agree that he wanted nothing to do with the choosing of a garment or styling his departed wife's hair for her final voyage. It was decided that the service would be held at the Westmoreland Funeral Home.

"Fine. Fine," Charles had said with a quick nod as he made a few notes in his ledger. All the while, Beatrice made her own mental notes from her unassuming position near the back of the room.

The children, three girls ranging in age from seven to seventeen, and a son of fourteen, had stood gathered behind their father in clean Sunday attire. The death of Mrs. Gold was foreseen as Harriet had been ill for some time, but the children still fought the turmoil no doubt roiling inside of their small frames. A hardy lot in many ways, they'd wiped at their tiny eyes and noses occasionally, but remained as quiet as field mice. It took everything in Beatrice to not offer her handkerchief to the babes, but she waited as Charles concluded the discussion asking Nathan if there was anything more he should note. At that time, the seven-year-old took a slight step forward and boldly said with a creak in her voice, "I would like to add that Mother would want a dignified burial. She valued cleanliness… and things that smelled nice. Cut flowers, never picked. She would want you to make sure to wash behind her ears before she is looked upon."

"I understand," Charles had said, remaining business-like in his attention toward the young ones.

"Mother was learned, too. She taught us all how to read," Madison Gold said out of her pursed lips.

"She was not all serious. She could be silly sometimes," added her son, Cody Gold. "Once, I spied her doing the two-step in the chicken coop when she thought herself to be alone."

The children released a small snicker, as did Beatrice.

Mr. Gold turned to his children with a scowl upon his face. "Hush now! All of you! That's quite enough."

"Right," said Charles, who had cleared his throat and asked Beatrice to fetch lemonade for the children so he and Nathan could discuss important financial matters.

Now, Beatrice's mind came back to center on her writing. The storm just outside her window broke. The rain settled into a soft rhythmic beat, and the winds calmed to create a soothing hum. A steady tapping began, which Beatrice recognized as the ivy vines climbing the trellis against the home just below. This cacophony was becoming more familiar and made her smile, because a settling sensation of her own was beginning to take hold as she found her footing in her role in her new home.

And though it wasn't a common approach for how departing announcements were written, Beatrice would not let go of the notion that the dearly departed were exactly that—dear to someone—and they should be recalled in such a way that reflected the sentiment, even if it ruffled the occasional feather. Writing about people who had traveled beyond wasn't simply a duty, nor did it need to slant toward the morbid. Her goal was to capture moments, no matter how glancing, of beauty in each individual, to account for a whole life lived, to express joy and sorrow, and to give a small bit of dignity as a final token. She could only wish that when her time came to pass, she too would be shown the same tiny gratitude.

The townspeople often made their opinions on the dead be known as well, though that could sometimes turn things askew. This had happened recently with Mr. Vandermeer, the town butcher. She'd discovered he was not a well-liked man and, having no family to speak for him, opened the ugly floodgates to the mortician and his wife. For days following his death—caused by his own mishandling of the cleaver when it fell from his carving table, thereby chopping his two toes clean from his foot, inviting a nasty and lethal infection—town folk trickled in to spout their feelings, masked in a thin veil of remorse, for the butcher and his parting. He had overcharged, did not attend Sunday services regularly, supplied spoiled meats, and had a poor disposition. That had certainly made Beatrice's job a burdensome one, but she managed to find a way to highlight some of Mr. Vandermeer's more worthy characteristics when she composed his announcement.

What if she couldn't do the same for Harriet Gold? What if she remained blocked by the immense pressure to get the wording just so? Her observations with the

Jody Wenner

Gold family along with input she received from friends and acquaintances at the women's auxiliary meeting just that evening should have told Beatrice everything she needed about Harriet, and yet, the parchment before her remained untouched.

Being bold in her stylistic choices and going against the grain was a new trait for her. Was this what held her back this night? Or was it the tone in which Nathan Gold had scolded his children for wanting to hold precious memories of their mother in their heart instead of unpleasant ones? Bea had no thoughts of being wild or of skirting norms, but what was so rash about cherishing the happier parts of a beautiful soul? How was this too unseemly? To Bea, unseemly was the coarseness more often found on the obituary page describing gruesome details of disease, brutal mangled words telling of tragic endings in fires, farm accidents or worse. Unseemly was final parting words with nary a mention of anything more than unpleasantries and sorrow, no expression of who Harriet Gold was in her heart. No. The woman who would be laid to rest before the town in three days' time was more than that. She was more than the dates she had been born and died. Beatrice would not be swayed by simple customs. This role as the writer was not one she took lightly. She had a responsibility to uphold to this mother of four precious children.

A writer—how one referred to themselves in a letter or even in something as unusual as a notice of passing. Beatrice thought the title sounded very satisfactory. Even if she wasn't producing great works of literature or imaginative children's stories, she felt this recent calling with a passion. It was quite a necessary one and gave her a purpose she had long been missing. Assisting her husband with the many duties in their home came with a contentment thus far in her young marriage, but being the writer gave her meaning in the way she had yet to experience. Of course, one day in the near future she very much looked forward to bearing her husband's children, as well. She'd wanted a family for as long as she could remember. But for now, she was quite satisfied, delightedly so, to think of herself as the writer, at least in the silent hours that the darkness offered.

It was late, and Charles had gone to sleep hours ago. He preferred the first part of the day to do his work, but Beatrice loved the ambience of the latter parts. She had not married for love, but Charles had much to offer her, even in their differences. She admired his confident and quiet reason. He'd built this stately home not far from the main streets of town which included rooms for his business as well as space that would be comfortable for a large brood they hoped to have, which was something they did have in common. His stability was the exact refuge she sought. A life of expected outcome. A home. Children. Happiness. That was all she could ask for after the turbulent and often lonely beginnings she had experienced.

A sudden energy burst forth in Beatrice and she, at long last, found the words she was concerned she never would. When she was done, she took a deep exhale and sat back to read her work.

Gold, Mrs. Harriet C. of Pine Grove, Minnesota. Born September 19, 1874; died May 29, 1912. aged 38 y. 7m. 10 d.

It is with great sadness to all who knew Harriet C. Gold that we announce her passing from this earthly sector as she moves into the house of the Lord. She was beloved by her four children and her devoted husband. Sickness caught her, but only because the heavens called out and she bravely answered, as if it were her duty. Harriet wanted all to remember her as a woman of faith, who cherished her children above all else. The writer notes she was a clever woman who danced when none watched, who made a delightful blueberry cobbler, who admired the simple beauties life had to offer. May she rest in eternal peace.

Interment on the Gold Farmstead. Twenty-four Oak Grove. One and all are invited to attend her mourning on June the Second at the mortician's home. Twelve Pine Street.

Pleased, Beatrice carefully folded the parchment in two and glanced at the fire, hoping that when she pushed the piece across the table for her husband's approval in the light of a new day, he would not toss her work into the blazing flame as he'd done on previous accounts.

Chapter Two

2022

Maddy Barton's husband veered the rental car slowly to the side of the road as pooled May rainwater sprayed the doors and side-view mirrors. He put the vehicle in park directly in front of Twelve Pine Street.

"Here it is!" Tim turned to look at her with wild, hopeful eyes, and asked, "What do you think?"

Through the drizzle, she looked past the *For Sale* sign stuck in the muck of the yard containing a massive two-story Victorian home that Maddy really wanted to love, but in the last hundred plus years it looked like the house had been converted into a duplex, turned into a triplex, gutted, burned halfway down, rebuilt, and then definitely gutted again. The aqua-marine blue paint was chipped in some spots and peeling in others, and the pale-yellow trim was extra pale from fading in the sun. The porch wood looked to be soft and rotting. And that was just the beginning.

Maddy wanted to ask her husband if he'd been drugged or held at gunpoint when he decided this was the house of their dreams, but the excitement on his face held her back. He always got so emotionally wrapped up in his big dreams, and though she hated to be the killer of them, she was pretty much exactly that. Practical. Sensible. The lone adult in the relationship.

"I know it looks rough," he said. "But try to see beyond that, Mads. Look at all the character. The potential."

She tried. She really, really did. "No, I mean...I get it. It has good bones and all that."

"Some fresh paint will fix up the outside," Tim said. "The roof actually looks pretty new, which will save us loads of money. And that turret is awesome, is it not?"

She nodded, still trying to see the vision. If it was to play king and queen, then Tim was on to something. As it stood now, she considered locking him up in that pointy circular room. He had one job. Find them a move-in ready house. This was not that.

"It's insanely rare to find a two-story Queen Anne for this price," he said, upping his enthusiasm a notch.

"That means something is wrong with it then. I'm guessing it doesn't have double vanities or granite countertops. I'm highly doubting there are stainless appliances, and it obviously is not the turn-key place I hoped for."

"No. Well, there were no pictures of the interior in the online listing, but—"

"That's a serious red flag, if I've ever heard one," Maddy said.

"If it wasn't pouring, we could take a peek, but I looked into the large front windows when I was here before and it didn't look that bad, I mean...I'm guessing it's gonna need *some* work, but hey, you did marry an architect, so..." Tim laughed.

"That's true," she said, still skeptical.

"So, you had to have known that when you set me free on my own in the wild to find us a new house that I would seek out something like this. I mean, Mads…just think of the cool history of this place. It's over a hundred years old. It's probably seen some shit."

"Yeah," she said. "It looks like it's been through some shit, too."

"I know it's not your dream home, but it's no worse than some of the dumps we've rented in the past. We know how to rough it. We'll inflate the air mattress and eat take out for a while."

"A while? Do you know how long it's gonna take us to gut this humongous house and renovate it? Even if we hire out a bunch of the work, it could be years!"

"We're handy. We can do a lot of it ourselves, and we can work in stages. We've got time."

"Do we? You'll be busy with your new job, the one we've relocated here for you to take," she reminded him. "And I can only do so much of it on my own." She let out a sigh. "I'm not even sure I want to take on such a huge project, Tim. I was hoping to spend my time working on my book."

Tim looked depleted for a second, but then Maddy saw his gears turning and he jumped back into the fight, firing off one of his sentimental, heart-tugging arguments that she could never say no to, and he knew it. "I just thought it would be fun to restore this place together. Make it our own. I really feel a connection. It feels like our home. I can totally picture it. Can't you just see it?"

He crouched a bit and pointed toward the top of the house. "We could turn the room with the turret into a cool writing space for you. Wouldn't that be amazing? It would for sure inspire you to churn out a masterpiece. And the listing said there are four bedrooms upstairs.

Four! So, I could have a separate office with my drafting table. That way, I wouldn't bug you while you're trying to write." He turned back to her and gave her a wry smile.

She thought about whether or not she had any real arguments left. "Four bedrooms? That might be a little too big for just the two of us, don't you think?"

"Well, I was also thinking maybe the fourth bedroom could be a…" Tim paused.

"A baby room?"

"I mean…can't you just see a few tiny terrors running past those huge front parlor windows?"

"If you're talking about ghost children in Victorian night dresses, then yes. I definitely can."

An awkward pause sat between them before Tim cleared his throat. "Anyway, don't say no yet. Just think about it for a little bit before you decide one way or the other. How about over lunch? A few blocks from here is the main part of town. It's super quaint and Mayberry-esque. I think you're gonna fall in love with it. Let's go check it out and see if we can find someplace to grab some food before we head back to the hotel."

"Yeah. Okay."

Tim smiled and took the rental car out of park and started driving.

As Maddy sat looking out the window, trying to forget the tension that lingered between them, she let guilt wrap around her, trying to find comfort in it. The conflicted feelings of being soothed by the tightness and also restricted by it somehow felt right in the moment. She and Tim had agreed before they got married that they both wanted children, but things had changed, things beyond Maddy's control. And now she was unsure, full of doubt, fear, and riddled with the knowledge that Tim still hoped for a boatload of kids someday.

Pushing it out of her head, she took in the scenes of their new place of residence. It felt so strange to not be living in Portland. Neither of them had been to Minnesota before Tim came for the job interview last month, then a second time after accepting the position at the architecture firm as a new junior architect. A friend who'd grown up in the Twin Cities told them to check out Pine Grove because he had fond childhood memories of visiting an aunt in the area. The town itself wasn't too far from the cities, and the houses were cheaper. Way, way cheaper. So far, it didn't feel all that different from Oregon except her family wasn't here, and everyone told her the winters would be brutal. She had the entire summer and fall before she had to worry about that. Besides, could it really be any worse than months of the Pacific Northwest's gloomy drizzle?

Within minutes, they arrived at the center of town which was in much better shape than the house they'd just seen. It was small, but it had an adorable café, an antique store, a cute little public library, a few shops, a pharmacy, a couple of banks, and the Pine Grove City Hall.

"It's so sweet," Maddy said.

"I knew you'd love it!"

They parked and entered the café called The Pine Cone. The walls were painted like a forest, and the front window had a ledge adorned with miniature evergreens in brown pots. They ordered lunch from the counter, then sat in a bright booth near the front with drinks.

Maddy saw herself walking over in the mornings, sitting at one of the tables by the window with a hot cup of coffee, pecking away at the keys on her laptop, and warmed to the idea. "I can see myself writing here," she told Tim.

He smiled. "Yeah?"

She nodded.

"Hey, uh, about the whole thing back there...I was being insensitive, you know, about the kid thing," he said.

"It's okay."

"It's just...I hope you aren't completely shutting yourself off to the whole idea of us having a family because of what happened. The chances of that happening to us, to you, are...I think it's pretty rare."

She clutched the glass in front of her and focused on the rain still coming down outside the window. "I know. It's just scary. The whole thing was...a lot. I need some time."

Tim grabbed one of her hands and held it across the booth. "I get it."

She turned from the window and looked at him. She knew he was going to propose something because this was a move he'd made a few times before—one of them was when he proposed. The last time he did it, he was trying to get her to agree to this move. She'd, of course, said yes to him both times, so why would this time be any different?

"How about," he said, "for now, we turn that extra bedroom into a guest room for when our parents and friends come to stay from Portland? We can revisit the kid thing at some point down the line, but only when you're ready?"

Maddy smiled. "Okay. All right. Fine. You win. You've convinced me. Let's do it. Let's buy the old house and bring it back to life."

Tim's baby-blues sparkled. He squeezed her hand. "Yeah? Are you sure? Because, I mean, we could buy a fully done suburban McMansion and call it a day, if that's what you really want."

"Shut up," she said, rolling her own basic brown eyes. "Don't make me change my mind."

"Right. Okay. So, we're doing it? We're buying the house?"

Maddy nodded. "I guess so."

Tim leaned across the table and kissed her. "Yes! You won't regret it."

She really, really hoped that was true.

Chapter Three

1912

The following day, Beatrice watched with bated breath as Charles held the parchment to his spectacled eyes, moving his lips as he read. When he was done, he set the paper down with a fraught look on his face and gave it a lengthy bit of consideration before asking, "Must it be so…wordy?"

"It must."

"Mr. Gold will not take too kindly to it."

"Mr. Gold cannot read. You told me so yourself when you went over the ledger with him. But do you know who can read? Those four poor babes, the children who are mourning the loss of their mother, the woman who lovingly taught them how to read. They will devour every word in the gazette, no doubt. Don't make the last, and likely only, words printed on parchment about their precious mother be…sour."

Charles looked down at the announcement and let out a long sigh. "I'll deliver it to the printer shortly."

Beatrice smiled warmly at her husband. "Thank you, Charles."

****

Later that same evening, Beatrice found herself once again at her writing table, yet this time she was writing for pleasure—a letter to her sister. She should have been in fine spirits, for her earlier victory with Charles was a true win, but the mood in the room had shifted dramatically from the previous night's writing session. It was once again late, as she preferred it, but there was no rain softly pelting the windowpanes, nor was there a soft glow from the embers, as the fire had gone out earlier on its own accord and Beatrice let it smolder to ashes. She considered getting up to stoke it but couldn't be bothered. Though the weather had dried and even warmed considerably, a peculiar and unwanted chill hung in the air. A heavy lace shawl lay across her shoulders but didn't seem to touch the coolness that permeated her surroundings.

A single candle flickered on her table, and even that was nearly wicked out. The small room in which she wrote was not stately, but she usually took comfort in the walls around her on any other night. Her husband had offered her the spired room as her own private sanctuary when she first arrived months ago, but it was at the front of the house and the surrounding windows did not provide the serene atmosphere she so desired. This room, with only a single window, had an exceptional view of the exquisite gardens in the back of the home. The space generally emitted the energy of a soft embrace and in some small way reminded her of her childhood bed chamber. It was perplexing to think that she would find any similarities between the two, having compartmentalized them into utterly distinct lives. The first being cold, sterile, and filled with turmoil and heartache, while her current one was full of hope.

Perhaps she was thinking too literally on the matter. Perhaps it was something simpler than all that.

Could it not be quite so that the hue on the walls was of a similar shade, or that the old books she'd carried along with her and placed on the shelves when she arrived filled the air with an aroma akin to her earlier days? It was more likely that she found comfort and safety in both retreats, but she didn't want to harp on the past. She was here now and that was all that mattered.

Positioned directly at the top of the staircase, the room's original intent was for purposes of sewing, but Beatrice's current position had no need for such work. She lived in relative ease as the mortician's wife. She kept busy with various activities, some simple and some unusual, but they were not those one might ascribe to a common housewife. She was afforded many luxuries here, as Charles had taken a servant in before she arrived who performed much of the work a wife might. Ester cooked and cleaned, while Beatrice handled affairs most often pertaining to funeral matters.

Besides writing communications, she attended to the finer details of décor, kept the gardens, practiced her music, and assisted her husband in dressing and presenting the deceased for the public or private viewings. Initially, this last task came with some adjusting, but Beatrice wasn't faint of heart. Ironically, when she first arrived, the heavy perfume of cut flowers wafting throughout every nook and cranny of the lower level was the thing that made her queasy. When she asked Charles if it could be lessened, he explained that the floral potency was concealing the permeating smells of death that would linger without masking.

This was no longer a concern as her nose and character had made the appropriate adjustments. She rather enjoyed the gardens behind the house and was learning the ins and outs of maintaining them. Each day, she would empty the myriad of vases in the parlor and adjacent sitting room, replace the wilted arrangements, and add fresh cuts and clean water. One could argue that it was a much finer task than emptying chamber pots.

She dipped her pen into the ink and thought for a moment before beginning a letter to her sister. How she missed her only sibling. Jane had been a perfect sister in every way, until she had fled, though Beatrice could not blame her for departing. Her talents were many. Not only was she bold and intelligent, but Jane also had a powerful beauty and a voice to match it, thus she set off with a vaudeville troupe to sing with the band. Since then, she had joined up with the most popular traveling carnival and toured the country with the act. With so much excitement, Jane didn't have time to write to Beatrice. It was understandable and Bea was nothing but envious of her sister. Yet, she often hoped for Jane to return to her someday. It was not likely to happen, but Beatrice could dream. She gathered that Jane had many suitors over the years, including a tiger trainer from the big top, a trumpet player, and a magician. None she fancied enough to settle down and marry, therefore a return to a civilized life seemed unfathomable. Even if she were to find love, she had become a worldly adventurer. This small town had nothing to offer Jane. She would likely not consider residing in such a place, much to Bea's dismay, as her sister was her only companion growing up. Jane was her only source of maternal comfort and guidance.

Pine Grove, albeit a simple Midwestern town, was

quite suitable for Bea. Though it wasn't as small as some and had begun to adopt more modern ways including establishing the funeral parlor. The town proper was nestled midway between the state's capital city of St. Paul and due west of Stillwater, the birthplace of Minnesota. Beatrice had been born and raised in Stillwater and though she missed the valley, the river, and the hustle and bustle of the larger town on occasion, she did not miss much else about the place.

While Bea was well aware that she could not send her letters off to Jane, for how would they find her in all of her traipsing train travels? She also knew it was imperative for her own mental grounding to continue to compose them. She had, after all, found her voice as a writer while creating these weekly letters.

My dearest sister,

If you are still on travel itineraries true to the circus schedule, I believe it would place you in Chicago at present, closer than you've been to home in some amount of time, yet still a greater distance than I would wish.

Yesterday, I had the pleasure of composing a notice for a farmer's wife. She passed from appendicitis that had festered for several months. How dreadful for her children and husband. One cannot bear to think of how things will proceed for them now. My heart will not allow it, I'm afraid, as I know it all too well having lived it myself, as have you.

I must apologize for of late my letters must seem to carry a heaviness about them, but in truth I am well. The mortician's treatment has been satisfactory, and I am happy here. The days are filled with a variety of fascinating new tasks, and I still learn more as time goes by. By way of reprieve, I'm making acquaintances with other women in town through the weekly auxiliary meetings. We pass the time with charity work, needlepoint, sewing, and of course a bit of gossip. It has also brought me more companionship than I've felt in some time.

Pine Grove cannot be expected to burst with as much excitement as you are likely experiencing in your adventures. Perhaps at some point in the future something interesting will take place that will liven up this writer's pen and inspire you to find your way home, if briefly. I do so hope you will consider a visit when your schedule allows.

Until then, your loving sister,

Beatrice

She placed the stopper back on the inkwell and sat for a spell, lost in thought as she watched the last bits of wick eat up the flame on the candle before her eyes. She folded up the parchment on which she'd composed Jane's letter then tied the bundle with a loose bit of red ribbon before getting up and slipping the stack alongside the books on her shelf.

Moving to the fireplace, Bea picked up a small, framed tin-set photograph of her mother and sister displayed on the mantelpiece. It was the only such picture she had of them. Looking at it tugged at her heart, yet she examined it often, searching for something new in each viewing. This tiny treasure invited in the few precious memories she had of her mother. She imbibed them like warm milk that comforted her until the emotions turned sour, and Beatrice was forced to thrust the photograph back down as though it had cut her sharply.

Just as the last ounce of light in the room sputtered, she heard the faint tinkling of the bells on the back door ring. Positioned beyond the kitchen, the intake room was initially slated as the pantry but was now the place where the mortician processed the patients on arrival. It didn't matter what time of day, as the dead did not keep time. In the evenings, Charles's younger brother, Francis, was in attendance to take in new guests to the house. He often slept on a fainting couch set up near the door in case someone should come calling or require his services as a transport in the late hours of the night.

Beatrice heard her husband's now familiar shuffling as he made his way down the staircase. It was followed by the faint murmurings between Charles and Francis. Not more than a few words of exchange took place between the brothers before Bea made out the sounds of what she also had come to know as the thing that happened next: a body being brought in and laid out on the cold table.

The discussion between the brothers never lingered. Charles rarely dallied, especially at this hour when there was work before him, but Beatrice couldn't help concerning herself about the siblings and the nature of their relationship. Perhaps she was wrong, but something about how the two men interacted felt stiff and unpleasant. Were siblings not meant to share more than work between them? Beatrice believed there must be a strong bond within them somewhere, but it was buried too deep for her to see. Jealous of what was unattainable to her, she set herself a small goal to help the brothers achieve what she did not and could not have. Perhaps the brothers' fondness for one another simply needed nothing more than a little coaxing.

She had only been in Francis's company on a few occasions, thereby did not know his temperament well, but he was perhaps a bit less refined than Charles. Being a woman who had mainly been brought up in the company of her sister and nursemaid, she had no real sense of what constituted typical behavior between two men. Yet surely, they must have at least a mutual respect for one another, or they wouldn't be in business together. Still, something didn't sit right with Beatrice about their conduct together. An idea broached her mind in regard to shaping the brotherly bond, which she would save to bring up with Charles at a later time.

Beatrice stepped out of her sitting room and stood at the top of the staircase. Though nothing out of the ordinary had occurred about this new remittance, something was different. She could feel it. And it then explained the mood cast early on, as though this dark presence had arrived in the home first before the physical being had entered and been set upon the cold table.

The voices of the brothers began to fade away just as her candle extinguished itself. As Bea stood in darkened silence at the precipice of the staircase, the bitter chill from the sewing room found her once again and worked its way through her shawl. She wrapped it around herself, but it did no good. The wicked cold had already planted itself deep into her bones.

It was then that the back door shut with enough force for her to feel the vibrations come up through the floorboards. Startled, she caught herself on the banister rail before tumbling down. What was this negative energy that flowed through the home on this night? Beatrice was perhaps not as practical as her husband.

She believed firmly that those who came through these doors and walls, the souls, were often frightened and lost. She sometimes felt the spirits of the dead linger, though she had yet to experience a charge of energy that carried with it anything resembling that which she felt on this night. Attuned to it perhaps more than others, she could not read if the spirit was simply scared or if it carried with it another emotion altogether. This one did feel different, jagged and harsh around the edges. It was perhaps less scared than it seemed to have an angry, vengeful energy. She stood for a bit longer attempting to connect to it more, but was unable to do so, until at last the chill abated and just like that, the presence that had squeezed her was no more. With a poof, it vanished, carried away down the staircase with the breeze.

Once Beatrice regained her composure, she retreated to her chambers and readied herself for sleep. When she climbed into her bed, she found that she was quite restless. She lay there for a long time waiting for Charles's heavy footfalls up the steps. She thought to perhaps inquire of the new arrival, though she wasn't sure why she felt a heavy burden as to stay awake. In the morn, she would be informed of all of the gruesome facts in order to wield her quill to compose an announcement for the gazette. Why she felt so ill at ease over this particular intake was the question. Death was the nature of the new life she had entered. Up until now, it had not been so troubling to her.

If anything, there were days when she felt more comfortable interacting with the spirit world than she did the land of the living. Some believed death to be a thing that, if around it long enough, could be caught much like an illness. Beatrice wasn't one of them. No. If this were true, she would have perished long ago. Clearly, this was nothing more than a silly superstition. Yet, she did believe the dead could be full of spite, and this notion worried her more than she cared to admit. Up until this point, she had only found comforted by those who had crossed over. Beatrice enjoyed the night for that exacting reason, but tonight a new type of darkness had entered her home, and for the first time since arriving, she looked forward to daybreak.

Chapter Four

2022

As Maddy lugged box after box into the front room of their new house, her arms burned, but she was feeling better about the place. It wasn't nearly as bad as she had imagined it would be on the inside. The hardwood floors had recently been resurfaced and sealed. The kitchen and bathrooms were dated but functional and would be fine until they were able to do the full remodel. The fireplace in the living room was actually incredible and looked like it was almost original except for some ugly eighties tiling. But that could be easily removed and replaced without much added expense. It would be an awesome focal point of the room. A few of the rooms even had decent paint on the walls.

Of course, the roughest room of all was the one intended for use as her office. Initially, Tim had offered up the room with the turret to her as a selling point, but upon seeing it, she realized it was too cold with all those windows, and the roundness of the room made the space difficult in terms of desk placement. They both knew Tim desperately wanted that room for his office, and she was more than willing to let him have it, so it worked out all around.

Her newly designated office space was the first

room to the right just at the top of the stairs. It was small, but there was something about it that Maddy loved when she walked into it for the first time. Sure, it had tacky, dated wallpaper that would be a huge pain in the ass to remove, but it was cozy and had a small, south-facing window that would get great sunlight during the day. Plus there was a spectacular floor-to-ceiling bookcase on the opposite wall. She had a ton of books, and her old bookcase was cheap and not the right style for this house. The built-in bookcase was rough, like most everything else here, but despite that, she could see the character under the layers of peeled paint. It looked like it might be walnut underneath. Why someone would paint over that was a mystery, but all she really needed to do was sand it down. With some elbow grease, she could probably get it back to the original wood in no time. A little varnish would have it looking polished and pristine. She was suddenly grateful that her parents had been so handy and had taken on lots of renovation projects in her childhood home when she was growing up. They'd taught her how to be a DIYer without her even knowing she wanted to be one. Hell, she *hadn't* wanted to be one until she saw this office space.

But the best part of the room, the thing that signaled to her immediately, was the window seat. It wasn't much, just a rectangular wooden bench built directly under the single window, but it still qualified as a reading nook. What shy, book-loving girl hadn't fantasized about having one all for her own? Maddy figured she would attempt to sew a cover for a cushion that would fit perfectly onto the bench so she would be ultra-comfy while she read.

All good writers needed to read avidly in their genre, and since she recently finished her writing program at PSU, she finally had time to spend doing just that. The only problem was that she didn't know what her genre was yet, though she was excited to figure it out. She'd read plenty of different books over the years in all the various categories: rom-com, literary, fantasy, hard science fiction, commercial, etc. But she hadn't quite found the one she was most drawn to, at least not the one she preferred as a writer. A writer? Was she? She didn't even dare call herself that yet. It felt too bold, too lofty, too confident. She was none of those things. She was…aspiring at best, but for as long as she could remember, she wanted to write a book. And now, she was finally ready.

The air in the house was stale after having been closed up for so long and the wet spring weather was starting to dry out and warming up. Now that they'd hauled all the boxes in, Maddy was tired and sticky. "I was thinking—" She hoisted open the first of five huge windows in the front parlor that looked out to the street. "—what about a mystery?"

"What about a mystery?" he asked, dumbfounded. He sat down on a short stack of cardboard boxes and wiped the sweat from his face.

"I might try to write one."

"Really?"

She tried not to let that subtle tone in his voice annoy her as she moved to open the next window. "Yeah. What's wrong with that?"

"No. Nothing. What kind of mystery?"

"I don't know. Maybe a murder mystery? I was sort of thinking I could use this creepy, old house as inspiration. Maybe it will take place in Victorian times or something."

"Do you know anything about Victorian times, Mads?"

"No. But, I do know how to Google."

"What would the premise be?" he asked.

She shrugged. "Maybe someone gets murdered here."

"Who?"

"I don't know. I haven't figured that part out yet."

"That sounds like chewing off a pretty big bite for a first novel."

"Thanks for having faith in me," she said.

Tim chugged from his water bottle for a second before he said, "No. I just mean…a mystery seems like a difficult feat for a first attempt, and then adding the historical element…I know I couldn't do it."

That was exactly why she wanted to do it. To prove to Tim that she could. He was the smart one who had, without much effort it seemed, followed his desired path to become an architect. He was the one who snagged a great job immediately after graduating from his program. He was fun and easy-going and everybody's friend. Maddy felt like a type A, socially awkward loser in comparison, which wasn't new.

Before she met Tim she'd lived in the shadow of her well-liked, talented, beautiful older sister. This was apparently a recurring theme in her life—replacing one rock star with another. She was a perpetual roadie for the band. She seemed to always be trying to prove herself, or at the very least, keep up, but in reality she was second fiddle on a good day. It had never really bothered her much. She liked having one best friend, staying in to read, being close with her family, but lately, something had changed. She had changed.

She was no longer living in her big sister's shadow. She was exposed, open to the elements for the first time. A part of her wanted to run and hide, but another piece of her was ready to stop sitting in the backseat. She was anxious to take some control over certain aspects of her future and find her way. Did she want to be a rockstar? Hell no. But she didn't want to be the one carrying the gear anymore either.

It was so hard without Jess. She had been a big supporter of Maddy's writing, always asking if she could read her latest short story, telling her how cool it was that Maddy could write so well. Now all Maddy had was herself to convince because her only fan was not here anymore to cheer her on, and that not only hurt, but it also made it difficult to have even the tiniest amount of confidence. Instead, it poured out of the holes in her heart like a sieve created by her sister's death.

It wasn't like Tim had directly said he didn't think she could do it, but he also hadn't ever acted confident in her abilities, even though she'd written tons of short stories, and some of them were pretty decent, she thought. Tim wasn't a big reader, but when he had read any of Maddy's work, he was mostly quick to point out typos or plot holes. He didn't seem to take her writing very seriously, and that really bummed her out because she'd been ultra-supportive when he came to her after they were first married and said he wanted to do an apprenticeship that would be unpaid after they'd agreed that he would work while she finished her creative writing program.

Maddy believed deep down she had what it took to be a successful writer, she just hadn't found her style or voice yet, but she also hadn't had much time to look for it. She had been busy working a full-time job to pay their bills while going to school, so Tim could pursue his dream. But now, finally, it was her turn to catch her breath. She was excited about the prospects of writing all day, or at least part of the day, when she wasn't scrubbing this place down, ripping out wallpaper, picking out new appliances, and on and on.

She looked around the place again. "Yeah. I like the idea of a mystery," she said with a surprising amount of confidence behind her words. "Something about it really feels right."

Tim got up and wrapped his arms around her. "Okay. Mystery it is then."

His tone was still a little too patronizing, but she wouldn't let that stop her. In fact, she would use it as fuel to fire her determination. Her professors had often asked what inspired them to write. She never had a great answer. She enjoyed it, but was that enough of a push to write an entire book? Probably not. Oddly enough, Tim was the dreamer of the two of them, while Maddy was the more practical one. Sometimes she wondered if she had enough creative juice to be a good writer. She thought she could do it with Tim backing her. She wanted to show him that she had what it took. That was a sad reality and probably not the inspiration people should have, but it was honest. She would prove to them both that she could do it. She could be a writer.

She was far less certain about how to tackle this house. She leaned back into one of the open windowsills taking in the fresh air from outside. "So, what's our plan of attack on this place? Are we going to work on one room at a time? And if so, which one? Also, should we unpack stuff and just work around it? Or are we going to live out of the boxes? Because I don't think we labeled stuff well enough for that."

Tim looked around the room. "Good questions. I honestly have no idea."

"But this was all your idea," Maddy said.

"I know. I'll figure it out. You focus on solving your mystery novel and I'll figure out how to turn this place into your dream home."

"Your dream home, you mean."

"How about *our* dream home?" Tim said.

"Yeah. Okay."

He smiled. "Let's start by ordering a pizza. I'm starving."

"Sure. I guess that means we have to find the plates." She moved to a stack of boxes and started to wedge the top corner of the cardboard open to peek inside.

She really hadn't done a great job with the labeling. At least she had remembered to do it for the first dozen or so boxes, and then she got lazy. And some of the stickers hadn't stuck, and she'd stupidly put them on the tops of the boxes instead of the sides, so now those labels were hidden by other boxes stacked on top of them. After rifling through five or so boxes, she still hadn't found the right one. Tim sat back down on one of the boxes and searched out a pizza delivery place on his phone. Defeated, Maddy gave up her own search and sunk back into the window to take a breather. The moment she did, the window, in revolt perhaps, gave a groan and then, out of nowhere, suddenly dropped. The heavy wood-laden frame came straight down hard and swift like a guillotine.

She jumped out of the way just before it crashed down into the sill. "Oh my God!"

"You okay?" Tim asked as he moved to examine the window.

"Yeah. I'm fine."

The pane of glass had not shattered, which was shocking considering how fast it fell and how loud the bang had been. But now a jagged crack ran straight down the middle of the pane of glass. It was the center most window making it extremely noticeable.

"Why did that happen?" she asked.

"Sometimes these old pulleys just need to have the sash cords replaced," he said, lifting the window back up to look at the inside track.

"Or maybe the ghosts don't want us eating pizza here." She laughed, but she also couldn't help but think it was an ominous sign. Then she glanced toward the top of the box that Tim had been using as a chair. Now that he was no longer sitting on it, she saw the label affixed to the top of the cardboard. It was clearly labeled: Dishes. "Oh, wait. I take that back. I think I just found the plates."

"See?" Tim said. "These ghosts obviously like pizza."

"Right. They were just trying to kill *me* then."

"Well, maybe we'll leave them a slice as an offering or something."

"If that's what it takes for them not to haunt us, then I'm game," Maddy said.

Tim laughed, but Maddy wasn't laughing anymore. She was looking at the crack, thinking maybe she would incorporate ghosts into her murder mystery somehow. Write what you know, right?

It seemed like she was about to get the full experience.

Chapter Five

1912

Seated at the dining table the next morning for breakfast, Beatrice sipped her tea and watched Charles eat a thick slab of buttered bread while working his ledger. He wasn't a handsome man by any means, but she found things to admire about him, like his quiet, assured nature. He was unlike her father in most ways and that suited her well. Instead of being stubborn and unmoving in his decisions, Charles listened and was rational in his words and actions. Even if his jawline was slightly asymmetrical and his hair was much too thin for a man his age, his eyes were soft and gentle behind his spectacles, and though he appeared rigid in his disposition. She saw a small spark of something underneath it all, an endearing quality. She believed she could trust him. It was a solid start.

In a similar manner, she didn't possess the kind of looks that her sister did. Her hair was terribly uncooperative in its wicked curliness, unlike Jane's which, in her mind, lay with perfect ease. And Beatrice's skin did not glow as her sister's did. It was often pale and dull. Her eyes were set in too deep, and her nose protruded more than she would have preferred given the set of her eyes. While Jane didn't seem to be the least bit concerned of her appearance, Beatrice attempted to overwork herself to look only half as nice as her sibling. And while Jane's voice was spun silk, Beatrice knew her words were best left on the page.

"Dearest," Beatrice said to her husband now. "I was thinking it might be nice to invite Francis and his wife to take supper with us. I'm coming to the realization that I do not know your family well and I would be very keen to get more acquainted with them. What do you think?"

Charles glanced up from his books for a brief moment and thought on the idea. "If you wish."

She smiled. "I do. Could you ask Francis when a good time might be for me to arrange it?"

"Fine. Fine."

"I appreciate it," she said with a doting look.

Charles finally set his pen down, gave her a glancing half-smile, and took up his teacup.

Beatrice decided this would be the right time to ask about the goings on of the last evening. "Was there…a new arrival last night? I thought I heard the bells ring."

Charles gave a slight nod. "There was."

She saw the look of distress cross his face but for a quick moment. "What is it? Is there something the matter?"

"No. No. Nothing."

"I can see that it is something." She had also felt it the previous eve, but she left those words out when she spoke.

Now Charles took a long, full drink from his cup and placed it down on the saucer before speaking. "It's"—he gave another great pause—"a child. From the orphanage."

"Good heavens."

She thought she'd steeled herself to this new way of life, but she had yet to encounter the death of a child. She had almost forgotten such a possibility existed for she'd been settled there now for several months, and she'd not come to experience such a dreadful event as of yet in all this time.

"There will be no announcement or service," Charles said in the most forthcoming manner she'd heard him take up.

"But why?"

"There are no funds for such a thing," he said matter-of-factly.

"Oh, Charles," she cried. "How dreadful."

They sat without words passing between them for a few moments, but Beatrice couldn't stop the questions from arising in her head, nor could she stop herself from asking them. "Of what age was the child? A girl or boy? How did it happen?"

"Does it matter? You will not need to write of it."

"I would still like to know."

He gave a curt nod. "A boy of twelve. It was an accident. I'm told he drowned while learning a trade."

"Drowned? What trade would involve having a child near the water?" It was a bit of a rhetorical question for she knew exactly what trade; she just didn't want it to be so.

"He was working along the edge of the St. Croix River."

"Please do not tell me it was…"

Charles's gaze fell.

Beatrice let out a sob. "Charles? Did this tragedy take place at one of the lumber companies?"

Charles cleared his throat and offered another nod.

Then Beatrice was sure. For she had seen such things with her own eyes during her time at the mills. Not all of the companies employed children, but she knew of one in particular that did. "Please tell me it was not my father's—"

"I'm afraid so."

"But surely, then there is a way for funding. W&W Lumber will provide—"

"I have already spoken with your father. He had offered a raw box and a small plot."

"That's less than adequate. What of a funeral?"

Charles shook his head.

"Perhaps I could speak to my father and inquire about a more generous offer—"

"No. It's done," he said, softly but firmly. Then while looking back up at her, he added, "I'm sorry."

She could see in his eyes the sincerity in his words, and it reaffirmed her happiness to be married to him, even as waves of disquiet passed through her. She smiled weakly at her husband as a returned gesture of good grace.

Charles got up from the table, collected his ledger, and gave her a peck on the cheek. "There's much to do to ready for the service today. We must get on with it."

Later, Beatrice stood in the gardens with her cutting shears as she clipped fresh baby's breath and added them to her basket. The sun was shining and lush greens were filling in nicely after the spring rains. Her surroundings were cheerful, if only she could stop herself from thinking about the death of a child at her father's mill. She knew accidents had occurred there many times before, but...a child! How cruel! How uncivilized! He was only a boy who hadn't reached the age of manhood. The very least her father could now do to make amends would be to offer the one thing he could give—a small sum for a proper resting for this young soul and peace for the living. It was the respectable and responsible thing to do. Alas, these were not traits her father possessed.

She hated to think poorly of the man of her own flesh and blood, but he often made it difficult for her to do anything but. He'd not been the most tender-hearted man, nor had he shown her much in the way of affection, though she tried not to blame him. It wasn't his fault, the situation he found himself in—the situation they all found themselves in.

Her mother's death had been the result of a new sibling Bea was to have. Clara had been everything a mother should be—the warmth and light of the family. She was nurturing and kind. Maternal. The devastation of the loss—not of the child—but of his wife, sat so far within her father, he was unreachable after that. If not for Jane, Beatrice would not have survived the years that followed.

After Jane vanished, Beatrice did not cast stones, as much as it had hurt her. Beatrice was twelve, the same age as the poor drowned boy, when her caregiver had also left. Ann, the hired caregiver, had taught her many skills but keeping a home or her father satisfied were not among them. Thereby, Beatrice didn't have time to wallow in her sadness, as she had much to do in learning her new role of homemaker as her father demanded. Her father often came in late smelling of wet timber and sour ales. He was gruff and short with her, barking his needs as if she were his personal servant and not his own offspring. It was at those times that Beatrice understood why her sister had gone, but she couldn't help but feel betrayal and self-pity.

Her one good fortune came when Charles asked for her hand in marriage. The timing worked in Beatrice's favor as her father had by now taken a second wife, another widow called Greta, who Bea wasn't altogether taken with, but she was making her father a tad more amiable. Suddenly, he no longer stayed late in the saloon, and he was ready and willing to let his daughter go for the cost of one contract of the sole lumber supplier to the Westmoreland Funeral Parlor in Pine Grove, Minnesota, which was where she stood now, glad to be basking in the beauty of the lush gardens. Yet she was unsettled, and though she hated going against her husband's wishes, she knew she had to speak with her father if she wanted to make things right, not only for herself, but for the boy and his family.

Hearing a rustling, Beatrice turned to see the neighbor, old Dr. Boyle, standing in his own unkempt garden across the way. A retired and now reclusive man, he'd never married. Disheveled, he was bent over his untamed flower beds, covered in black soil while working a hoe in his hand. People in town said that he'd lost his mental wherewithal, probably caring for patients at the sanitorium all those years, but Beatrice had had some delightful conversations with him regarding the flowers and other such pleasantries as the weather. For as tattered as he and his yard appeared, she'd found him to be knowledgeable and a fine conversationalist.

She called over to him. "Good morning, Dr. Boyle."

Still on bent knees, he tipped an imaginary hat to

her. "Mrs. Westmoreland. How do you do?"

"I am well. Thank you."

He smiled and returned his focus to the earth.

When Beatrice's basket was plum full of greenery and other colorful cut flowers for the parlor vases, she went inside and began to prepare the space for the funeral service for Harriet Gold taking place later that day. There was no more time at present to ponder the tragic and untimely death of a small boy, for there was much work in front of her today to put another soul to rest. Her own inner turmoil would have to wait until she had a moment to spare in order to hatch a plan to make peace with the child and ease his wary spirit. At least now it was clear to her what was causing the darkness, and she knew what was needed to do in order to quell it. It would involve confronting her own dark past, but so be it.

Chapter Six

2022

On Monday morning, Maddy was alone in the big
Victorian house for the first time. Tim had left bright
and early for his first day of work. Their car had arrived
from Portland over the weekend, along with the moving
container with the boxes they'd lugged in. Their
furniture wouldn't be there for a few more days. They'd
decided to sell their second car because it would have
been too expensive to ship, and it was getting too old to
justify the expense. That left Maddy without any means
of transportation. Pine Grove wasn't like Portland. It
didn't have a light rail or a city bus she could just hop
on. She could probably do a rideshare if she really
needed to, but for now, she had wallpaper to strip.

She stood in her office trying to figure out a good
approach. The sooner this 90s taupe paisley was gone,
the better. She ran her hand along the wall until she felt
a seam in the paper, and then she jammed her fingernail
underneath it to dislodge a section of it from the wall.
She pulled it until a small chunk ripped away.
Repeating the process, she managed to rip another
small piece from the wall, and then another. At this
rate, she'd been here most of her natural life before one
wall was complete, but she was impatient. She
continued this way until she had a section slightly

larger than a bread box revealed. And she realized then that she was looking at…another complete layer of different wallpaper beneath this top layer. She groaned. The paper underneath was a glossy, bright-orange and looked to be from the disco-era of the early seventies. Was there seriously going to be ten layers of paper to peel off? One for each decade this house had stood? This was not going to be as simple or straightforward of a task as she had hoped it might be. She needed a new plan.

She went downstairs and into the front room and began digging again through the pile of boxes in search of Tim's tools. She found one labeled "garage crap" and dug around until she found a putty knife. It almost looked older than the house, coated in various colors of dried paint splotches and a bit of rust, not to mention the black plastic handle had a crack in it. If they were going to renovate this entire house, they probably needed to buy some new tools. For now, this old putty knife was going to have to work because it was all she had.

Back upstairs, she threw on a pair of cut-off jean shorts and a T-shirt, and put her hair up, preparing for battle. The sun was already pouring into the small room attempting to bake her alive. She very carefully opened the window to avert another near-death scenario. Since it was the only window in the small space, there was no cross breeze, in fact, there was no breeze whatsoever. There was nothing she could do about it. If she wanted to have the room ready by the time the movers brought her desk and chair, she had to get to work.

As she did, she realized how quiet it was. The only sounds she heard were from the old house creaking and groaning, and though she was starting to recognize some of its various chatter, she wasn't exactly comforted by it. She was still thinking about the ghosts that didn't want her there. She imagined the noises were part of their extraction plan. She'd obviously watched too many cartoons as a kid.

As she scraped wallpaper near the window, she peered outside and saw straight down to the backyard. Though the house sat near the end of the block, it wasn't completely isolated. There were a handful of homes fairly well spaced out on the street, though most sat not near the street, but toward the back of the lots, hidden by trees. Their house was the opposite. It sat close to the street and the backyard extended a good distance with some tall hedges on either side of a fence creating privacy. From this vantage point, Maddy could see the house on the next lot over. So far though, it looked to be dark and possibly vacant. It wasn't old, at least not as old as this one. It looked to be built in the seventies or eighties. It wasn't as big as this house either, but it was a decent-sized split-level. It was odd because it appeared well-kept overall, but the windows were all covered with thick drapes, and she hadn't seen any lights on inside, nor had she witnessed anybody coming or going from the house since they'd moved in.

It was sort of eerie that she hadn't seen very many people around the neighborhood in general, or that nobody had stopped to introduce themselves or just say hello yet. No pies on the porch, no welcome wagons. Minnesota was known for its niceties—or so she had heard. She tried to remind herself that she'd just moved locations, she hadn't gone back in time. People in Portland generally kept to themselves nowadays too.

Hell, Maddy generally kept to herself. She would much rather be writing than socializing. She'd always been a bit of an introvert, but the move and this big, empty house had her feeling lonely. She missed her parents and her best friend already and she'd only been in Minnesota for a few weeks.

Change had never been something she handled well in general, at least initially. She just needed to give herself some time. Eventually, she'd get used to this new state, this new town, and this new/very old house and being alone in it. At least that was what Tim kept telling her. Besides, if she wanted to be a successful writer, she would be spending a lot of time alone.

A few hours in, Maddy had finally scratched the surface, at least on the one section she'd been tackling, and she was ready to kiss the wall in victory. Her battle was won. She peeled back what had to be the final layer of paper, only to see…more wallpaper. "You have got to be kidding me!"

The newly exposed paper was a tad macabre. Off-white with an inky black print, it reminded her of a Rorschach blot. Wanting to see more of it, she glided the putty knife along the seam of the current top layer and was able to peel another large section away. She stepped back to look at it from a wider view. It wasn't an ink blot after all, but more like a fleur-de-lis pattern. It was a little creepy, but also interesting in a cool, gothic sort of way. It couldn't possibly be original to the house, could it? It did have a Victorian feel to it. She grabbed her phone and snapped a picture of it to send to her mom who would definitely be able to help her identify it. Then she dialed her mom's number.

"Hey, hon!" her mom said. "How's Minnesota?"

she asked, drawing the o out long so it sounded like Minnesooooda.

"It's not as good as Oregon," Maddy said, saying Oregon like Or-a-gone as opposed to Organ, which was the proper way to say it if you were a local.

"No," her mom said. "Because you or-a-gone from here."

"Wow. Nice one," Maddy said with a laugh.

"Like that?"

"Have you been waiting to use that?"

"No. I just came up with that."

"Really?"

Chuckling, Kathleen said, "No. I've been waiting."

It was good to hear her mom's voice. It was also good to hear her laugh. She hadn't done much of that lately, not since Jess died.

"So, hey," Maddy said. "Can we video? I want to show you the house!"

"Yes! It's early here though, honey. I'm still in my robe and I haven't brushed my hair."

"It's fine, Mom. Really. I'm just excited to see your face." Maddy dialed in the video call and there her mom sat in her robe at the kitchen counter with a cup of coffee in her hand as promised.

Seeing her face made Maddy want to burst into tears, but instead she pointed the camera outward and walked around the house, starting on the main floor, first pointing out the highlights like the cool fireplace and going quickly over the less cool parts, like the cracked window and the dated appliances in the kitchen.

Then, as she climbed the stairs, she said, "Okay, so I want to show you the room that's going to be my office. Did you see my text?"

"Yeah. I wasn't sure what I was looking at."

"It's the wallpaper. What do you think of it?"

"It's definitely different," her mom said.

"Different good, or different bad?"

"I'd need to see it again."

"Okay." She walked into the room and moved her phone around the space to show her mom. "So? What do you think? It still needs a ton of work. I plan to strip the bookcase, but once that's done, I just have to make a cushion for the window seat."

"It will be a perfect space for your writing."

"Right? Oh, and check out the view of the yard from here."

"Wow! Is that a flower garden?"

"Yeah. I guess I'm going to have to figure out how to garden now." Maddy turned the camera quickly and sat down on the window seat.

"Hey," her mom yelled.

Maddy gave a little jump. "What?"

"Turn the camera back. What was that?"

Maddy turned her phone slowly around the room again.

"Huh. I dunno what I saw. Maybe it was that thing." Her mother pointed her index finger. "What's that jutting out there?"

"This?" Maddy asked, pointing the camera toward the spot where the wall had a slight protrusion.

"Yeah. For a second, I thought a person was standing there." She laughed and took a sip of her coffee. "What is it? Is it an air duct of some sort? Did they convert the radiators at one point?"

"Nope. There's no central heating or air in the

place," Maddy said with a groan and pointed the camera to the old radiator in the back of the room.

"Oh, boy. No central air?"

"Nope. No air conditioning at all. It's already so hot in here too. Anyway, Tim said that weird protrusion is likely the chimney. This room is directly above the fireplace downstairs. It was maybe brick at one point, but he thinks it was probably plastered over during one of the many renos over the last century. It's a little weird, but I guess that's what gives these old houses character, right?"

"Absolutely," Kathleen said, and chuckled again. "Who wants four boxy walls anyway?"

"Not me!" Maddy laughed. "So, about the wallpaper…what do you think? It looks old, right? Like it could be original to the house, maybe. Is that even possible?"

"I suppose it could be."

"So, what do you think? Keep it or tear it out?"

"I don't know, honey. It's your call. Keeping it means you have less work to do. You won't need to paint."

"I like that option," Maddy said.

"Well, whatever you decide, I think it's so great!"

"That was such a Mom answer."

"I know."

"Okay, well, I better get back to it then. When I finish, you and Dad have to come and visit and see it in person. K?"

"Can't wait. That will be before winter though, right?"

"Ha ha. Very funny, Mom."

"I'm kidding. Dad and I will be there whenever

you invite us."

"K. I already miss you guys so much."

"We miss you too." Maddy's mom puckered her lips and blew her a virtual kiss and Maddy did the same back.

After she hung the phone up, she stayed seated for another minute, still deciding whether or not to keep the wallpaper. She scanned the room, trying to envision the whole thing with the black and white paper. As she did, she wondered again about her mom seeing something in the camera that wasn't there. She worried about her. It was horrible timing—this move.

When Maddy's sister died, her mom decided to retire from her job as a nurse in the neonatal unit of the hospital. It was probably for the best, but it also gave her ample time to do nothing but be sad. Maddy had originally been opposed to moving across the country, and it had caused a bit of a rift with her and Tim for a time. Maddy's dad sat her down and told her she had to go and live her life. This was a great opportunity for Tim, and it could be a nice change for her, for both of them. What had happened with Jess was done. There was nothing they could do about it and staying wouldn't bring her sister back.

She knew her dad was probably right, it was just really hard. She had lived in Portland her whole life. The timing was terrible, but Tim argued that a move might help with the grieving. He obviously won the argument, like always. He wasn't entirely wrong. She definitely needed a fresh start. Maddy could admit that everywhere she went after Jess died, all she did was think about the times she'd been there with her, what they'd done, how much fun they'd had, how she would never get to experience that again, and the pain and hurt started all over.

Maddy stood up and decided she was in love with the black and white paper. What would Tim think of it? She caught herself wondering. Wait. No. This was *her* office. It didn't matter what Tim thought. She liked the wallpaper, and it was going to stay regardless of what her husband thought. Because she already knew Tim would hate it. This was not his style at all. He was not into dark and spooky, which was a little weird because this house that he so desperately wanted was nothing but dark and spooky, but he didn't see that. He saw the quality craftsmanship and the detailed woodworking. If he could, he would have painted the whole house in pastel colors. He liked bright and bubbly. Sometimes Maddy thought of him as a happy-go-lucky toddler. That was often the thing she found charming about her husband, but lately, she wasn't feeling it. Instead of bright and happy, she was feeling this wallpaper vibe— a little dark and creepy.

Chapter Seven

1912

The service for Harriet Gold went swimmingly.
The day was bright and cheery, and Beatrice felt an
aura of warmth spread out inside the home as they
made their final preparations. When it was time to
begin, Beatrice and Charles stood at the propped front
door and greeted the guests as they arrived. More and
more people continued to shuffle inside until the rooms
filled to the seams. Shortly thereafter, Beatrice sat down
at the baby grand piano in the sitting room and played
some soft tunes while those in attendance milled about
talking in hushed tones. It was during this time that
Beatrice overheard two women talking quietly nearby.

"I have not seen Mrs. Gold in some time, but I was
reminded of what a delightful woman she was when I
read her notice. I had not intended it, but suddenly was
compelled to pay my respects."

"Why, I felt exactly the same," said the other.

Eventually, most made their way to the casket to
pay their respects directly to Harriet. The coffin sat
upon a low pedestal in the front of the parlor with a fine
linen draped upon it. Harriet looked lovely, as the sun
poured in from the row of windows and hit her face just
so, for she had been a beautiful woman, though
Beatrice was also pleased with the work she'd done in

presenting her well before the crowd.

Once the family pastor was ready to give a few words, Charles tinkled a small bell and people sat down in the two rows of chairs placed earlier by Francis. Mr. Gold and the four children sat nearest the front, while the remaining guests, perhaps thirty in total, filled in the remaining seats.

At that time, Beatrice stopped playing and got up from the piano. She stood at the back of the room and guided anyone who needed assistance during the service. It was a lovely sermon and from her position, Beatrice saw many of the guests pull handkerchiefs from their pockets, being discreet, as they stanched their tears during the short speech.

Once it was through, Charles closed the casket and three burly men, likely farmers, along with the young Cody Gold, Harriet's only son, surrounded and carried the coffin through to the back of the house and out the kitchen door where Francis waited in the carriage to take Harriet to her final resting place, the small gravesite on the Gold farm.

When the Gold family exited, Bea was a bit nervous about the possibility that Nathan would be upset with her with regard to the notice, but he kept his head low and did not speak to her. Just as the last of them had gone, the youngest daughter of the Golds, the bold seven-year-old, rushed back in and threw her tiny arms around Beatrice just below her waist. She did not speak a word but buried her head into Bea's dress. Beatrice's heart felt it might burst and she squeezed the child back with everything she had before the girl released and rushed off to catch up to the family.

As Beatrice tidied up the parlor after everyone had

gone, she felt a sense of peace, for though Harriet had not been a strong presence to her, that was a good thing, as far as Beatrice believed. It meant Harriet had led a nice life and had no need to be known in the wake of her passing. And now there was a calmness in the air, at least in this portion of the home.

Exhausted, she and Charles finished out their day with a light meal and then took to their bed where they had an equally light chat about rather mundane things such as the weather and news that had been printed in the daily gazette. When the candles were extinguished, Beatrice fell fast asleep alongside her husband only to be woken with a start well after midnight. She sat up in bed, listening. Had the bells jingled below? No. She did not think so. All seemed quiet within the home, though her skin was pricked with cold bumps now and her heart beat quickly.

As she lay, tuning in to the disturbance more closely, she knew that in the morn she would have to confront it, for she was no longer distracted by another soul's parting. The young boy downstairs was back, begging for her attention, that much was clear.

****

She woke earlier than usual, knowing that her husband was out of the house on a business call, for he would not understand her need to see the boy. Beatrice stood over the body of the young child laid out flat on the cold table in the intake room. The day was dreary, hot and humid, and the room was cast in shadowy light. The door was propped open near the kitchen, but the air hung thick like a blanket and didn't do much to stanch the death soaked into the walls of the tight space.

Under normal circumstances, she would not be

here until it was time to dress the departed, but this was not a normal circumstance. It was unlikely that Beatrice would be able to soothe this tiny spirit in front of her now, but it would not hurt to try to reason with him.

Her other need for the earlier viewing was that she was uncertain what kind of emotions might take hold when she did. Not that she was inclined to hold back her tears, but she preferred to release them in a dignified manner. Charles would likely not be comfortable with such a display of hysterics, if one was to spring forth, given the mortician's profession being what it was, and Beatrice couldn't trust her emotions given the nature of this death. So here she stood.

Peering down at the sunken cheeks of the little face before her, she did not shed tears as she'd assumed she might. But she did have a renewed thirst to do right by it, to change the heavy and stagnant air stirring around the room. She tried her best to reconnect with the tiny soul, letting her mind quiet initially. When she didn't get anything in return, she took his limp hand in hers and she directed her own energies into his, speaking calmly in her head, but there remained silence.

So focused as she was, Beatrice hadn't noticed that her brother by marriage had slipped through the open back door until she heard a tinny sound behind her. Alarmed and a bit embarrassed, she quickly let the dead, cold hand she'd been clutching go. She turned to find Francis rifling through a drawer along the back of the room, clearly in search of something. The wall was lined with cabinets and drawers filled with Charles's equipment needed to perform embalming procedures such as hoses and pans, scalpels, and the like, while the shelf above held the various containers and jars, some holding liquids and others waiting to receive them.

"Oh, Francis, you startled me," she said. "I didn't see you come in."

She had been aware that he was in the carriage house, as she'd heard the aggressive sounds of a casket being assembled echoing out from that direction when she'd entered the room. As much as he'd given her a start, she was also relieved to no longer be alone with her thoughts and the corpse of the unresponsive child. She had grown accustomed to Francis's presence in the home, as he often seemed to be in and out at all various times, not only in the day, but also at night when he attended to late callers. While she was used to sharing the home with a third party, no matter how often he made an appearance, she had not yet felt a sense of ease with the mortician's brother. She did not know why.

While Charles could be pensive, Francis was more assured in his mannerisms. If she had been an outside observer, she might assume that Francis was the oldest brother in some ways. He had a bit of a bark when he spoke to Charles that didn't sit well with her. Beatrice assumed that had mostly to do with Francis's less refined ways. Charles was more educated. He had attended the School of Mortuary Science in Cincinnati, Ohio to study the sciences of embalming. He was a learned man, while Francis had worked at a sawmill and now handled the laborious aspects of the business.

Beatrice sometimes wondered why Charles let his brother dictate as if he were the man in charge of the whole operation, as if he owned the funeral home outright, as if he were the older sibling. Perhaps she would learn more about their shared history at the upcoming dinner party. She hoped it might shed light on some of the behaviors of these two siblings. There had to be a reason behind their character. Surely, if anyone were to observe her and Jane's interactions, they would likely find things to be a bit peculiar indeed, so she did not want to cast any judgment of yet.

Now, Francis stood looking at her, as though he was more alarmed by her presence in the room than she was of his, though surely he saw her standing in the middle of the small room when he had entered. He was more squat than his older sibling, but his build was far more steady and strong. Had he witnessed her holding the dead boy's hand? Unsure, she smiled at him, searching his eyes. They were dark, though handsome, and reflected a boldness that lacked in her husband. He held her gaze as they both searched for something in the other. Finally, he tipped his head while still looking at Beatrice and said, "Pardon," as he closed the drawer and began to back out of the room as though he'd interrupted a gathering he had not been asked to attend. Bea supposed in some ways, he had.

"No need to leave," she said. "I was just…" She searched for words to make sense of what it was she was doing there, but Francis didn't offer her time.

"I have found what I was searching for," he said hastily, and exited through the door as swiftly and silently as he'd entered.

Stymied, Beatrice saw nothing in his hands, yet this felt no different than the other times Francis had stumbled upon her while she worked. It seemed as though the man was not comfortable sharing the same space with her. Perhaps it was out of courtesy? Perhaps he did not care for her presence there? Was it possible he was not comfortable with the dead? She did not know. Again, she did hope the meal might change her confusion about the man. For now, she stood alone again with only the lost soul of a child before her and while she still did not feel his presence in the room, she communicated to him her plan going forward regardless.

****

My dearest Jane,

The evening before last we had Charles's brother here at our home for a meal, along with his wife, Elizabeth, whom I hadn't had the pleasure of meeting yet. I was delighted to find she is a wonderfully interesting lady and quite well-spoken too. I believe you would like her very much. She is the head nursemaid at the Elmwood Home for Orphans. Elmwood, in case you have forgotten, is the town mid-distance from Pine Grove and Stillwater. Unlike our own childhood nursemaid, Anne, Elizabeth is abundantly warm, and I do believe she must make a marvelous caretaker for the poor orphaned souls for whom she is charged.

In fact, while in discussion with Elizabeth after sup, I inquired of a child from the orphanage. He was brought here late one eve not but a few nights earlier having perished tragically while laboring at Father's mill. She was able to provide me with facts of the child's narrative. I must say, Jane, I was quite aghast. The child's name was Henry Davis and his family had been established in Pine Grove for decades before they both succumbed to their own tragedies. Mr. Davis had been well loved as the general shop-keep for many years. He fell on a patch of ice outside the store one early morning while bringing in supplies and was knocked cold, only to be found later in the day frozen to death in a snowbank. Mrs. Davis took ill that same hard winter of pneumonia, leaving three young babies behind.

There is to be no formal service for the boy, who plunged to his death while hooking stray logs at the water's edge for the sake of building materials. That the child died under our father's care has been a source of deep discontentment for since hearing the news I can't stop stewing upon it. The orphanage has no funding for final arrangements, and it shall not surprise you to learn that our father has only agreed to a small pittance for the child who perished under his supervision. Charles has advised me against discussing it further with Father, yet I can't help but feel a sense of obligation toward the orphaned lad.

My apologies, as this writer has once again steered her words toward the morose. I do so wonder about the adventurous life you must be leading whilst I am here fixating on those who have no more life to lead. Though you mustn't pity me for I do feel this is important work. If I do not speak up for the dead, who will? I am content to do so whilst I sit and dream about the wonders of your own life, dear sister.

As ever,
Beatrice

Chapter Eight

2022

Maddy was still in her office when Tim got home from his first day of work. She heard him call out to her. "Mads? Hello? Anybody home?"

"Upstairs!"

"Hey," he said, stepping into the room with a box fan in each hand. He set one down in front of the outlet and plugged it in. "I come bearing gifts."

She let out a squeal, moved in front of the fan, and stood with her sore and sweaty arms stretched out while basking in the coolish air blowing on her. "You're a lifesaver."

Tim sat down on the window seat. Maddy watched his face as he examined the newly exposed black-and-white wallpaper. She could tell by his expression that he definitely did not like it. It did not surprise her in the least. What did she expect from a guy who was wearing light tan khaki pants and a button-down, lemony-yellow shirt?

"What do you think of it?"

"It's super creepy," Tim said, staring at it. "You're going to tear it out, right?"

"I think it might be original to the house."

"Okay. And?"

"Why did you want to buy this house if you don't

like the style of the era?"

"I didn't say it all had to be restored back to the original period," Tim argued.

She sighed and set the putty knife she'd held in her hand on one of the shelves of the bookcase, and put her hands on her hips, looking around the room. "Well, I'm feeling it. I'm going to keep it."

"Really?"

"You don't have to like it. It's my office. I'm not telling you how to decorate your office space."

Tim's eyes went wide, but he put up his hands in defeat. "Okay. Okay. I'm just surprised. That's all."

She shrugged. "Oh! How was your first day?" she asked him, turning her face to the fan, blowing loose, sweaty hair from her face.

"It went really well."

"Yeah?"

"Uh huh. I'm starving. You wanna go find someplace to grab dinner and I'll tell you all about it?"

"Like this?" She looked down at herself. She was covered in sweat and sticky wallpaper paste. "I don't think so."

"Go shower then. I gotta change out of these work clothes anyway."

****

Since they didn't know of any other eating establishments around the area yet, and they were already sick to death of pizza delivery, they found themselves back at The Pine Cone Café. Standing at the menu board, the guy behind the counter stood ready to take their order. About their age, maybe late twenties, early thirties, he had sort of a bohemian/surfer dude thing happening. He was tall with shaggy brown hair, dark eyes, and long shorts and a hoodie on. He reminded Maddy desperately of home. He was exactly the type of person she would expect to see working at a place like this in Portland. While it made her homesick, she was also pleasantly surprised to see someone like him in this small town.

"I don't think I've ever seen you guys in here before," he said. "I'm guessing you're not from around Pine Grove?"

"No. We actually *are* from Pine Grove," Tim said to him, giving Maddy a wink.

"As of Saturday," Maddy added.

"Ah. Newbs. I knew it," he said. "Well, for better or worse, welcome. I'd recommend the pine groovy burger or the pine coney dog. Both are excellent. Oh, and there's an amazing grilled trees sandwich."

Maddy smiled at the goofy food names. "Thanks. It all sounds great." She wondered if he was the owner of the place, though he seemed a bit young for that, but he also seemed a bit old to be just working the front counter. He was giving a pretty hard sell for a part-timer though, except for that better or worse line.

"I'm Frankie, by the way," he said. "Take your time. There's no rush in the Grove. Just give me a shout when you know what you want. Also, welcome drinks are on the house."

"Thanks, man," Tim said.

After they ordered, they looked for a spot to sit. The place was actually quite a bit more crowded than when they'd come for lunch the previous time. There were probably only fifteen tables in the whole café in total, but most were taken up by a mix of families and some older couples. The atmosphere was super casual, which was great, but looking around, Maddy noted there weren't a lot of other people remotely the same age as them in there, well…except the guy behind the counter. She felt a pang of regret. Had they made a huge mistake moving to a sleepy, small town? What if they didn't make any friends? What if they became an old, boring married couple with nothing interesting to do except come to the same little café for the daily special?

Two people got up from a small table toward the back and Tim and Maddy sat down. While they waited for their food, Maddy said, "I wonder if this place feels a little old for us."

"Old? What do you mean?"

"Like…it has a family feel."

Tim looked around as if he was just noticing this. That didn't surprise Maddy at all. Tim wasn't the most observant person in the world. "I guess maybe a little. Is that bad?"

She shrugged. "No. It just feels a little out of our element."

"We're not really young hipsters anymore, Mad. We're almost in our thirties. In fact, we might be older than that dude running the place."

"True," she said. "What do you think he meant when he said, 'welcome…for better or worse'?"

Tim shrugged. "Who knows. Either way, I like it here. I like the idea of us having our little place. I even like that it's a family place. I mean, look at that table over there with the two little kids coloring. It's sweet. That could be us someday, bringing our kids here for dinner."

She gave Tim a look, and he backtracked. "Not

right away or anything, but maybe someday."

Maddy turned to look, even if she was annoyed. She had really hoped Tim would lay off pushing the family thing for a bit after their last discussion, but apparently not. It was an adorable scene though, she could admit. She shrugged her shoulders. "Okay, yeah. It's sweet. Anyway, tell me about your first day at work. It went okay?"

"It was great. The people were nice. And I've already been assigned to a project, so I guess I'm hitting the ground running."

"Wow! What's the project?"

"Just some senior housing, but I sort of expected to get assigned to the boring jobs for a while."

Maddy nodded.

"Oh, except…they're already sending me on a work trip."

"Really? Already? Where to?"

"Oddly, back to Portland."

"When? For how long?"

"I leave in the morning actually."

"What? You're traveling on your second day of work?"

"Yeah. I guess I have to meet with the developers who just so happen to be based in Portland, and there are a few places they want me to tour that they've already built there. I'll be back on Saturday night, so it's just five days."

"A week? Well, maybe I'll come along and see my parents."

Tim looked down at the table. "I have to go with my work team, Mads."

"Oh. Right. Of course. That makes sense."

"Sorry." He reached across the table and took her hands. "It's my first work trip. I can't really ask if my wife can tag along yet. Also, our furniture should be arriving by the end of the week and one of us needs to be here when it does."

She pulled her hand back. "No. I know. You're right. I wasn't thinking. I get it."

And she did. She really did. She just wasn't thrilled at the idea of staying alone by herself in the house for the next four days. But she was a big girl. She could do it, even if she didn't want to do it. She could do it. The time would fly by; she had so much work to get done. Besides, what was the worst thing that could happen? Maybe the house would succeed in its mission to kill her, or maybe she would somehow make friends with it. She hoped for the latter.

Chapter Nine

1912

While Beatrice sat with Charles and sipped her morning tea, a queasiness resided deep within her. Surely it was because she did not like what she was plotting to do. She decided if she wanted to rectify the ugliness that swirled about, she would simply have to venture forth and speak to her father. There was not enough time to post a letter, nor did she trust her father to reply if there were. A visit was the only way to make things right.

She hated the notion of going against her husband's wishes, especially so soon into their marriage, so she decided it best to not tell him of her plan. Instead, she said, "Dearest, I was considering making a short trip to Stillwater to take afternoon tea with an old friend if it's not too much of an inconvenience."

Charles shifted his gaze up from his paper, pushed his spectacles up, and said, "I don't see why not. It's quiet here at the moment."

She smiled. "Thank you."

"I'll have Francis ready the carriage."

"It's settled then." And it was settled, so to speak. Everything was settled except her insides, which churned with waves of guilt about her deceit and also with turbulence in the prospect of seeing her father shortly, but she knew the trip was imperative in order to restore harmony to her home which was where her heart now resided.

Shortly thereafter, Beatrice readied herself and rode the distance to Stillwater on a horse and buggy with Francis at the reins. She reiterated that she was to have tea with an old friend and Francis did not question such motives. In fact, he did not ask a thing of her along the route, which made for a long journey, giving Bea too much time to ponder and dread the visit ahead.

She knew she would find Jakob Weber at his home on this day for it was a Saturday and Jakob being a German man of ritual, it was routine for him to sit and be waited on for much of the day, while perusing the paper and smoking his pipe.

His family had come to America and settled in the small southwest town of New Ulm several decades earlier and had worked the land there, but Jakob and his father didn't see eye-to-eye, so Jakob set off to become his own man when he was a youngster of fourteen. All he carried was a rucksack and the notion that he did not want to be a toiling farmer.

When he reached Stillwater in 1888, the lumber industry was at its peak. Hundreds if not thousands of tall white pines were floated down the St. Croix River and were caught at the Boom Site where companies sorted the logs based on trademarks cut or stamped into the felled trees. Jakob happily took to this trade as it was not what his own father did. That it was still back-breaking work no longer mattered, as he believed he could find profit down the road from it.

He first labored at one of the biggest and most

successful mills in the area, the Stillwater Lumber Company where they turned logs into lumber quicker than any other company for great distances. As a young, strong lad, he did much of the back-breaking work for small wages, but he saved like a thief and soon had a modest-sized bankroll. By the time he married Clara, Beatrice's mother, he had enough to acquire a more than modest shingle-style home in the vein of a colonial American revival. It wasn't as grand as some of the others in the area, but what it lacked in size and character, it made up for in locale, as it had been built on prime ground on the upper banks of the St. Croix River with a glorious view of the green valley below, especially once many of the tall trees had been cut away.

As Jakob got older and had experience and skill under his belt, his frugal and calculated character allowed him to rise the ranks, unconcerned about stepping over some to do so. He purchased half of his own mill. The Walker and Weber Mill, W&W as it was known, was established just after losing his wife and unborn child. Though that babe was a girl, Jakob had hoped to have many children; this dashed that dream. It was not because he had loved children, but instead because he had aspired to one day bring his sons into the business to keep the family name and legacy, so that he may continue to build his fortune without having to break his own back. He believed he deserved that, and had been robbed of it, though he had never stopped to consider how he had fled his own family legacy without looking back. This conclusion was not lost on Beatrice, however.

She stood full of dread as she knocked on the door

of her childhood home with great reluctance, but also with a desire to have it be all over and done with so she could return to the place that felt more cherished to her than the one before her. Her stomach coiled into tightly woven knots. She contemplated pivoting and simply walking away, but then she saw her father's face in the leaded glass window and knew it was too late. Jakob was forty-five years of age. Not only was it the tail end of his life, but also of the lumber boom and his success as a lumber baron. Things were no longer going his way and his constitution reflected this even more than when she'd fled from him just a short time ago.

"Father," Beatrice said when he opened the door. Her gloved hands wrung themselves tightly around a small handbag she clutched.

He nodded.

"Might I come in?" she asked.

Jakob grunted and allowed her to pass through the threshold. He went back to his high back leather chair in his sitting room and Beatrice removed her hat and gloves and sat on the davenport across from him. Being in the home again brought up more strife than she had anticipated—and she had expected a fair amount—so, she sat for a spell, not speaking, and she breathed in and out deeply from her diaphragm, doing everything she could think to quell the churning in the pit of her gut.

As she took in air, she looked around. The place had not lost its cold sense about it. The furnishings were utilitarian at best and the décor was non-existent. Anything that had been a reminder of Clara or the girls was long since put out of eyeline or even disposed of— even the portrait of Jakob and Clara on their wedding day, which had been mounted on the wall opposite where Beatrice sat last she'd been inside the home. It should not have shocked her since a new wife now resided there.

"Greta? Is she well?" Beatrice inquired.

He shrugged. "*Ja*."

Her father still held onto a mix of English and German, but he often brought out his German words when he was feeling uncomfortable. She could relate to this. She repositioned herself in an attempt to soothe her anxiety before pressing on.

"Is she in?" Beatrice asked, looking about but not seeing Greta, which was peculiar since a guest had arrived. She was not offered tea or water, which was made all the more obvious by her parched throat.

"*Ja*. She's resting in her chambers."

Beatrice could only assume this to mean that Greta did not care to see her. So be it. The feeling was mutual. "You look well," she said, tentatively.

Her father did not respond to this thin compliment for he could see through it. He did not, in fact, look well at all. His beard had gone stark white and bristly, and his face was puckered with too much age and toiling in the beating sun on the river's edge for many years. His once muscular and robust frame had begun to wither considerably since Bea had last seen him, and his forehead was permanently set with lines that made his scowl deep and harsh.

Beatrice felt even more nauseated now that she was face-to-face with him than when she just imagined it while enduring the bumps along the rutted path from Pine Grove. She'd been rehearsing her words throughout the journey, but now her tongue felt too large for her mouth and she wanted to retch. She knew it was best to simply get it over with than to prolong the niceties any longer. Her father would not be taken in by it anyway. She decided to push straight ahead.

"I'm sure you must know why I've come today, Father," she spoke. "Charles has told me of the child, Henry Davis, who perished at the lumberyard. I would like to hold a dignified service for him and have come to ask for a small bit of funding to do so."

"Already I have told the mortician I will pay for his pine box."

"But what of the rest? A short service? A gathering and a burial? You are a well to do man. It's the least you can offer given the circumstances of the boy's demise."

"No," Jakob said without missing a beat, in a tone Beatrice knew well.

If she hadn't thought better, she might have turned and run to seek shelter in the only safe haven she knew in this abode, her childhood bed chamber she had shared with her sister. But her things were no longer there, nor was Jane. All she would find inside the sad space would be her stepmother, and she was more than certain this woman would not offer up any resemblance of comfort to her. Beatrice sat as if naked, an overwhelming vulnerability taking hold, but she knew she must keep trying for the mission was important or she wouldn't have made the trip. She had to stay strong even if she knew what she was doing was likely impossible: changing the mind of the thickest man she had ever known.

Her own mind reeled. She wished she were more clever, had a stronger argument to make, but nothing came forth in the moment except a buzzing in her brain.

She swallowed and said, "Is there anything I can do to make you reconsider? I beg of you. Just a few dollars. It is but a small price to pay for salvation."

Her father did not look at her but picked up his pipe and paper on the table beside him and directed all of his attention to them. She was all too familiar with this act. He refused to give her another moment of consideration. She had failed.

She replaced her hat and gloves and left without another word. Her father did not look into her eyes again or show her out. Because the visit had lasted far less than the intended time, Bea sat down on the stoop and cried softly into her gloves while she waited for Francis to return.

On the bumpy trek back to Pine Grove, Beatrice continued to feel ill. She thought once she'd departed from her father's company it would alleviate the extreme discomfort she held, but it did not. Each pitch of the wheels from the rutted path made her stomach feel worse. By the time she'd reached Twelve Pine Street and was back on solid ground, her whole being was so sour she retched onto the ground near the carriage house before going inside. She hoped Francis hadn't heard such an undignified act, but it seemed more than likely that he did given his presence just around the corner as he unhitched the horses.

There was nothing she could do about it. It was done. Yet nothing was resolved. Perhaps that was why she continued to feel so out of sorts. She'd not been able to persuade her stubborn father, and she'd failed to bring peace to the child and her home. What was to come of such upheaval now?

Chapter Ten

2022

After Maddy filled her mug with coffee, she drank half of it while sitting on one of the cardboard boxes in the parlor. All she wanted to do was get to work on her novel, but she couldn't do that until she had a completed workspace, meaning a desk and a chair that was not a cardboard box. Looking around the room made her cranky. Ties, socks, boxers, and belts were strewn about the parlor floor. It looked like a businessman had been sucked into a tornado and only his clothes had been spat out.

Instead, it had just been Tim packing for his trip in the frenzied last minutes of dawn before heading to the airport. And now it was just her and the house until Saturday.

She got up and stood gazing out the front windows as she finished her coffee, looking, but not really seeing anything in particular until a group of about six young kids, all boys, stopped their bikes on the sidewalk directly in front of the house. A couple of them got off of their bikes and they huddled together as close as they could. A few even took a step or two into the yard. Maddy, curious to know what they were up to, moved her body off to the side a bit so they wouldn't see her watching them.

They peered at the house as if it were haunted, and for all Maddy knew, they were right to assume so. One of the bigger kids whispered in another's ear. It reminded her of playing a game of telephone when she was little. The secret went down the line, tallest kid to shortest and stopped at the smallest boy on the end with tight curls peeking out of a blue and red Minnesota Twins' baseball cap at least two sizes bigger than his little head. His finger pointed up toward the turret. The older boys nodded their heads in a synchronized dramatic fashion. Maddy highly doubted these kids were admiring the craftsmanship of the hand-cut fish scale shingles or the turned spindles, as her husband had so excitedly pointed out to her. She could only think of one good reason for little kids to ogle at a house in such a way, especially an old, spooky house such as this one.

On impulse, she set her coffee down and swung open the front door. She stepped out onto the porch. "Hi," she said, smiling widely, leaned into the railing trying to appear extra friendly. She didn't want to scare them, but her curiosity had gotten the better of her and she had to know. "I'm Maddy. We just moved in. Do you guys live in the neighborhood?"

The boys looked around at one another. Nobody spoke. Maddy knew she was being stupid. She shouldn't have come out. She wasn't sure what she was trying to accomplish besides looking like a crazy adult. She felt like one too. "I was just curious what you were talking about. I happened to see you pointing at my house."

The tallest boy's eyes went wide. He looked ready to jump back on his bike and pedal away, but the youngest boy bravely took a small step closer to her and hollered, "They say that someone was murdered in your house. Is it true?"

She tried not to react, but her mouth definitely dropped open. "Murdered?" Maddy shook her head. "Uh, no. I don't think so."

The little boy turned back toward the older ones and puffed out his chest. "See! I told you!"

She watched them as they got back on their bikes and pedaled away with lightning speed without another word or even a quick glance back. Maddy stayed put long after they'd gone. She wasn't sure what to make of the whole thing. Were they just kids being kids on a carefree summer day, using their imaginations, having some fun? Or had someone really been murdered here, in her new house?

She went inside, picked up her coffee mug off the floor, and she retreated back upstairs. She couldn't think about it for too long because it gave her the creeps, but also because she had no way to verify if it was true, or did she? She grabbed up her laptop and Googled the address of the house, unsure of what might come up. Scrolling through a dozen or so pages, the only thing she saw was real estate listings. She laughed at herself as she put the computer back to sleep, feeling stupid for thinking she would find something online that would clear up information she had gathered from a bunch of little boys on her front lawn.

She put her hair up, set to finish the last few sections of wallpaper removal. Scanning the room looking for the putty knife she'd been using previous day to scrape the wallpaper, she came away empty handed. She moved to the bookcase for a closer inspection because that's where she thought she'd put it down last. Not seeing it, she poked around in the waste bin where she'd been chucking the old paper, figuring it may have gotten tossed inside by accident, but it wasn't in there. It also wasn't on the floor, or on the step stool, or on the window seat, and that didn't leave many other places to look in an otherwise empty room.

"What the hell?" she said out loud. "It was here yesterday."

She blew a loose strand of hair from her face that had already managed to escape the hair band in her frenzied search. She was once again annoyed, but she wouldn't be deterred. Instead, she went back downstairs and found the mop bucket and filled it with hot water and threw a sponge in. Then, she found an old spatula in the box with the kitchen stuff and headed back up.

In the middle of climbing the staircase with the water bucket in one hand and a kitchen utensil in the other, her foot caught the edge of a step weirdly and she lost her balance. Attempting to not spill the entire bucket of water sloshing around, she tried to right herself, but her ankle twisted. The water in the bucket flirted with the edge as it teetered in her hand. Maddy had to make a quick choice. She could let the water go in order to regain her balance, or she could keep a hold of it and tumble down the stairs to her death. Either way, the water was going down, so she released the bucket.

Her other foot, the one that had been planted securely, slipped on a few measly drops of water that had already escaped, and in catching herself for a second time, her shin banged hard on the front face of one of the steps. She let out a wail that echoed down the walls, but she did not fall.

She sat down hard on the middle step putting pressure on her shin as she cursed to herself while watching the contents of the bucket cascade all the way down the staircase like a waterfall. It seemed like a sad metaphor for something, though she wasn't sure what. A part of her wanted to cry, so maybe that was it— something about spilled tears. She didn't cry though because that would have only added to the water she now needed to sop up from the newly redone hardwood stairs before she ruined those too. She turned and looked back up at the stair above and ran her hand over the surface of it trying to figure out what had tripped her in the first place, but she felt nothing but smooth, polished wood.

"I don't believe in ghosts," she yelled down the stairwell, as if saying it out loud actually made it true.

As she got up and went back to the kitchen, her mind replayed the event. This could make an interesting plot point in her book. Drying off the water from the steps, she pondered how she might incorporate such a scene. Might the killer push their victim down the staircase because they wanted them gone from the home? There could be something there. Maddy only hoped she lived long enough to be able to write it.

Back in the office after the minor hiccup, she got back to work. The last section was the weird spot that jutted out where the chimney came up from the living room. Removing the top layers of paper on it revealed that this area did not have any of the original black-and-white wallpaper covering it. Instead, it was just white plaster and stood out even more than before like an eyesore. Maddy was disappointed. She highly doubted she would find a place that sold this print of wallpaper. Maybe she could get Tim to remove the plaster altogether so the original brick could be exposed? She added it to Tim's ever-growing chore list.

She pushed on and removed the final section of old paper near the floor.

"Hmm…what's this?" she asked out loud. She bent down and got closer. "Looks like some kind of stain." She scratched at it a bit, but it wasn't going anywhere. It was definitely soaked in well. Small, dark blotches were splattered across the gothic wallpaper. As she grabbed the sponge from the bucket and scrubbed at the stains, her mind wandered back to the kids and the idea that someone had been killed here. Could this be blood? No. She wouldn't let herself believe that. Besides, they were pointing toward the front of the house, at Tim's office. Surely nobody had been murdered in Maddy's sanctuary.

She was clearly losing it. Maybe she was inhaling too much wallpaper paste. Or it could have been the fact that she hadn't spent this much time alone in a very long time. Not that being alone was a bad thing. But if Maddy was being honest with herself, she had sort of forgotten how to be just her and not Maddy and Tim, the couple. They had been together for almost a decade, having met toward the middle of their undergrad programs at Portland State University. And while they hadn't moved in together for a few years after that, they were still almost always together. Granted, they'd been busy doing their own things for much of the years they had taken the leap to move into an apartment together. Tim was pursuing his master's degree in Architecture, while Maddy worked full-time as an administrative assistant for a non-profit to pay rent. Maddy ended up pursuing an online creative writing program so she could continue to work full-time.

It only bothered her in that she didn't feel as though she'd gotten as much out of the online program as she would have liked, but she let it go because it was over and behind them, and now she was ready to focus on what mattered for her future now which was to actually write a book.

She was just recently coming to the hard realization that she always took a backseat. It wasn't Tim's fault, per se. He never pressured her; she was always willing to go along with whatever he asked, because she knew his dreams were important to him. But what about her own needs? What she needed was to stop letting Tim dictate her life. All she wanted was to feel like they were working on an even playing field. That they were equals.

The problem was that Tim didn't ever waiver in things. He just decided something and went after it. Maddy always played the what-if game. What if she hated it here? What if she failed at writing? What if they had kids and it was a disaster? Or worse? What if she didn't always go along with Tim's choices for a change? She needed to find a backbone somewhere. Although, if her backbone was anything like the putty knife that had apparently vanished into thin air, she was doomed.

That afternoon Maddy got a text from her best friend, Ellie, who was studying in England.

—*How's the new place?*—

Maddy responded —*That depends…*—

—*On what?*—

Considering her words for a moment, Maddy responded —*On the fact that I've just spent twenty minutes shopping online for a sage kit*—

Ellie's reply was fast and full of questions. —*Huh? A sage kit? For what?*—

Maddy—*To remove the bad mojo from my new house*—

—*Oh. Wow*—

—*Yeah*—

Chapter Eleven

1912

To my darling sister, Jane,
I write to you with news that is not of death and dying for a change, but of the thing furthest from it. Let me begin first by saying that I visited with our father, and it was most unpleasant in every way possible. I believed myself to be ill in spirit and mind from the journey, but several days later, I was still quite stricken and overcome with a feeling that I could no longer attribute to the ugliness that transpired upon my visit.

Charles's brother sent his wife Elizabeth to call on me in my bed chamber where I lay resting, too ill to do anything for the turmoil within was such. If you recall from my previous correspondence, Elizabeth is the head nurse at the children's orphanage, but also practices midwifery in the community. That is how I gained the knowledge that I am with child.

I cannot tell you the shock and elation this writer experienced upon hearing the declaration. What with all of the excitement of late drawing my attention away from such matters, I hadn't even stopped to consider this prospect. Of course it was to be expected, yet it came as a joyful surprise. You know that I have longed to have a family. I am to be a mother! Imagine that. It is a wonder to me each time I recount it throughout my day and I cannot hold back a grin. Charles is also in good spirits about the news as he has longed for a family as much as I have. Together, we are in awe of our good fortune.

Additionally, I pray, dear sister, that you will be afforded the opportunity to visit when the babe comes. How I would love for you to meet the little one. With much to look forward to in the months ahead, I may not have the time to write quite as often but know that you are always in my heart.

Yours,
Bea

Chapter Twelve

2022

Later that night, Maddy lay on the air mattress in the big, empty house and contemplated getting a dog. It seemed like a more sure-fire thing than burning an herb and wafting it around the air in hopes of smoking out the evil spirits from the place. She'd always had pets growing up but hadn't been able to have one living in apartments that didn't allow pets. A dog would definitely make her feel safer about being here alone, especially if Tim was going to do a lot more traveling for his job. She wondered if he would agree to it.

As far as she remembered, they'd never discussed the topic. Did he even like dogs? The fact that Maddy didn't know was a little startling, but she did know that having a pet would be a good precursor to kids, a warm-up period. If she and Tim survived a puppy, maybe they could handle a tiny human?

She tried to read, but she kept hearing an odd, hollow tapping noise. It didn't seem to be coming from inside the house, so Maddy took that as a good sign. Eventually, she set the book down and got up to look out the window. At first, she saw nothing out there, but once her eyes adjusted, she could make it out. An overgrown branch scraped methodically against the house from the light breeze. She added it to the list of chores, but first she would need to buy some pruning shears because she didn't even need to dig through the boxes to know that they had none. In fact, they had no garden tools at all because they had never lived in a place that had a yard.

She checked the time, wondering if Tim would still be working or if he might be back at his hotel. It was two hours earlier in Portland, so she doubted he'd be settled in for the night, and though she was in, she was definitely not settled. She was tired from the work she'd been doing on the house, and from the lack of decent sleep she'd gotten overall these last few nights.

Unwilling to admit she'd become completely dependent on Tim for her ability to sleep comfortably, she blamed it on the air mattress instead. She held out a while longer, then she called her husband. She told him about the kids on their bikes in front of the house and what the little one said.

"He said someone was murdered in the house?" Tim asked.

"Yes! Do you think it's true?"

"Nah," he said. "They would have had to list that on the property disclosure statement."

"Then why would those kids say that?"

"Sounds like they were trying to spook the youngest boy."

"Maybe," she said, still skeptical. Tim made a decent case, but Maddy wasn't entirely convinced he was right. "Oh, hey, before I forget, did you happen to move the putty knife I was using on the wallpaper?"

"Me? No. Why?"

"It's the weirdest thing. I can't find it anywhere. I swear I set it down on the bookcase, but it's not there anymore. I've searched every inch of this place, twice. It's nowhere. The only logical reason I could come up with was that maybe you had used it before you left for some reason."

"Nope," he said. "It'll turn up. You probably set it down somewhere weird. That's what always happens to me, and then I find the thing a few days later and remember that I actually had left it there."

"Yeah. You're right. It's just that I was sure I set it on the bookcase."

Tim made a spooky, haunting noise. "*The Case of the Missing Putty Knife*." He laughed and then said, "That could be the title of your book."

"Hilarious. Maybe I'll use the putty knife as the murder weapon…"

"Oh, that's good," Tim said. "*Spackled to Death* by Maddy Barton."

She laughed. "Remind me not to let you help me with a real title when I finish the book."

"What? Why not? Those are both amazing titles!" Tim said, playfully.

"Well, a title might be all I end up with at this rate."

"You know you don't have to do all of the house projects in the first week, Mads. I was thinking of this remodel as a long-term project."

"When the furniture comes, it's going to be harder to get stuff done. Besides, you know I hate half-finished projects."

"I said long-term. I didn't say half-finished."

"Mm," was all Maddy could say about that without picking a fight, because Tim wasn't always great at seeing projects through to the end.

"Listen, once I settle into the job, I'll have more time to focus on the projects."

"Okay, fine. But we should shoot for at least having a plan in place for getting some of this stuff done. The list is getting longer by the day."

"Agreed. Anyway, how was your day? What did you do?"

"Besides almost being the next murder victim?"

"Huh?"

"This house hates me. It keeps trying to kill me."

"Explain."

"Oh, I smashed my leg on the stairs and almost fell to my demise."

"Damn. Are you okay?"

"I'll be fine. It's just a bad bruise."

"You don't seriously think the house is out to get you, right?"

"What? No," she said, sarcastically.

Tim sighed. "You aren't cursed, Mads."

"Well…that's debatable at this point. Either way, my luck is total crap."

"Sure. You've had some bad things happen lately. Everybody does now and then."

"They say these things happen in threes, so, by my math, I still have one more major catastrophe to occur. It's like waiting for lightning to strike. I'm just keeping my guard up. That's all."

Tim laughed. "Maybe the thing today on the stairs was it. So, you're probably done now."

"This little bruise? No. I don't think so."

"Okay. Well, that whole rule of threes things is just dumb superstition anyway. Try thinking optimistically for a change."

"For a change?" she asked, surprised. "You think I'm a pessimist?"

"I mean, not all the time, but you've definitely been pretty negative lately."

"That's because my sister died!"

"I know. I know. I just…I want you to be happy, that's all."

"I'm trying," Maddy said. "It's not that easy. I think about it all the time. I miss her so much. She was my big sister, and it's hard to sweep it under the rug and act like it didn't happen."

"I had hoped the move would help a little."

"The move has actually been sort of stressful, don't you think?"

"Well, yeah. But it's done now and as soon as the furniture arrives, we'll be more settled. So, the tide's gonna start to turn."

"Maybe," Maddy said.

"There's that positive attitude," Tim said.

"Sorry."

"I believe that if you think good thoughts, good things will happen."

She suppressed a laugh. "Hey? Do you like dogs?"

"Dogs? Uh, sure."

"Do you want to get one?"

"A dog?"

"Yeah. A big one. Maybe a husky or a German shepherd."

"I didn't know you liked dogs," he said.

"You didn't?"

"No."

"Well, I do. Besides, we have plenty of space and a decent sized yard for a big dog."

"True," he said. "Let me think about it."

"Why? You just said you like them."

"I do. I've just never really considered owning one. I don't know what that even involves."

"You never had a dog growing up?"

"No. Did you?"

"Yeah," she said. "A couple."

"Oh," was all Tim said in reply. He switched the topic to tell Maddy about his day and the subject of getting a dog never came back up by the time they ended the conversation. Maddy let it go for now knowing they both had a lot on their plates at the moment.

She thought about what Tim had said about good things happening if she started projecting a more positive attitude. She wished life were that simple, and maybe she did think that way at one point, but she was older and wiser now and she didn't buy corny sayings like that anymore. Life could be amazing, but it could also be cruel, and that wasn't being pessimistic, it was simply being realistic. She didn't tell her husband this because he wouldn't get it. Nothing terrible ever happened to Tim.

Maddy picked up her book and tried to read it again. It was the second one she'd started since they'd left Portland, and it was the second book she would set aside. Either she'd just not found anything that grabbed her lately, or she was still too distracted since the move to fully engage. Either way, it was so unlike her. She loved reading. She'd been a voracious reader since she could form sentences. And being type A, she almost never just gave up on a book, but here she was, closing another one and setting it aside, and she couldn't help but equate it to failing. Maddy pushed the guilt aside and tried once again to quiet her mind and sleep, but she failed at that too. Her body was sore and beaten up, and mentally she was exhausted. She really wanted to drift off and not think or feel anything for several hours, but she couldn't.

She got up and went to the bathroom and contemplated going downstairs to find something to eat. The box of chocolates her mom had given to her as a going away gift was really calling to her, but as she stood at the top of the dark staircase looking down, she got a chill.

Going down the stairs suddenly hit her as an absolutely horrible idea, which was so stupid. She was being ridiculous. She wasn't afraid of the dark. She was a twenty-nine-year-old woman. Yet, she stayed put, unable to make her legs move. She turned the flashlight on her phone on and shone the beam downward. There was nothing there, obviously. Maybe it wasn't the ghosts that scared her, but the near-fall still lingering in her head, with a tender bruise still evident as proof. Whatever the reason for her sudden spook, she decided chocolate wasn't worth the risk. She would save it and have it first thing in the morning for breakfast instead. Clicking the flashlight off, she turned on her heels and flopped back onto the half-deflated air mattress in utter defeat waiting for morning to come, hoping for it to bring her a new attitude along with it.

Chapter Thirteen

1912

The Women's Auxiliary meetings were something
the ladies of Pine Grove had held weekly going back to
at least a decade before Bea had taken up residence in
the town. Held each Thursday evening in the aptly
named *Our Lady of Hope* church basement, the purpose
of the auxiliary was two-fold. It was meant as a time for
the ladies to gather informally, in a social manner, but
also for them to come together and think of ways to
better the community and help their neighbors in the
spirit of the church, and of course, God.

Beatrice believed in the mission, of course, but she
was also interested in gaining something else from this
group of women who were older, wiser, and indulging
in the most delectable desserts she'd ever laid eyes
upon. What better way was there for a younger,
recently wed woman who had no mother, aunties, elder
sister, or mentor of her own, to acquire the necessary
knowledge needed to bring a new life to the world? Bea
wanted nothing more than to do it correctly. Though
still a bit shaky in her constitution, knowing the reason
for the upset made her able to tolerate it enough to get
up from her bed and attend a meeting. She was not
ready to share news of her condition with these new
friends just yet as it was early days and there were other

women within the group whose time it was to shine, and Beatrice happily let them have the spotlight. She was simply there to absorb all that went on around her like a sponge.

The room thrummed with life, and Beatrice reveled in it. These ladies were not dour or mousy, as one might assume from a church group. No, indeed. They were a good-natured and driven bunch, but in this setting, they took their hats off and loosened their corsets. Things could even get a bit boisterous at times, as the women shared high-spirited gossip and laughs, all the while fixed properly in their seats with their needlepoint in their lap or their tea in hand.

The ages of the women varied greatly. The oldest was Miss Fanning, who was nearly seventy-four. She had been the headmistress at the local schoolhouse for many years. She'd never married or had children of her own and now lived all alone in a modest residence just next to the church near the schoolhouse and the Pine Grove Central Cemetery. Miss Fanning still had all of her wits about her and was esteemed for her vast knowledge, but she was not revered as being the most jovial of the bunch. She could be frank and outspoken at times when she felt strongly about a subject, but she was always fair. Beatrice rather liked Miss Fanning right from the start. Decorum and etiquette and all things proper were generally better tolerated by the majority of the group, but they made an exception for the most senior of members, such as Miss Fanning.

Miss Fanning sat next to Bea stitching a binding along the edge of a quilt she'd no doubt painstakingly sewn in its entirety all by her own aged hands. It had to have taken her months if not years to work, for it was covered in embroidered details finer than Beatrice had ever seen. Her needle and thread weaved in and out of the fabric draped across her lap in a slow but unwavering pace. When she paused on an uptake, she so casually turned to Beatrice and asked, "My dear girl, do you not sometimes find your husband's work to be a bit melancholy?"

Beatrice hadn't anticipated the question, for she had only planned to listen and learn from the group, and while she was not taken aback by it, she was a bit stymied by how to answer it. She decided honesty was the best approach. "In fact," she stated to Miss Fanning and the others around the circle who listened with intrigue, "I believe it to be quite the opposite."

Miss Fanning set her needle down and gave her a distasteful look before Beatrice went on to explain herself. "When I was just a girl of four, I lost my beloved mother and unborn baby sister. My father became disobliging as he refused to accept the situation. Therefore, we did not have a bereavement period. We did nothing of the sort. This alone has haunted my days since—or perhaps my sweet mother and sister are the ones who haunt me, unsettled in their purgatory, as they were never given a proper send-off." Beatrice took a small sip of her tea before she continued. "All I have is a portrait of the two on their deathbed. It's something, but it wasn't enough to honor them, in my humble opinion. That is a long wind for me to say that I feel rather strongly that the job my husband provides, for which he has trained so thoroughly and diligently for many years and received a certification through the new medical association of morticians, is a necessary and noble one. And the services I've attended with him have been so warm and sincere, they have wholly restored me of the thing that left me marred as a child. I'm quite prideful of the work being done at the Westmoreland Funeral Parlor." She looked down and added, "Forgive my boastfulness."

When she gathered the nerve to look back up, nearly all of the ladies in the circle had stopped working their needles and were slack-jawed with attention to her words. Looking around at them, seeing the full audience, she thought it an opportune time to bring up the young boy, Henry Davis, who still weighed so heavily on her mind. Again the ladies gave their full attention, and when she finished speaking of the terrible event a few dabbed at the corners of their eyes with their silk handkerchiefs.

"So tragic," Miss Fanning said. "I knew the young lad from earlier school days. He was a good boy, smart as a whip, too."

"I knew his mother," said Mrs. Engebretson. "She was a dear friend. She would be saddened to know her boy wasn't sent off with dignity."

The other women in the circle nodded or verbalized their agreement of the matter.

"Perhaps," Mrs. Goodwin said, "we could start up a collection plate, as is done in the church service, only during the funeral proceedings?"

"Oh, that's a wonderful idea," another added.

Beatrice thought on it before saying, "I do believe it may work if we could get enough people to attend."

"Most in the town were quite fond of Mr. Davis. He was a generous merchant," Miss Fanning said. "And with your skilled hand with words, Mrs. Westmoreland, I do believe if you wrote up one of your most elegant announcements for the gazette, I imagine the town would show in spades and be willing to give a few loose coins to the collection plate."

Yes. Indeed. This just may work. How had she not come up with this course of action on her own? She would use her writing to bring people together. She thanked the ladies profusely for the marvelous suggestion. All seemed pleased to be included in the plan.

And so it came to be. Beatrice continued to gather more information about the family in the way she always had—by listening to the people of the community, friends and family, open up about the Davis family when asked. The family was very well respected in Pine Grove, it turned out. So, the next night, Beatrice sat down and wrote up another death announcement, her first for a child, but sadly, not her last.

She was of yet a bit leery to discuss the whole thing with her husband, so before she did, she decided it best to compose the announcement and present it to him for his judgment. Like before, she sat with her writing tool in hand while all of the various bits she'd collected about the family circled around in her head. There was some pressure to get this one just right, as it would dictate not only whether Charles would allow a service to be held for young Henry, but also if the announcement itself might propel the townsfolk to attend and contribute to the cost of the services rendered. The idea of collecting contributions was so new, and she wasn't confident that it would go over as well as the ladies thought it might. So much was at stake with just her words alone that Beatrice's hand shook as she began to put pressure down upon the parchment.

****

Davis, Henry of Elmwood, Minnesota (formerly Pine Grove). Oct. 12, 1900; died June 02, 1912. Aged 12 y. 8m. 2 d.

Young Henry only intended to learn a trade when he sought employment with the W&W Lumber Company of Stillwater, yet instead of felling trees, what befell was a ghastly accident that took the dear boy to be once again reunited with his parents and God. He was a bright child with exceptional marks in school. He was strong and willful with a full future in front of him. He only wished to contribute to the wellbeing of his younger siblings who he now leaves behind: Margot and Emery.

The town will undoubtedly recall the Davis family as this writer was told they were kind-hearted, gentle, hardworking members of our community. They would want nothing more to see their boy brought home to rest in a civilized manner.

Please join us at the Westmoreland Funeral Parlor for some parting words, a prayer, and a proper burial for young Henry on June the Six at Twelve Pine Street. A small donation will be accepted from those in attendance for the purposes aforementioned, parted between the funeral home and the remaining Davis children.

****

The next morning, Beatrice slid the parchment toward Charles as they feasted on their mid-day meal. She likely should have been hesitant to do so, but fear did not reside within her, only a conviction that what she was doing was the right thing, and she felt that her husband, being sensible, would see things the same way as she did. She hoped for it, for she did not want to go into any further detail explaining to Charles how this spirited boy may affect them if he chose not to lay him to rest properly.

"What's this?" Charles asked, holding the paper out in front of his specs.

"Dearest, I know you were not so inclined to do further business with my father with regards to the young boy, but I spoke with the women of the auxiliary and they persuaded me that funding for Henry would be no problem to come by; that the town would generously donate to the funeral service and contribute to his remaining siblings by means of a collection plate set out here in the parlor if we were to decide to host his parting service."

"A collection plate? At a funeral?"

"The ladies assured me this would bring in adequate payment, and if it does not, they would be willing to take up the remaining monies by holding a charity event."

Charles read the death announcement before him and thought upon the idea for a goodly amount of time before finally speaking. "And this shall make you happy? To lay this boy to rest?"

"It shall, very much indeed."

"A viewing will not be possible given the conditions and the lack of procedure put upon the body at this point. Would the town accept a closed casket, do you believe?"

"I believe they would. Seeing a lifeless child is not for the weak hearted so a closed casket might be best."

Charles nodded. "Then I will arrange for it if it's

what you want." He folded the parchment and placed it in his stack of paperwork. He opened his ledger up and went back to his work.

Beatrice got up and went about her tasks as well, but now she did them with ease for the weight she'd been carrying around with her, dark and burdensome, all at once lifted from her shoulders as if she'd just removed a thick and heavy shawl. She breathed in air that seemed to offer new and clearer possibilities.

Her husband's actions pleased her beyond measure, though she realized he was perhaps being so agreeable because he did not want to upset her in her state, and that was perfectly wonderful for Beatrice for she did not want that either. And as she carried on with her day, she no longer felt the presence of evil being held just at bay, and what a satisfying thing that was, for now she was convinced that with this problem resolved and done, all would go swimmingly from this point forward.

Chapter Fourteen

2022

Maddy realized Tim was right about one thing. She didn't need to renovate the whole house in a week. It was time to reward herself by putting some ideas she had for her book onto the page finally. The next morning she packed up her laptop and headed over to The Pine Cone Café. Getting out of the house was exactly what she needed, she realized the second she started walking. The sun and fresh air rejuvenated her, and when she arrived, she was excited by the possibilities of writing something new.

The café was relatively empty except for a group of four old ladies who sat chit-chatting at a table in the middle of the room, and one middle-aged man in a suit on his laptop near the back of the café. This was great. There would be very few things to distract Maddy here.

A chipper-looking, middle-aged woman who kind of reminded her of her own mom was behind the counter today. She wore a plum-colored blouse with slacks and had a sweet, roundish Mom-face. Maddy ordered a coffee then found a seat near the front window just as she had imagined when she and Tim visited there the first time. It was sunny and quiet. Perfect. She turned her computer on and did a little internet surfing, then she responded to a few emails.

Her coffee was half gone when she finally got around to opening up her Word document. She took a deep breath and stared at the blinking cursor and the big empty box on the screen for a few minutes. She just needed to decide on her plot. She had a bunch of ideas swirling around, but she wasn't sure where to start. She typed a few random opening sentences, but they sounded stupid, so she deleted them.

As she sipped her coffee, she tried to let her mind free fall, but she suddenly had nothing, not a single idea. Okay. Fine. She didn't need to write by the seat of her pants. Maybe she should start with an outline. She jotted a few plot points down that she'd thought of throughout her week, but nothing really connected together or had any frame of reference.

She looked up from the screen trying to generate some ideas. Frankie, the guy who had been working the counter the last time they were there, was wiping down a table next to her.

"Hey, you're the newbie, right?"

"Hi. Yeah. I'm Maddy."

"Where'd you say you were from again?"

"Uh, Portland. Oregon."

"Right on," he said. "I'm a fairly recent transplant myself."

"Oh, yeah? Where from?"

"New York."

"Oh, wow. What brought you here?"

"A girl." He laughed. "Didn't work out, but this place is a lot cheaper than the big apple…" He stopped wiping and stood up straight. "You aren't a writer, by chance?"

"Oh, uh. Yeah. I mean…sort of…aspiring. How'd

you know?"

"I recognized the expression of anguish on your face," he said with a laugh.

"Last year I finished up my master's in creative writing, so…"

He nodded. "So, the next logical step is to write something. I get it. I'm a writer, too. I worked for a small literary press in NYC. So when I'm not cleaning tables, I'm usually sitting at one doing exactly what you're doing."

"Oh, yeah? What do you write?"

"I mostly write short stories, flash fiction, that type of thing. Haven't worked up to the big ole, scary novel yet. Maybe someday. You?"

She nodded coyly. "I'm attempting a big, scary novel, actually."

"Oh, nice! What genre?"

"I'm just getting started, but…it's a mystery."

"Very cool! What do you have for a plot so far?"

"Not much. Just something taking place in the turn-of-the-century in a big Victorian house."

"Sounds good. Who's your main character?"

"A woman named Hattie Hatterby. She's a hatter from the early 1900s."

He nodded but didn't say anything. Maddy's cheeks flushed, because as soon as she'd said the words out loud to someone she barely knew, she could tell they sounded really, really dumb. "It's stupid. I don't think I'll use it. I'm still just brainstorming."

"It's not stupid at all. Though I think they called them milliners," he said. "And maybe the name is a bit too…satirical? Unless you're writing satire. Are you?"

"No. It's supposed to be a historical murder

mystery."

"Ah." Frankie went back to wiping down the next table.

Maddy lowered her head down onto her arms, but she refused to give up this easily. She resurfaced and thought for a second. "What if her name is Mrs. Somebody the fourth or something along those lines. Does that sound a bit more realistic or is the fourth a stretch? Maybe the third would be better? Like Mrs. James Thereby the third?"

"You could do the fourth," he said. "I'm actually a fifth, believe it or not."

"Really?"

"Yeah. My family is extremely rooted in their ways, for better or worse." He gave an annoyed laugh and then added, "Anyway, it works...and I like it better than the first one."

"Thanks." She sighed. "This is so much harder than I thought it would be."

"It is definitely hard, but you can do it. Getting started is the worst part, I think. Just push through it."

She smiled at him. "I'll try."

"I'd love to read it when you're further along...I mean, if you want a second set of eyes on it."

"Yeah? That would be great."

"Anyway, I'll let you get back to it."

Shortly thereafter, Maddy gave up and walked home. On her walk, she thought about how Frankie had used the same phrase he'd said the last time she talked to him. For better or worse. She had no idea why it stuck out, but it seemed sort of odd, like he was trying to warn her about something. Maybe it was her pessimism kicking in again. She was likely reading into it. Maybe Frankie simply had a clutch phrase that he spoke when he was nervous. She knew people who did that. It was probably nothing.

Just before she arrived at Twelve Pine Street, she passed by the house next to hers, the one that looked vacant. As she did, something caught her eye. The heavy curtains hanging over the front windows ruffled. Or did they? Maddy slowed her stride. Was she seeing things? She swore she saw the curtains swaying. Was someone in there? Were they watching her?

Picking up her steps, she was almost to her porch when she looked again and saw the curtains part more fully this time. She stopped just as a sleek, black cat appeared from behind them, almost like a magician parting a curtain at a Las Vegas show. The cat gave her a coy look before curling up into a ball on the window ledge, the whole time keeping his green eyes affixed on Maddy as if he had something to tell her.

She shivered and raced up her steps. After she unlocked the front door, but before going inside, Maddy took another look over in the direction of the cat who had closed his eyes and was now sleeping peacefully in the sunny window bay. Did someone live there after all? Or was the house just full of feral cats? Either way, Maddy was sufficiently creeped out.

Inside, she tried to forget about the cat and her failed attempt at writing. In order to do that, she decided it was best to stay busy. It was time to tackle the bookcase. If she couldn't write books, she would at least have a place to store the ones other people wrote. She wanted to get the old, chipped paint scraped and sanded away, so she could have the mess all cleaned up before her office furniture arrived.

She located her tools, put on a mask, and started to have at it. The paint was cracked and peeling, so she sincerely hoped it would come away easily, but she wasn't going to hold her breath knowing how uncooperative the house had been already.

With no putty knife, she opted to use a large flat-head screwdriver, though it would make the work slower going as she had to be a bit more delicate with her touch if she wanted to keep from gouging the wood too much. Thankfully, the chipped paint had flaked right off with minimal effort on her part, and after an hour or so, she was able to move on to the sanding portion of the project. A lot of the original wood was now visible, and it was glorious. Finally, something was going in her favor. She started to feel, dare she say, positive. Were things finally turning around for her?

She climbed the step ladder to reach the top shelf, the last section. Since her mood was better, she decided to put some music on. Twisting slightly to pull her phone out of her back pocket while standing on the top of the rickety step stool was maybe too much for the old ladder because it made a loud, cautionary cracking noise just before the rung below the one Maddy stood on gave way. She froze with her phone in hand, still curled up like a pretzel. If she slowly undid herself and stepped down, maybe she could...nope. The step she was standing on collapsed and as Maddy fell with it, she dropped her phone. It reached the floor first, so instead of both feet landing on the ground, Maddy's right foot found the phone.

Her body slid out from under her and Maddy hit with a thud, flat on her back. Stunned, she lay there for a second in utter resigned silence. Her ego was bruised, but she was okay otherwise. The same could not be said for her phone. The screen was shattered, and it wouldn't turn on.

"Come on!" she yelled.

That was it. The final straw. She was convinced now more than ever that the house was evil. She dropped her phone to her side and lay there with her eyes closed, breathing deeply to keep from sobbing. When she regained her composure, she opened her eyes. From this new vantage point on the floor looking upward toward the ceiling, or in this case, the bookshelf above her, she saw something black poking out from the bottom of the middle shelf, something wedged between it and the wall. Maddy knew exactly what the something was too. She recognized the old plastic handle with the paint drips. Her missing putty knife.

She stood up and went over to it. She knew she'd set it down on the shelf before she and Tim had left to go have dinner the other night. How it had managed to fall behind the shelf was a mystery, but at least it hadn't been ghosts after all. Maybe it was the breeze from the box fan? She doubted it could have been so strong as to blow a metal object, but who could be sure? It didn't matter. The case of the missing putty knife was now solved. Much to her dismay, Tim had been more or less right. The tool was pretty much where she'd left it.

Now she just needed to figure out how to get it out because as she yanked on it, she found it to be wedged in tight. She tried to grab a hold of the bit sticking, but it was really jammed in there, and the rounded edge of the plastic handle made it hard to grasp. She grabbed the flathead screwdriver nearby and attempted to push it from the side, but that didn't work either. And just as she was about to see if she could pry the shelf off by lifting from the bottom, her hand felt something that didn't belong—something hard and metal, almost like a small lever. Feeling around, pushing and wiggling it with her fingers trying to identify it, something popped, and the lever released. Like a springboard, a drawer just below the shelf shot open toward Maddy's face. She let out a small yelp. She had luckily managed to avoid being hit by it.

"Aha, you missed me!" she yelled like a small toddler taunting her sibling during a fight, only in this case, she was talking to a house.

"What's this?" she asked. But it was a dumb question because it was was obvious. It was a hidden drawer built into the wall that sat between the shelves. She had likely freed it while sanding away the old paint, but she wouldn't have known it was there without releasing the lever. It was that camouflaged. The more interesting question was what was inside of it?

Maddy felt inside and came away with a stack of paper that was thin and fragile and tied together with a delicate silky ribbon. It appeared to have once been red, but the color had faded and was now a shade of light rose. She very carefully undid the ribbon and separated the first piece of paper from the bundle. It was folded in thirds. Slowly, she opened it and read what appeared to be a letter addressed to a woman named Jane, written by someone named Beatrice.

Letters? As she held the bundle in hr hands, a tingle shot through her entire body. This was like a scene from a movie. She wasn't sure yet if this discovery was good or bad, but it felt significant in some way, as if this was the climax of the story. And, if she was the main character, the question was, was she in a love story or a horror film. There was only one way to find out. She took the letters over to the window seat, sat down, and got as comfortable as she could before she started to read.

Chapter Fifteen

1912

Dearest Sister,
The proceedings for the young boy, Henry, I wrote about in my last letter went off so spectacularly, there was not a need to hold any further charity events to cover the expenses of a well-crafted casket, a beautiful service, and even a modest headstone with engraving, with enough left to take care of his younger siblings. My heart was so full. I do believe even Charles was surprised by the outcome, as were Francis and Elizabeth. I had invited them personally as I hope to get closer to them if we are to all be one big family now. I do believe that Elizabeth was wonderfully inspired by the rally of the women's auxiliary. I asked her to join us at the next meeting, but she seemed mildly reluctant to do so. I will have to inquire again at another point.

The one person who was not utterly charmed by the outpouring was our dearest father. He may not have been aware of the affair if not for my announcement of the event in the gazette. Charles relayed to me that he had harsh words for him in a meeting he called him to, and in fact informed him he will no longer be supplying wood to Westmoreland Funeral Parlor or have anything else to do with him or me.

I do not think I will ever come to understand

Father's ways, as I was certain my actions were pure and done in good conscience. Charles explained that it's all transactional for Father, that my words shed a harsh light on his company and will cost him. What say you, dear Jane? Was I wrong? I only wanted to help this poor family. Now it seems I've made a bigger mess. Charles tried to console me, but it seems he is also quite affected by Father's decision, as he was giving Charles a good cost on the supply of the coffin wood. So he is now fretting for the future of the business. All because of me! I had so hoped that once the proceedings were complete and the child was laid to rest, so too would be my feelings of discontent, but it is not the case.

You must know how dreadful I feel. If only you could advise me, dear sister. It has been such a long time since I've last heard from you, Jane. I do so wish you'll communicate soon. I think of you often, and hope this letter finds you in good health and mind.

I remain your devoted sister,
Bea

Chapter Sixteen

2022

After Maddy finally came up for air, she'd read through a handful of the letters. She wanted to keep going, but she also wanted to savor them like a good book. She wondered if they were real, though judging from the condition of them, they certainly seemed to be authentic. So far Maddy had gathered that the writer of the letters, Beatrice, was the wife of a mortician. That in itself was pretty damn interesting! Had a mortician and his wife lived in their home? Or rather, did she and Tim live in theirs? Holy cow! No wonder the house was haunted.

She immediately thought to call her mom or her best friend to tell them about her amazing find, because both of them would be as fascinated with the whole thing as Maddy, but her phone still wouldn't turn on. That was more than a little alarming. Now she was in a haunted house alone without means to communicate to the outside world. Wait. That wasn't completely true. She still had her laptop. She grabbed it and sent an email to Tim and one to her mom to let them know what happened, then she placed an order for a new phone to be delivered.

Since she no longer had a workable ladder to finish the work on the bookshelf, and with her computer perched on her lap, Maddy decided to try to get some more words down on the page. Feeling inspired, likely by the old letters, she didn't want anything to stall her motivation. The only problem was that she'd been seated on the hard bench for the better of an hour reading the letters. Without a cushion, her butt was completely asleep.

She got up in search of a good spot to do some writing in a giant house with no chairs. She started out on the floor in the parlor with her back against the wall and her laptop on her…well…lap, but the hardwood was…well…hard, and the room was stuffy and intolerable from the sunlight streaming in through the big windows which lacked curtains.

Relocating to the air mattress, she found it way too squishy to balance her computer and her mug of tea while trying to concentrate on writing. She got up and went back to the window seat feeling a little like Goldilocks, except this one wasn't just right either. It was the best option, but still not comfortable. After several more minutes of attempting to begin a story, she typed a few words then deleted them, tried a few more, and backspaced them away too. She shifted in her seat, determined to not fail at this. That made her think of her sister, who had never failed at anything she tried, except the last thing she did—the thing that actually killed her. At least writing a murder mystery would not kill Maddy, though not writing it would definitely break her spirit.

She wasn't ready to give up, because if she'd learned anything from her writing program was that writing wasn't magic, much to most people's disbelief. It was hard work, determination, and perseverance.

There were rules and formulas. It wasn't all fun and games, even if that was the joke Tim liked to make, which Maddy felt was at her expense. She just needed a new game plan. While the letters were a strong motivation, there was still a lot of background research she needed to do. She'd decided to write a murder mystery, but when was the last time she'd read one? That's when she remembered there was a public library in the town center.

Maddy packed up her bag and headed out, walking back to town. Outside, on Pine Street, the wind was picking up and clouds quickly filled in filtering out the sun. She was used to overcast days, but this wasn't the same as a typical Pacific Northwest day. This looked like a Midwestern thunderstorm was rolling in, but Maddy figured she could get in and out of the library and be on her way back home before that happened. She briefly wondered if she'd remembered to close the window in her office, but again, she would have time to do that after grabbing a book or two.

The Pine Grove Public Library was so small Maddy laughed out loud when she stepped inside. The town was not large, but the size of this library seemed comical even in comparison. The space wasn't even as large as the downstairs of her new home. Granted, the house was ridiculously big. Still, this was more like entering someone's personal den with their private book collection on display, not a public library. Did nobody in Pine Grove read? That didn't bode well for her future career as an author.

A woman at the front counter greeted her. She was not all that much older than Maddy, if she had to guess. Not the stereotypical looking librarian either. She had a cool, edgy vibe. Again, Maddy saw this a lot in Portland, but she really hadn't expected to encounter many hipsters in the small town of Pine Grove. A librarian in a tiny one room library with purple hair and a septum piercing was definitely unexpected. She wore jeans and a black T-shirt with the name of a band that Maddy didn't recognize. Not that she was super cool or anything, but she did loosely follow some current indie music. It was sort of shocking, in a good way. Maybe this town wasn't as stuffy and old as she kept thinking it was. She considered asking the woman about the band, but she didn't want to sound dumb and naïve, so she didn't.

"Hi, there," the woman said when she finished typing something into her computer and looked up at her. "Welcome. What can I help you with today?"

"I'm a new resident, and I was hoping to check out some books, so I guess I need a library card."

"Excellent. Welcome. So, we don't actually use library cards here."

"No?" Oh, God. They still used those little paper cards tucked into the books, didn't they? Like in elementary school? Where you just signed your name to it and they crossed it off when you returned it. The honor system. Wow. Okay, maybe it was as old-timey as Maddy was thinking.

"Nope. I'll just need your email address and I can give you one of these bad boys." She held up a circular, plastic disc about as big as a nickel. "When you leave, it will track the books you've taken with you. Same with when you return them. We'll email you to remind you when they're due."

"Oh," Maddy said. "That's actually super high-tech. We didn't even have that in Portland."

The librarian laughed. After Maddy gave her her email address, the woman said, "By the way, my name is Kirsten. You're from Portland? Oregon?"

"Yep."

"I love it there."

"Me, too," Maddy said, longingly. "But it's nice here, too."

Kirsten smiled. "Okay. Here's your chip. We actually call it a token because it sounds a little less scary to people. They don't like the idea that I may be watching them when they leave here." She laughed again. "I tell people to think of it as a library card they don't need to show me. That usually helps. Anyway, just keep it in your bag or your wallet or wherever. Just remember to bring it with you when you come back."

"Cool," Maddy said, taking the library token. "Thanks. Um, where can I find your mystery section?"

"Ah, mysteries. Those are housed on the negative thirteenth floor, so just head to the back and take the elevator down."

Maddy's jaw fell open. "Are you serious?"

"No," Kirsten said, trying to stifle her laugh. "It's just a dumb joke. Sorry. The mysteries are in rows three and four over there," she said, pointing to a case not more than six feet from where Maddy was standing.

"Oh. Wow. You totally got me."

"Sorry. I couldn't resist. Anyway, let me know if you don't find what you're looking for. I can look anything up for you and have it transferred from a nearby library in Washington County that's a little larger than this one...the Stillwater Library has practically everything you might want. Have you been to Stillwater yet?"

She shook her head. "Stillwater? No."

"You should definitely check it out. It's only about fifteen minutes or so to the east of here. It's such a cute little town. A lot of it was built in the early-to-mid 1800s and it's right on the St. Croix River. Some fun touristy things to do and see there, or if you like architecture, they have a ton of old buildings and houses. There's a trolley tour you can take that'll give you the history of the town. It's considered the birthplace of Minnesota because it held the first county seat. Sorry. I'm rambling. I get a little too into history sometimes. Anyway…"

"No. That's great. My husband is actually an architect, which is why we moved here—for his job, so he'll be very interested in checking it out. Thanks."

"No problem. Oh! And one last thing before I let you head to the thirteenth floor…ha-ha…I actually host a book club here on the second Friday of every month. We read widely. I'm not sure if you like other books besides mysteries, but this month we're actually tackling something from the Mistress of Mystery." She held up a book to show Maddy the cover and title. It was a classic. Maddy had always wanted to read it but hadn't gotten around to it yet.

"Oh. Yes. I'm definitely interested." Maddy took the book. "This is perfect."

"Great! This Friday then. I hope that's enough time for you to read it, but even if it's not, please still join us. We won't mind if you don't finish the book. And you can give input on which book we read next. Anyway, I hope I don't sound desperate, but we'd love to have you. It's really a great group. It starts at seven."

"This is cool. Thanks very much for all of your help, Kirsten."

"Yeah, great to meet you, uh…sorry, what's your name?"

"Oh, it's Maddy Barton."

Kirsten smiled. "Okay, Maddy Barton. Hopefully, I'll see you at the book club meeting."

"You will!"

As Maddy perused the small mystery section she couldn't believe how stupid she must have come across to the cool librarian. She had no idea why she'd blurted out her full name except that she wasn't sure if she needed that info for the coin thingy too. It had been so long since she'd had to try making new friends, it was like she'd forgotten how.

After pulling out several books and reading the back blurbs, she finally settled on a few, and then waited until Kirsten walked away from the desk to leave so she didn't have to make a fool of herself again by more awkward conversation. She didn't think she could bear it and luckily with the high-tech library coin, she didn't actually need to. As she exited, she wondered when this move would start getting easier. Instead of feeling adjusted and settled, she felt like she was living someone else's life.

Chapter Seventeen

1912

Beatrice spent all of her time now attempting to keep her mind and body busy as she awaited the arrival of her first-born child, but she also knew to rest more often. As she sat taking tea in the garden one late afternoon, she wanted nothing more than for the calendar to advance quickly so she could nestle her first born babe in her arms. She wondered what the child would look like. Would it resemble her late mother, or would it be a boy taking on characteristics of her husband? Would it have curly hair like her own or fine like that of Charles? She imagined herself rocking the little one to sleep as it cooed softly, smelling sweetly as babies did. If only she could sing like her sister Jane, who had the voice of an angel. No matter, she would instead walk with the little one and bounce it gently in her arms. She could not wait.

As it stood, time crawled to a halt. In part because Charles was out of sorts, full of new worries. Money was suddenly tight; and his mind could not focus on anything but, so he worked his ledger under the assumption that by moving or changing the written numbers, it would solve their financial quandary. Shortly after her tea, Bea found him late that afternoon in his study with his head buried deep into his books doing just that. Concerned for his mental wherewithal, she asked him to come for a stroll down Pine Street before the evening meal to look in on the mercantile for a few items needed for the nursery.

"How will we afford them?" he asked her.

"We do not need to purchase them at once. I just wish for a little fresh air, a nice stroll to town would perhaps be good for us both."

"You go on. I have more to work out here."

"I would love the company," she begged.

"Good company I would not make, I'm afraid."

She nodded in defeat and headed out onto the cobblestone path that led to the shops alone. Dr. Boyle's home looked dark and unlived as she passed by, so Bea was given a good start when the old recluse offered a greeting from his porch as the sun began to dip lower.

"Fine day, is it not?" he asked from his chair. He wore his bed clothes and slippers. His hair was tussled, and he held the gazette in front of him, reading by the day's fading light.

"Tis, indeed," she replied, though she was not in the highest spirits.

Lowering the parchment before him, he said, "Everything well? I see a heavy burden on your face. Might I lend an ear?"

She considered momentarily speaking with the doctor about her husband's current state of mind. He would likely have some guidance to offer, having cared for people in the psychiatric facility for many years, but she decided not to inflict him with such melodrama, for surely that was all it was. "I appreciate the offer, Doctor," she replied. "The only burden I carry is a child." She gave a nervous laugh.

"Oh, well…I'm afraid my expertise is null in that department. In such a case, I can only offer my congratulations."

"I accept. Good evening to you," she said as she continued on her way and left him to his reading.

As the sun plunged over the horizon, the heat of the day burned off, making for a pleasant walk. The air smelled rich with hints of mid-summer grasses and wild blooms. With the fair weather, Beatrice crossed paths with many others out enjoying the evening. Some rode bicycles with large baskets transporting things from the shops. Women carried parasols to block what remained of the sun from their fair skin, while small children ran amuck, whooping with joy, tossing sticks and balls or other such toys. Their high squeals and unfettered laughter delighted her heart. She smiled and greeted a few acquaintances as she journeyed along the short route. A few automobiles puttered along the cobbled path, honking their horns in warning of their approach, as the pedestrians parted the sea and ogled at the newness of the machines.

The walk did wonders for Beatrice's spirit, though the lingering guilt of what had occurred with her father and consequences of his awful bitterness her poor husband was now stuck dealing with remained with her. Her father was a man of substantial wealth. As part of her family, he should be someone they could turn to when in a financial crisis; he should not be the person who put them in one. Charles's parents were no longer alive. They had perished in a fire in their home in the middle of the night when the boys were both in their late teens. Francis had saved Charles's life by carrying him out of the blaze. They'd lost everything, and could not afford a burial for their parents, so they dug two graves on the meager homestead, and they marked them with stones. It was this that had prompted Charles to set off and work hard to be able to attend mortuary school in Ohio. Beatrice had no idea what type of people his parents had been for Charles did not speak much of them, but she had no doubt they had been better people than her own father, leaving her with twisted emotions on the unfairness that good people were gone while bad ones carried on.

When she arrived in the town proper, Beatrice peered through the glass in several shops before going into the mercantile. She perused the cribs of varying cost and material. Many were made of iron, some had wheels, some had intricate designs carved into the wood frames. A beautiful walnut crib caught her eye, but she dare not dream of such a lavish purchase. It was more practical, she decided all at once, to ask Francis about making something simple out of pine. It did not crush her spirits. All she was concerned about was the child itself. She would give it so much love and care, it would not want for material possessions.

****

Dear Jane,

Because of the man I am not proud to call father, Charles had been obliged to sign a new contract, not for raw materials as he'd hoped, but with a new coffin maker entirely. Up until this time, his brother had been constructing the boxes themselves, but there is more interest these days for polished pieces of more elaborate and decorative coffins. These changes are bringing considerably rising costs to the company as a whole. All of this has caused Charles the loss of much hair on his already thinning head, not to mention his disposition has gotten even more jittery than usual.

He doesn't blame me, though I cannot help but feel terribly upset by the situation as a whole. He says it has more to do with him not having the notion as a new businessman to realize the expenses involved in keeping up such a large home. The cost of goods and services are more than he'd planned for when he began the venture. My attempts to assure him that we will not fall into despair have been failed ones. He has asked the hired servant to take her leave and for me to forgo my role as writer and to take up new duties in the kitchen in the meantime. I had only managed to get by putting food on the table for Father, though as you know, he required very few meals to be provided on the regular. German food is far simpler to prepare in some ways than that of Scandinavian or American varieties that Charles is accustomed to, I've come to find. I am up for the task, though I find myself getting more easily tired as the babe inside grows. Nonetheless, we are making do and splendidly at that. I must have faith that we will find a way out of all of this before the child arrives.

Again, I do not know why I bother you with some domestic concerns. You are more likely to be dancing in ballrooms and attending fine galas during your leisure time. I'm afraid in my own haze, I have lost track of your current route, but surely if you do get any time away, a visit would make this writer ever so gleeful.

With love and admiration,
Bea

Chapter Eighteen

2022

When Maddy stepped out of the library with a pile of books in her hands, it was black as night. She took all of two steps down the sidewalk toward home before thunder boomed out and the sky opened up producing torrential rain. She quickly tucked the books into her bag and tried her best to protect it as she sprinted the few blocks home so the books didn't get ruined.

Many of the tall trees lining the boulevard helped shelter her from the rain, but she still managed to get thoroughly soaked by the time she reached the front porch. Standing under the mostly dry awning, she dug around in her right pants' pocket in search of her front door key. She didn't have a key ring for it yet, so she'd simply been sticking it into her pocket so she didn't lose it. Except now, the only thing her hand found inside the pocket was a few loose coins and her newly acquired library token.

She set the stack of library books on the porch and used both hands to dig around in her bag, thinking maybe she'd absentmindedly dropped the loose key into the bottom of it, which she realized now to be a mistake. But as she felt around, weeding through the random items, she came up empty-handed. Growing more frantic, she tried looking inside the two small, inner purse pockets, hoping the key had slid into one of them, but no luck there either.

Maddy sat down on the top step, still sheltered from the rain for the most part, and she began to pull stuff out of the bag one by one. When the bag was emptied out and there was no key anywhere, she shook it upside down. She didn't understand. It had to be in there somewhere because she'd obviously used the key to lock the door when she left. She stood back up and frantically checked her pants' pockets again. Nothing but some lint emerged.

She went to the door and turned the knob to see if the door was even locked. It was. Maybe the back door was unlocked. She didn't think that it would be given that she hadn't used that door at all since Tim left, and she had been checking the locks every night before she went to bed. Regardless, she walked around and double-checked anyway. Just as she suspected, the back door was locked. Now what?

Walking back to the dry porch, she pulled her cracked, dead phone out of her bag and prayed it would turn on so she could call Tim. He wouldn't be able to help all the way from the west coast, but he might have some ideas for how she might get in that she hadn't thought of herself. She pushed the power button down hard on the phone and held her breath. Nothing happened. She wanted to throw the cracked phone through the front window, but she didn't. She did, however, glance at the cracked window wondering how hard it might be to bust through it, though once she got inside, she'd have a gaping hole and if she thought she was having trouble sleeping now, she would definitely not sleep with a wide-open window. Not to mention, given how things were going, she could just picture herself cutting her leg or arm off in the process of crawling through the broken glass to get in.

It was windy, and she was soggy, hungry, and if she was being honest with herself, she was also scared. She slumped down below the front parlor windows. "You're probably happy about this, aren't you?" she said to the house, spitefully.

At least she was sheltered from the rain for the most part. All she could do now was wait until it let up. Then she would walk back to town and see if she could use a phone somewhere to contact a locksmith. Someone at the café or even Kirsten at the library would be willing to help. She felt mildly better now that she had a plan.

She looked down at the stack of books beside her. She may not have a phone to look at, but she did have something to read while she waited. She cracked open one of the books, but it didn't hold her attention, so she closed it and started the next one. Again, she quickly lost interest. She was about to give up, but she picked up the book club selection Kirsten had given her and decided to see what all the fuss was about. She was embarrassed to admit she'd never read anything by this author. If she was going to be a good mystery writer, she'd probably better read a book written by the best mystery writer of all time.

Before she knew it, she was sucked in. She'd been reading so intently, she almost didn't notice an old man was standing on the porch next door at the house she thought was abandoned. He leaned over the rail and began to shake out a small rug. Dressed in shorts and a flannel shirt, he wore a pair of socks with his slippers.

Maddy jumped up to face him. "Hey there," she said. "I'm your new neighbor, it seems. My husband and I just bought this place and I've already somehow managed to lock myself out. You wouldn't happen to have any thoughts on what I should do?" She smiled awkwardly at the old man.

"Have you changed the locks?" he asked, somewhat gruffly.

"Changed the locks?"

"Since you moved in? Have you had them changed, or are they the same ones that were there when you moved in?"

"Um, they're the same ones."

He nodded. "Then I've got a spare key."

Excitedly, she said, "You do?"

"Yeah. Come on over and I'll see if I can scrounge it up for you."

Maddy hesitated for a second because this seemed like a good way to be found under the strange neighbor's basement stairs, rolled up in a newly shaken out rug with no signs of life. That would surely constitute the third bout of bad luck she'd been waiting for, especially since she had no phone, and therefore no way to call for help if things went downhill once inside. She glanced at the old man with socks and slippers on again. She decided to risk it. He was a pretty old dude and also looked fairly harmless. He wasn't entirely out of shape, but she thought she could probably take him out if she really had to.

She followed him into his house. It smelled like pickles but was otherwise normal. Framed pictures that appeared to be a family—hopefully his own family—hung on the wall so she felt better about her decision.

He took her through the living room and into the kitchen where he placed his rug back down on the floor near the sink. Maddy noted a ham and butter sandwich on white bread sitting on the table with an open paperback lying beside it. A broken pickle jar sat in the sink. He must have dropped it on the rug, which was why he was shaking it out just now.

He turned toward her and said in a scolding voice, "Now, first things first, you really shouldn't make a habit of going into a complete stranger's home alone unprotected."

Maddy tensed up. "No. I know, but I—"

He turned his back toward her before she finished speaking and he began to dig around in one of his kitchen drawers. "I have daughters not much older than you," he said, as things clanged around. "They'd probably do the same thing as you, even though I tried to drill this stuff into them a million times."

She saw him shake his head as he continued to grumble, shoved the drawer closed, opened another one, and fished around in it for a while before repeating the process with another drawer.

"My dad taught me the same thing. And you're right. I just—"

"I'm John, by the way. How rude of me not to introduce myself. Now that we know each other, we're not total strangers anymore, I guess, so maybe it's okay."

He turned and gave her an expression that may have been a smile, but it still had a hard edge to it like he wasn't ready to fully let her off the hook. Then, he twisted back around to the drawers and continued his digging. Silverware, pens, screwdrivers and small pocketknives came out and were then strewn about the countertop.

"I'm Maddy," she said. "My husband is Tim and he and I just moved here from—"

"Ah ha!" John interrupted again, whipping around toward her. This time with a key ring dangling from his hand. "Here they are. I think it's this one." He started to wind it around the ring to remove the solitary key from the bunch. "The last owner rented the place out, and he got tired of driving over to let people in all the time when they didn't have their keys, so he gave me the spare. I probably should have charged him for the service."

"How long have you lived here?"

"Oh, let's see…Helen and I bought this place in 1974, so what's that then? Forty-eight years, I guess that would make it."

A large black cat with glowing green eyes and white paws peered at them from the edge of the doorway. Maddy recognized it as the cat from the window she'd seen earlier.

"Helen is your wife, I take it?"

"No. That's Helen," he said, shifting his gaze toward the cat.

Maddy tried not to react, but she sensed the old man was staring at her. "I'm teasing," he said finally with a smile that was much softer than the last one. "That's Boots."

She returned the smile. Did everybody in this town have the same sense of humor? It certainly seemed like it. Boots cautiously came nearer and she reached down to pet the cat, but it pulled back, instead preferring to bump his head against her leg.

"And, yes," John said. "Helen was my wife. I lost her almost a year ago."

"Oh, I'm so sorry."

He nodded. "Me, too."

"I lost my sister last year. I understand."

"I'm sorry to hear that."

"Thanks."

"Anyway, I didn't mean to cut you off before. I can only focus on one thing at a time. Now that I've found the key, I'm ready to hear about how you and Tim are from Portland," John said. "He's an architect and you're remodeling the old place next door."

"Yeah. How'd you…"

"I met Tim a few days ago in the back by the garage. You think I'd let a complete stranger in my house? No way, Jose." He chuckled again and handed Maddy the key. "It's yours now, but you should probably think about changing those locks, especially if you misplaced your key."

"I definitely will. Can I ask you something?"

He shrugged. "It's a free country."

"Is there something not right about our house?"

John nodded. "I imagine there's a lot not right about a hundred-and-ten-year-old house. Why? You having some issues over there?"

Maddy laughed. That was the understatement of the century, but she wasn't about to tell a virtual stranger about her accidents and how she was sure they were caused by ghosts who'd roamed the house in the past. "No," she finally said. "Just dumb stuff, I guess. Like things going missing."

"Well, homeownership can be a real burden sometimes."

"Yeah. I'm realizing that. Anyway, thank you so much for the key. It was so nice to finally meet you. I wasn't even sure if anybody lived here."

"Boots and I, we like the quiet."

"I'll make sure to keep the noise down then," Maddy said.

John's expression didn't change.

"That was a joke."

"I got it," he said with a straight face.

"Anyway, thanks again."

****

Back inside her own house finally, Maddy threw herself on the air mattress and let out a sigh of relief before she got up and changed out of her wet clothes and toweled off her damp hair. While she did, she thought about the tongue lashing she was going to give Tim when he got home for not telling her about meeting the next-door neighbor, and also for not getting the locks changed. If this house had been a rental property, there could have been an infinite number of people who still had a key to the place. She shivered even though she was finally warm and dry again.

She went into the office to check the window she thought she may have left open and saw that it was actually closed, which was incredibly lucky because sitting below it on the bench was the stack of old letters she'd found. If the window had been open, they would now be ruined by the rain. This was the first thing to go right for her in so long she could hardly believe it. She'd been certain she would walk in and find a pool of water ruining her new window seat and the found letters.

Downstairs, she fixed herself a quick lunch of

leftovers, and took her book back into her dry office and sat on the dry window seat to read the murder mystery while she ate. She was torn between the book and the bundle of letters, but if she wanted to have the book finished in time to attend the book club at the library, she had to set the letters aside for the time being.

Chapter Nineteen

1912

Beatrice found herself seated amongst the ladies of the auxiliary once again. This time, there was much talk of babies as one of the other members, Mrs. Aldrich, was nearly due for her own delivery. This prompted Beatrice to impart news of her condition. The women were jubilant at the announcement and began offering her insight and wisdom on the subject henceforth, though not all of it was perhaps what one might consider reasonable or even worthy of consideration.

One may have thought Mrs. Engebretson, a woman who had a full brood of eight, would dispense invaluable knowledge on the subject, but instead, she told Beatrice, "Do remember, dear, to sleep only with your feet covered. This will allow the child to grow strong and healthy within. And do avoid consuming heated food. You will find that it does not agree with the babe and may even harm the growing child."

Mrs. Aldrich looked practically ripe with hysterics as she listened, red in the face, fanning herself rigorously. The more wisdom that was dispelled, the faster her fan fluttered. Beatrice couldn't help but notice the temperature rising a bit herself as she took in the facts. Some of the women said it was best to bathe in milk after the birth in order to regain her bodily contours, while another said that a poultice of bread should be wrapped around the mother's stomach for similar effects. The ladies went round and round on this particular thought and it was never agreed upon what method was best, though both seemed a bit inconvenient and foolish in Beatrice's mind.

"And one mustn't forget about the babe and how to manage it when it's made its arrival," Mrs. Engebretson said, smugly. "When they fuss, it's best to undress them as fresh air is so good for their little minds. In warmer weather, I always found leaving them on the porch had great benefits. Oh, and do make sure to always put them facing north to sleep."

"North?" Beatrice said. "Why is that, exactly, Mrs. Engebretson?"

"Oh, well…to keep them aligned with the earth."

A few of the other women made noises and bobbed their heads in agreement. Beatrice had come into the meeting feeling elated to share her bit of news, but now something akin to fear was taking hold. She hadn't stopped to consider all of the knowledge she needed to know, not only to grow the babe, but also to have the child out and keep it safe. Remembering all of the various bits was getting to be more than Beatrice had expected. She almost wished she'd brought her parchment and pen along with her.

The final bit of advice struck a dark chord. "Do remember," said Mrs. Bloomsted, a woman who had lost her husband to influenza the previous winter and had been in a dispirited way ever since—or so Beatrice was informed by the group, "it's quite imperative to compose your final will and testament before the time of birthing arrives."

With this, the talk on the subject was promptly halted when Mrs. Aldrich let out a loud gasp and became much too over-heated to continue on. Another of the ladies volunteered to assist her in getting some fresh air. It was rather stuffy in that church basement, Beatrice noted.

During all of this, she couldn't help but notice that Miss Fanning, the old schoolmarm, remained quiet during the discussion, which was mildly unusual for her. Given she had never been a parent herself, she likely thought it unwise to offer up her own thoughts on the matter, but Beatrice knew she was an educated, practical woman and she wondered about her thoughts as some of these ideas didn't stand to reason with her. Later, while Miss Fanning was getting a fresh cup of lemonade at the table toward the back of the room, Beatrice approached her to find out her position on things. Miss Fanning took a long, slow sip of her cool drink before answering. "Well, I'm no expert on the subject myself, but I have observed the phenomenon many times throughout the course of my life. I'm certain it's all overwhelming, but I do think, dear, that good sense is best. Eat and drink what provides good nutrients, get extra rest, try not to fret, and all will be well. I can tell you have a good head on your shoulders. Try not to worry." She gave her a soft pat on the shoulder and went back to her seat. This comforted Beatrice a good deal and she was glad she'd decided to ask for the woman's opinion on the subject.

Returning to her own sitting room later that evening, Beatrice once again worked her pen, but this time it was to compose a list of the things she required for the babe. While she did so, she also noted a few of the more useful tips she'd acquired from the women. She pondered the last suggestion made by the Widow Bloomsted with regards to writing a will and testament before delivering the child. What a dreadful thought, yet, knowing how things had transpired with her own mother, she couldn't help but feel as though it was perhaps also necessary. Of course, what did she, a newly married, young woman have to testify? She could think of not one thing, yet the idea stayed with her lodged in her mind and would not loosen its hold. Beatrice took up a blank piece of parchment and sat with it for some time before she began to write again.

Chapter Twenty

2022

Maddy became fully engrossed in the book club selection and was pleasantly surprised by the writing. She hadn't read a book with such maturity and depth for a long time. If she could write a murder mystery half as complex, she would be satisfied. A few more loosely defined nuggets of potential ideas for her own work surfaced now and then as she read, and she paused to jot them down in a small notebook she'd found in the box of office supplies.

She'd been sitting on the window bench for too long and her legs had gone numb, so she was forced to get up to stretch them out and move around a bit. She wanted to keep reading, but she couldn't sit on the hard, wooden surface any longer. It lit a fire under her to get going on making the cushion for it.

Downstairs, she dug through the moving boxes once again until she found her sister's sewing machine. Jess had been an amazing clothing designer. She'd started sewing clothes when she was only eight years old, and by the time she was twelve she made all of her own outfits and they were not bad. Some of them were quite spectacular and other kids at their school started asking if she would make clothes for them, too. By the time she'd finished college, she'd already sold several designs to major fashion houses. Maddy had never sewed a thing in her life. Well, except for the pillow she had to make in Home Economics class in the ninth grade, but truth be told, Jess had helped her with so much of the project, Maddy had barely touched the thing. Her big sister wasn't here to do it for her this time, so it was all on her.

Along with the machine, she also had a stack of fabric from her sister's stash. She went through it and found a print that would work perfectly in the room paired with the black and white wallpaper. It was a nice, muted orange, but it would definitely add a pop of color. For the stuffing, Maddy pulled some foam out of a few old decorative pillows she had packed, and she lugged all of it back up to the office.

"Now what?" she said aloud, after she got the machine plugged in and unfolded the fabric and spread it out on the floor. She tried to channel her sister. *What would Jess do?* She'd watched her sister sew from afar for years growing up but had never paid much attention. Now she wished she had. It wasn't something she cared about until now.

She picked up the foam and set it on top of the material, folding the fabric around it trying to envision how she could stitch it up, but she was at a loss. YouTube was the obvious solution here. When in doubt, consult the experts on the internet. Maddy grabbed her laptop and opened it on the floor next to the sewing machine. Sitting cross-legged, she did a general search for beginner sewing tutorials, and as she scrolled down the various thumbnails of videos, she stumbled upon one that almost made her heart stop. "Jess," she whispered. Her cursor hovered over the box, but her finger wouldn't let her click on the still frame of the ghost of her sister staring back at her.

Of course her sister had posted sewing tutorials. Why wouldn't she? It made perfect sense; it was just shocking that Maddy had never bothered to go and look for them until now. Here was her big sister, ready and waiting to offer her support and guidance from beyond the grave, the same as she'd done when she was alive.

Tears fell from Maddy's face as she clicked the play button and watched her sister teach her how to sew for a second time in her life. The only difference was that this time she paid attention. The sewing machine her sister used to demonstrate was the one Maddy now had in front of her. She had no idea why, when her mom asked her what, if anything, of Jess's belongings she might like to have, she picked the sewing machine. Maddy did not sew and had no use for the machine, but it was such a symbol of who Jess was that she had to have it, even if it ended up being a very heavy paper weight. The talent her sister possessed in turning out beautiful things from squares of material with just this machine had always been intriguing if not mysteries to Maddy, so much so, she'd brought the dang thing with her literally across the country. It felt good attempting to put it to use.

She sat, watching every last video her sister had on her channel, even the ones that had nothing to do with what Maddy was trying to make. Just seeing and hearing Jess again was so heartbreakingly comforting, she didn't know how to process it. When the videos were all done, the day was almost over and Maddy hadn't even turned the sewing machine on yet, but she was now ready to give it a try.

After measuring, cutting, and pinning, just as her sister had instructed, Maddy put the fabric on the faceplate of the machine and took a deep breath. This was it. She pressed down with her foot like she would a gas pedal on a car. The needle went flying through the fabric at an alarming speed. "Whoa! Too fast."

It turned out, this was not like driving a car at all. She let up on the gas and looked at her work. She had sewn the wonkiest line imaginable. It looked no different than when she was in middle school Home-Ec.

She sighed and thought about giving up, but instead she pulled open one of the little drawers on the machine and found the seam ripper. She knew it was there because she'd seen her sister pull it out a few times in the videos. If Jess had to rip stitches out, Maddy shouldn't feel bad about having to do so. After ripping out the thread, she tried again. This time she eased the pedal down and the machine slowly moved the fabric forward while also stitching it together. Yes! She was doing it. She could hardly believe it.

"Check it out, Jess!" she said out loud. "Bet you never thought you'd see me sewing."

After stitching her way around three sides of the rectangle, she left one short side open to turn the fabric out, remembering to clip the corners for crisp, clean edges just as Jess had advised. She turned the material right side out now and shoved the foam piece in and she was floored. It actually fit! She couldn't believe she'd sewn something. It wasn't perfect, but it would definitely work. When it was finished, she sat down on it to claim victory.

By the time Maddy picked her book back up to start reading again, the sun was going down outside. A faint knocking sound hit her ear. She twisted to look out the window behind her, assuming it was the same tapping noise she'd heard previously—the branch scratching the side of the house, but the night was calm with no breeze at all.

She heard it again. Where was it coming from? Maybe downstairs? She got up and went to Tim's office to get a full view of the front of the house. She saw nothing except a car parked in the front of the house.

The knocking came again. Was someone at the front door? Who could that be? Her pulse raced. What should she do? Instinctively, she grabbed for her phone, and then she remembered she didn't have a phone. It had died. Her new phone was supposed to be delivered…today. She watched from Tim's office as someone left her front porch and got back into the car and drove off, that someone presumably being a delivery person.

Maddy went downstairs and unlocked the door. She looked down and saw a small package sitting in front of her. She was embarrassed, but not for long because she was no longer without a phone.

As soon as she got it all set up, she snapped a picture of her new cushion and sent it to her mom, then she called her and told her the whole story of how it came to be. They cried and laughed together. Even if making one cushion was all she got done today, she didn't care. It was so worth it to feel connected to her sister again.

Chapter Twenty-One

1912

Beatrice spent much of her time in the kitchen now that the servant was gone. She also continued changing out the vases each morning and tidying up the parlor even though there hadn't been a funeral for weeks. In addition to these chores, she'd begun to make a nursery out of the spare room. She had no idea if the babe would be a boy or a girl, but with the rest of the house feeling drab and possibly bent toward darkness, she had selected a new wall covering. She wanted something with more cheer.

She was concerned that the child would grow to be odd being surrounded by all of the death, so she selected a soft yellow hue. It had no floral pattern, nor any pattern at all, in fact. It was not pale nor dark. She had a difficult time convincing the shopkeeper at the mercantile that this was to her liking, and when he pushed back explaining that this was simply not done, she did not let up in her conviction. With Charles too preoccupied with his books, once the new paper was in, Bea herself pasted it up onto the walls in the small room that was to be the nursery.

The days dragged on this way for what Beatrice felt might be indefinite, as she performed perfunctory tasks, waiting impatiently for the child to arrive. Certain that the tides of good fortune would change when the babe was at long last here, she did not let things weigh her down. Even while Charles was notably absent in mind, when he was not locked into the intake room at his desk, he paced about the home pensively. Beatrice knew the child was going to make an arrival whether the business was flourishing or not, so she pushed onward in making preparations herself. Unable to wait much longer, she decided to speak with Francis about the crib without consulting her husband. She entered the carriage house unannounced one evening after supper for she had witnessed him slip in while she was cooking the meal near the kitchen window that faced out toward the carriage house.

"I do not need anything more than what is practical," she told him. "It can be a small pine cradle if that is best. Some place for the babe to sleep. Anything will do, really."

He wore a white shirt and suspenders. A heavy tool belt hung about his waist. He looked up at her but did not speak.

"Can you do that?" she asked. "I would be quite grateful."

He seemed to be pondering her request, and it was the first time she thought she recognized anything in the way of similarity between the two brothers. When he nodded to her though, it wasn't the kind she might expect from one agreeing with an arrangement, but rather his expression was one of hesitation, doubt, and if she wasn't so observant, she might have said she saw fear in his eyes. Beatrice did not know what to make of it or how to proceed. Flustered, she turned and left.

She found Charles at his desk in the intake room. "I

have asked your brother to build us something for the babe to sleep in. I told him something simple would be to my satisfaction in order to keep the cost low. I am entirely unsure if he accepted my request. Why that may be, I do not know, though I wish to know. It may be possible that the order will need to come from you."

Charles looked up at her. His expression was hollow. He appeared as though he had not slept in days. His tie hung askew, and his top button was undone. Beatrice did not know if he had even registered the words she had spoken. She was used to waiting for him to reply, but now his eyes were dull and unresponsive entirely.

As she stood at the threshold, she considered repeating her words. A small fury began to bubble within her. Did no one in this home respond to anything she said? Just as she opened her mouth, the mortician looked back down and began to scribble new numbers into his ledger.

Resigned, Beatrice turned and walked through to the parlor. It was as if she were a ghost in her own home of late. The somber mood seemed to be swallowing them all whole. She stood and fretted in front of the cold hearth in utter despair. Charles was not behaving in a manner becoming of his usual dignified self. Things were unsettled. She must make them right again. She simply could not live with constant negative auras in her new home; she'd done that in her previous life and did not care to do it ever again. She'd promised herself that when she brought children to this life, it would be a happy one.

Something must be done to fix their troubles, but what could she do now? This was an entirely different beast than the one she'd tackled prior, and Bea realized that she was more understanding of how to handle situations with the dead than she was capable of dealing with those of the living.

****

A fortnight passed and summer gave way to unexpectedly mild weather. Beatrice attended to the gardens, not only harvesting the late blooms but also preparing and planting bulbs for the next season. All the while, she gained more and more roundness in her belly which took away some of the sting of their current troubles. In fact, it gave her great delight. But as it did so, the mortician grew more and more unhinged, which cast a tension on the couple that had not previously existed. Beatrice did not have many trusted companions to consult in the ways of marital bliss, so she kept it to herself for the most part, expecting it to pass.

Though, as she visited with the midwife, her sister by marriage, one afternoon to check on her progress, she decided to ask for Elizabeth's confidence in such matters. Beatrice lay on a fainting couch in her bed chambers with Elizabeth at her side in a hardback chair. She took the pregnant woman's pulse and then felt around her midsection with her bare hands. While doing so, Beatrice felt calm. She'd gotten more and more familiar with her sister by marriage these past months and had nothing but admiration and respect for the woman. She was kind and patient, and Beatrice was overjoyed in this new companion. And though Francis was the younger sibling of Charles, Elizabeth was a few years older than Beatrice herself. Her manners were well-refined, and she had shown Beatrice nothing but care and attentiveness regarding her condition. They

Jody Wenner

had even met a few times to have tea together in town. It was splendid to have someone to talk to who was so intelligent on so many topics. It was almost as good as having her real sister back in her life.

Beatrice had not planned it, but it was at the forefront of her mind, so as Elizabeth continued with her examination, Bea asked, "Is it common to find husbands coming across rather…impertinent during such times, do you suppose? For I believe that nerves are getting the better of Charles. He is consumed with the slowness of the business and won't allow himself an ounce of happiness for the child."

"I can't see how the two are connected," said Elizabeth.

"Nor can I. Only that he feels it's best to bring the child into stability. I feel the same, but surely this funeral company had been afloat for long enough now to be a good and constant service to the community. The fashion in which people are perishing is not to change anytime soon."

Together, the two women snickered lightly.

"It can't be good for the constitution to keep up the constant worry," Elizabeth added. "Though Francis is much the same, brothers cannot be too different. Now, dear, how have you been? Are you well?"

"Yes."

"Any unusual feelings to report, upsets that do not appear normal?"

"No. None."

"Delightful. By my terms, I believe you will deliver sometime in the early part of winter, just before the season's tidings."

"A most astonishing holiday it shall be then!"

Beatrice exclaimed.

"Indeed."

"Will you and Francis celebrate with us? I would like to invite you for a festive meal before the child arrives."

"That would be wonderful. We graciously accept the invitation."

****

Later that night, while reading in her bed chambers, Bea reflected upon the conversation with Elizabeth. While she hadn't learned much in the way of making sense of her own husband, she was now more confused than ever with regards to his brother, for Elizabeth had suggested that the brothers were similar. Beatrice had always considered herself to be adept at reading people's character, so this new information confounded her. In fact, if at all, Bea considered Francis to be quite the opposite of the mortician.

Perhaps she had got her brother by marriage all wrong? Or was it her own husband she did not know as well as she believed?

Chapter Twenty-Two

2022

Maddy sat at the café early the next day eager to take another stab at writing, but after an unsuccessful attempt, she closed her laptop in frustration, took her book out, and began reading. She got so lost in it, she hadn't noticed Frankie come in and sit down at the table across from her until he spoke.

"Morning," he said. "How goes the writing?"

"I'm not really sure," she admitted. "I've got some bits and pieces down, but it's still lacking something. I'm not finding that one thing. The spark. You know?"

"Ah. I know that thing you're talking about."

"Where do your ideas come from?"

"Hmm…" Frankie said. "All sorts of places, I guess. Usually, it's when I'm not trying to think of an idea that something will pop into my head. Probably my best short story came about when I was walking my dog."

"Yeah? I was just thinking the other day that I'd like to get a dog."

"It was totally irrelevant to the walk; it was just something kooky that came out of nowhere."

"Right. So, what you're saying is that I should stop trying to come up with ideas. Got it," Maddy said, smiling across the table at him.

"Exactly. Although, other times I've come up with ideas by going to the library and reading old newspapers on the microfiche."

"Really?"

"I've been known to borrow an idea or two from an odd headline or an old, bizarre crime report I stumbled upon. You never know what might spark your imagination."

"That's a really good idea. I hadn't even considered spring boarding off of a real event, but why not, right?"

"Exactly. I mean, as long as you change the names and the specific details, you're free to riff off of the general concept."

"Huh." Maddy's thoughts were interrupted by her phone sitting on the table next to her that started to ring. She glanced down at it. "Oh. That's my best friend. I should probably take this. Excuse me."

She stepped outside the café and spoke to Ellie on the sidewalk for about fifteen minutes before returning to her table. "Sorry about that," she said to Frankie. "It was sort of an emergency."

"Everything okay?" he asked.

"Yes and no. Ellie's in Cambridge finishing up a Ph.D. program in history. She and her boyfriend broke up so that required urgent discussion," Maddy said with a laugh. "But the good news is that she's coming home next week and she's going to stop for a quick visit on her way back to Portland."

"Oh, nice."

"Anyway, I'll let you get back to work," she said to him. "Thanks for the inspirational chat though."

"Anytime," Frankie said, as he started clacking

away on his keyboard.

Maddy was about to try again herself when her phone buzzed for a second time. This time though it wasn't a social call. It was a message that the movers would be arriving shortly with the truckload of their furniture.

She grabbed up her things and practically ran back home to let the movers in. It took them less than an hour to haul all of their things into the house and put them in position. When it was done, Maddy couldn't believe how great it felt to finally have furniture. She spent the next few hours unpacking some of the boxes and getting her office set up. She wasn't ready to say that it felt exactly like home yet, but the air had shifted somewhat.

Maddy sensed a change, like the house was happier somehow, and might possibly no longer be wanting to kill her. She was fully aware that this notion was incredibly ridiculous, but she didn't even care. Sure, maybe it was just that the house finally felt lived in or something, but since she'd found those letters, she had noticed a different overall mood shift in the place. Maybe it was a coincidence, but Maddy didn't think so.

It was late afternoon when she texted Tim to let him know the furniture had arrived. He was on a lunch break, so he called her. When he asked what she was up to, she told him about the book club and how excited she was about it.

"Yeah? That's great. You definitely sound happier than last time we spoke. And making friends too, it sounds like."

"Just a few. That reminds me, why didn't you tell me that you met the neighbor, John?"

"The old guy? I dunno. Why?"

"It would have been nice to know someone was alive nearby, I guess."

"Sorry. I didn't know you wanted to know about the curmudgeon next door."

"He's not that bad," she said. "If not for him, I'd still be locked out."

"What happened to your key?"

"I have no idea. It vanished into thin air. Though, you were right about the putty knife. I found it, so maybe the key will turn up, too. But, thanks to John, I have the spare now. Still, we need to change the locks."

"All right. I can do that when I get back."

"I went into the little drugstore this morning for the first time on my way to the café and picked up a little gift for John in town this morning and left it on his porch as a thanks for helping me, and, you know, for not murdering me."

"What did you get him?"

"A jar of pickles and some cat treats."

"Huh?" Tim said.

"I guess you had to be there."

"I guess. Okay, I better get back to work, but I'm looking forward to seeing you tomorrow."

"Me too," Maddy said. "What time does your flight arrive?"

"Sometime in the evening."

"Okay. See you then."

****

After Maddy got off the phone, she went up to her office and stood in the doorway taking it all in. Her new writing space looked great now that her desk was in place, the bookcase was finished, and the cushion was on the bench seat. She couldn't get over how great the wallpaper looked. It really was the defining quality that made the whole room feel special, like an actual writer might work here. Now she just had to get something written. She had no more excuses, no more distractions. It was time to focus.

Full of worry, she stepped in the room and sat down on the window seat. Maybe focusing was the wrong approach. Maybe she'd been focusing too hard. Based on her conversation with Frankie at the café, if she wanted to get the juices flowing, it seemed like the best thing to do was to not focus. Instead she needed to ease up a little, try to be more of a dreamer. She wasn't good at that.

Turning to look out the window, she put her knees up and wrapped her arms around them and tried to rein in the sinking feeling. What if she failed at it? What if Tim's subtle comments were all his way of gently telling her that he didn't think she was good enough? After several false starts this week, Maddy was starting to believe it was true herself.

Chapter Twenty-Three

1912

The amusing remark Beatrice had made to Elizabeth about death not going out of fashion turned out to be less humorous and more sedate than she had cared to ever dream. For things did seem to change, and for most this might be taken as a welcomed change. But for Bea's husband, a mortician who was on the verge of a collapse in more than one way, this was anything but good news, especially one who had a very pregnant wife who required a good many things now that the baby was due to make an arrival into this world soon. Why was this happening now, of all times? Beatrice did not care to speculate, and since she was not the superstitious type, she would not give in to the notion that she was being cursed with poor luck.

Surely the weather played a part in their current misfortunes, as it remained downright balmy that fall, and even in the early part of winter, the conditions were not as brutal as they could often be for Minnesota. It may or may not have been a factor in the way in which diseases carried; but, for whatever reason, life expectancy rose a percentage or two in Pine Grove, and the business of handling the dead, and burying them, came to a complete crawl, for there seemed to be no one dying.

It wasn't entirely true; there had been one death in town—an old spinster who lived alone in a small abode on the edge of town. Unfortunately, her brother and nephew could not be talked into having their business handled by Westmoreland Funeral Parlor. It was difficult for Bea to know if it was simply that they were solidly set in the old traditions, or if Charles, in his ever-increasing desperation, had lost his flair for persuasion. His manners had become so sour that even she was avoiding his company of late. When he did speak to her, during their shared meals or in their bed chambers, his words were often terse and unkind.

Things continued on in this downward spiral, but Beatrice refused to give up for the most part. She firmly believed that a sour disposition in her own self would somehow leech into the child and cause concern, whether it be in the birthing process, or in the character of the child later. She did not want either of those to occur, and though she still fretted to a small degree about the birthing process—not ignorant of the perils that existed—she cast those sinister and vile thoughts aside the moment they surfaced.

She continued to write to her sister, and though she had noted in one letter she may not have the time to do so, she found herself writing with possibly even more regularity. In doing so, she found some solace, just as she had when she was a lonely and troubled child.

Dearest Jane,

You would not recognize me if you saw me. My belly is swollen beyond measure and my bosom is unfathomably no longer my own. I am now wearing loose gowns and housecoats. My sister by marriage has been a great source of comfort for me throughout.

We've met regularly for check-ups, but they generally result in tea and good conversation. You would be surprised to know that she and Francis are not equipped to have children of their own. I imagine that is why she has chosen to tend to the children at the orphanage. When I questioned why they did not acquire a babe or two from the ones there in need of a good family, she confided that she did not believe them to be strong or smart enough and were from lower stock, which I do not think is true and argued thusly with her for the first time. I was shocked that a woman with such high intellect herself would believe that. She invited me along with the women from the auxiliary to come and see the orphans for ourselves and we did. It was a delightful experience. We brought them some necessities from the church funds, but also candies and trinkets. The children were pleased as punch by the gifts, and it brought all the ladies smiles as well. We did not see any that were infirmed or sickly as Elizabeth had indicated.

It is not my place to cast judgment on Elizabeth, as I have found a lovely companion in her. I do believe she will make a wonderful and attentive aunt. I cannot remark on Francis as he isn't one to offer his opinions outright. I do often feel as though he does not care for me. I have asked Charles his thoughts on the matter for which he is not inclined to divulge, leading me to trust my first instinct on the subject. Nevertheless, I do often wonder what it is that Elizabeth finds redeeming in her husband. I should be so glad as to not have him as my own.

Goodness me. The unseemliness of the words cast by this writer today are not appropriate and verging on gossip. It is with good reason that this letter will never be posted and therefore will not see another set of eyes upon it. Regardless, I do feel somewhat better having written them down.

Yours,

B

****

During this time, to quell the mind from the worry and negative energy floating about the home, Bea took refuge in the temperate weather, spending many hours sitting on the window bench in her sitting chamber. She so enjoyed feeling the fresh air from the open window on her face, listening to the rustling of leaves on the trees as the breeze pulled through them. The gentle smell of the dying garden below rose up and hit her nose in earthy and autumnal tones. All the while, she worked her thread and needle. The ladies auxiliary had begun a baby quilt for her. The child would need warmth if it was to be comfortable during the inclement winter weather that would inevitably arrive at their doorstep before too long.

The piecing of the blanket squares had been all stitched together by the ladies, but the hand-quilting that held it together was Beatrice's responsibility. She struggled with the task at hand as she had not been taught these basic life skills growing up. Anne, her strict caretaker and teacher, was the reason Beatrice wrote as eloquently as she did. Anne taught her well in the way of refinement, books, music, and the like, but she left much to be desired in the practical ways of the home and even less in the department of love. A mother she was not. A homemaker she was most definitely not. Yet Bea wouldn't let that stop her; she was focused on giving her child the things she lacked which included a beautifully hand-sewn blanket.

With her hoop in her lap, she attempted to replicate the motions she'd observed from Miss Fanning during the women's meetings. It was while she was doing exactly this one fair afternoon that she witnessed an unusual scenario occur just below. Francis pushed through the back gates and rushed down the path in such a crazed fashion that he stumbled on an uneven patch of cobblestone under his feet but dusted himself off and continued to march straight into the mortician's office and slam the intake door shut.

Beatrice felt the reverberation directly into her bones and she paused her stitching to listen to the brothers' raised voices pouring up through the window, though as much as she strained her ears, she could not make out their exact words. She had never heard Charles's tone so harsh.

What could they possibly be spatting about? It had to be the matter of money as it was the only thing seeming to occupy them at this present time. Beatrice thought there surely must be a way to solve this dilemma in a more civilized manner, and as she pondered it herself for another short while, she thought perhaps she'd come up with a way.

Chapter Twenty-Four

2022

Maddy decided she couldn't sit wallowing in self-pity forever. She had to redirect her negative thoughts and the best way to do that was to dive back into a reality that wasn't her own. So, she finished reading the murder mystery with just an hour to spare before heading over to the Pine Grove Public Library to attend her first book club. Walking over, she was nervous and apprehensive. She'd always wanted to join a book club, but never had the time while she was working and going to school. The idea of discussing books with people who were also fond of reading was probably stupid to other people, but Maddy didn't have anybody else in her life that harbored the same love of books as she did—not Tim, not her best friend, not even her parents. So, while it might sound like a little thing, to Maddy it wasn't. It was everything.

When she got to the library, there were a dozen or so chairs set in a circle in the middle of the room. Maddy was clearly excited about the meeting because she got there incredibly early. She was the first one there, or maybe the only one? Kirsten, the librarian, was standing behind the front desk, but was talking on the phone. She gave Maddy a warm wave and pointed to the chairs. Maddy noticed that Kirsten had changed her hair color from purple to jet black since she'd been there last week.

She sat down, and with nothing to do but wait for others to arrive her nerves raged. It was like being the new kid in class. She pulled the book out of her bag and paged through it, skimming some of the pages as if she were about to take a test on it. She closed it and was about to put it back in her bag when something fell from the pages and landed on the floor near her feet with a clank.

She picked it up and stared at it indignantly. It was her missing house key. She was glad to know she was still in possession of it and that it wasn't floating around somewhere for anybody to find, but she was certain she'd shaken the books out one-by-one on the porch that day.

"Howdy, neighbor."

She turned to see John take the seat right next to her and relief washed over her. She actually knew someone else in the book club already, or at least she sort of knew him. It shouldn't have surprised her all that much that he was there. He'd had a book open on his kitchen table the day she was in his house. "Hi. I didn't know you were in the book club," she said.

"I didn't know you were in the book club either," he replied.

"This isn't your first time here though, is it?"

"Nope," he said, flatly. "Did you enjoy the book?"

"Are we allowed to say that before the rest of the group shows up? Or is this the whole group?"

"It definitely varies from month to month, but no. There will probably be a few more people here. And...yes. You're allowed to tell me if you enjoyed the book before we get started."

"Okay. Then, yes. I did. Very much. How about you?"

"I think I'll save that information for the group."

"Hey!" Maddy felt like she was finally getting the hang of this midwestern sense of humor. It was basically like non-stop dad jokes.

"No. In all seriousness," he went on, "I think it was a little overwrought and unrealistic in some places, and I may have stumbled upon a few plot holes. There were too many characters, in my opinion, but all-in-all, not bad. Very well written overall. A solid mystery to be sure, though I solved it before the end. I'd give it an eight."

"Oh. Wow. I guess I need to up my analyzing skills if I want to be part of this discussion."

Just then, another member joined them and sat down in one of the empty chairs. She was a middle-aged woman who didn't have many discernable physical traits, medium-length straight brown hair, brown eyes, brown slacks, brown shoes, and a light-blue blouse. Maddy was sure she had never seen her before, though she was a pretty normal looking lady, if a little brown, in Maddy's opinion. Not that Maddy was anything special herself. She also had medium-length brown hair and brown eyes. She was wearing jeans and a gray sweater, so maybe a tad less brown, but just as boring, now that she thought about it.

Kirsten made her way over and sat down. She checked her phone. "Okay. Should we get started? We may have a few others trickle in, but I wanted to do introductions today because we have a new member. Maddy, would you like to go first?"

As Maddy said a few basic things about herself, such as recently relocating from the Pacific Northwest for her husband's job, another person came in and sat down. She glanced over and was surprised to see that she actually knew this person too. It was Frankie from the café. What were the odds that she would know two of the five other people in the group? Well, maybe pretty good given the size of the town, but it did help her relax somewhat.

The middle-aged lady introduced herself next. Her name was Pam. She had two sons and she worked at the pharmacy. Then John introduced himself. "I actually met Maddy last week when she locked herself out of her house, because she's my neighbor to the west. Anyway, as the rest of you know, I'm a retired homicide detective with Washington County, I make ship models in my spare time, and I like to read Westerns."

Maddy's jaw nearly detached itself. John was a homicide detective? No wonder he'd scolded her about going into a stranger's home. And her gut had been right about him all along. He was a good guy if a bit on the crabby side, when he wasn't making dumb dad jokes. She now felt ever better about having him as a neighbor.

Then Frankie introduced himself, but she didn't learn anything new about him. He'd said basically the same things he'd told Maddy a few days prior about himself and then added a bit more about his writing. "I write poetry, short stories, and the occasional screen play. My favorite genre is science fiction, but I enjoy light fantasy once in a while too, or really anything that isn't laced with too much reality."

Just as Maddy hadn't said anything about being a writer, Frankie hadn't said anything about working at the café, though it was probably already a known fact to everybody there. Maddy was not ready to share with the group that she was trying to write a book for whatever reason and Frankie did not bring it up during their conversation either, which she appreciated.

Kirsten went last. "I'm Kirsten. I'm a history nerd, I collect old books, and my girlfriend and I like to go antiquing on the weekends. Contrary to everything else I just said, we do not own a single cat." The group laughed at that, but John interjected, "Hey! There's nothing wrong with owning a cat."

"I didn't say there was. I just wanted the record to state that I do not currently own one."

"Your loss," he said.

Everybody laughed.

"Okay. Thank you all for coming tonight. Let's get cracking on the book, shall we?" Kirsten held up her copy of the book.

Maddy's nerves picked back up as the discussion of the book got rolling because this group was small, but they were also incredibly smart. She was more than a little intimidated and spent more time listening than talking, which was fine with her. She realized she hadn't gotten nearly as much out of the book as the rest of them. They'd gone deep, but it was all really valid criticism. She felt like she'd learned more about writing and reading in the two hours there than she had through much of her grad program, which was exhilarating and also a bit disappointing. It dawned on her that she needed to start reading like a writer if she was going to learn about the craft. And hearing what people liked and disliked would go a long way in helping her formulate what might work from a reader's perspective when she really got into the meat of her own writing.

At the end of the meeting, they talked about what they were going to read next. John advocated for a Western, while Frankie had a science fiction title in mind. Pam wanted to read a work of literary fiction, and Kirsten had a historical fiction title she'd brought to the group. "What about you, Maddy? What's your preference?"

"Oh, uh, I hadn't thought to come up with a book, but these all sound great. I'm happy reading whatever you guys pick."

"Okay. Well, let's go with Pam's book for next time," she said. John groaned and Pam clapped.

"What's the title and author again, Pam?"

"*The Life We Bought* by Alexandria Jennings."

John groaned again and Kirsten gave him a scolding look before she said, "Great. I'll get some extra copies in and have them at the desk in a few days for you to pick up. Thanks, everyone. Great meeting! See you next month." She got up and started putting the empty chairs back where they belonged.

"Thanks for having me," Maddy said to Kirsten before she left. "I really enjoyed it."

"I hope you'll join us again!"

"I will."

She asked John if she could walk home with him. He nodded and they were off. On the way back, she asked him about being a detective. He gave blunt answers, but she'd come to realize that was just his way. Yes, he liked the job. No, it wasn't at all like what you see in the movies. Yes, he'd been haunted by a few of the cases, etc. Then, he thanked her for the gift she'd left for him and Boots. Before she knew it, they'd reached his front porch.

"Okay. Have a good night, Maddy," he said.

"You, too."

"You ever need anything, don't hesitate to give me a holler."

"Thanks," she said.

Once she stepped inside her own front door and locked it, she realized how exhausted she was from the week. As she got ready for bed, she was happy about one thing at least and that was to be sleeping in a real bed again—her own even. Dozing off, she felt bad that she had hardly missed Tim all week. She definitely did miss him, and she was excited to have him return, but she was also proud of herself for managing independently without needing to call or text him constantly, not that she could have since she was without a phone, but she felt good about meeting a few people on her own and finding her own way in a new place.

Maybe, just maybe, she was stronger than she'd been giving herself credit for all this time.

Chapter Twenty-Five

1912

Later that evening, Beatrice sat with the mortician at the dining table, but it seemed as though he was once again unaware of her presence. Deeper in thought than normal, Charles swished his silver spoon mindlessly around in the stew she'd prepared for him.

"I was thinking—" she spoke between bites of bread "—perhaps we should consider selling the piano? It would bring in a little extra monies until things get sorted."

Charles threw his head up and looked at her as if he really hadn't known she was there. His eyes behind his spectacles looked a bit like when a canine had succumbed to the mad disease. It startled her, but none more than when he thrust his fist down with such a force that it caused the stew to splash from the tureen which lifted from the table and bounced back down with a clatter.

"We cannot get rid of the piano. It is necessary for the business when it regains strength," he hollered. His eyeglasses now sat askew on his face.

Beatrice covered her mouth with her napkin, but she pressed on if a bit quieter and less assuredly than before. "I do not believe it to be entirely essential. We can do without it."

Pushing his spectacles back up the bridge of his nose, he sighed. "This is not your concern. I will not have you worrying over it."

"I only thought to help…"

A long and tense lull stretched on between them for a time until Charles spoke again. Now his voice was softer and rife with anguish. "There is something with which you might be of assistance."

"Anything, dear. What is it?"

"There has been another death. I will need you to write up the announcement."

"Oh, Charles! I don't understand. Isn't this the news you've been hoping for? Doesn't this take the burden off? Why are you so full of agony over such things?"

"It's another child, just a fresh-faced babe really. From the orphanage. Francis brought her in just a short time ago. I didn't think it good to tell you, given your condition."

"I see," she said, though she didn't really. She had been seated with a clear view of the path all afternoon and had not seen Francis bring anything but himself through it.

"Again, there will be no viewing, but I will want you to write up an announcement." As he spoke the words, it was as if being forced to do so against his better judgment. "I would encourage you to add your usual…flourishment."

"But, Charles, you've never encouraged this before." She was astonished and even proud, but for only a moment. "What do you know about the child?"

"I know nothing beyond it being a very young girl and there is not more to be gathered. Please, just do what you are so skilled at. Write up something that will tug at the town's hearts and open their purse strings."

Then she understood. "What is the child's name? How did she come to pass?"

He sighed. "I do not know. She was orphaned. You'll have to come up with something."

"But that is deceitful," she said.

He sat for a moment longer before setting his spoon down on his napkin and getting up from his seat. He stood over her in a rather frightful way. "We are not deceitful," he bellowed. "We are good, honest people who have fallen on hard times." He began to walk away and Beatrice heard him mutter, "I will do what I must for the sake of this family."

She sat at the table pushing her own stew around for a long while. A sourness had risen in her stomach and the food no longer appeared or smelled palatable to her. Something was off, but she couldn't make right or wrong of it. How could she write a death announcement that stirred emotions if she had nothing to go on? And why wouldn't her husband give her more information? Why Charles was acting so strangely was perplexing.

Was it simply that he could hardly bear the idea of taking in more donations? Or did this all have something to do with the argument she overheard earlier this afternoon between the two brothers? Or was it something else entirely? She let it sit without thinking much more about it, because she could see the bind the mortician was in and that he only wanted to do right by her and their child. The one thing alone was more than Beatrice could have hoped when she married the mortician, but was doing right by her also doing right by all? The lines were clouded. Her father had only done right by himself and that was unappealing too, but she was learning that things were not always black and white.

After clearing away the uneaten supper, she went up to her sitting room and stared blankly at a parchment for much longer than she'd ever done before. Unable to produce what Charles had asked, she instead began a note to Jane hoping to transfer her negative energies onto the paper and out of her soul.

Dearest Jane,

The business has been suffering of late, and thus it seems so has my marriage to the mortician. Though I fear I am befuddled as to this latest development— recent bouts of children from the orphanage dying. It would seem that in some regard this would ease the burden on the business but has only hastened to make things worse. I simply do not know what to do. I seek your guidance, dear sister, for I am frightened by the revelations I fear I have uncovered. I wonder to inquire with Elizabeth about such events, for as it sits, I fear that something ugly is happening between Francis and Charles. But I do not think it wise to point a finger. Without guidance from Elizabeth, I do not have a friend to confide in. I have thought about discussing it all with the old Dr. Boyle who lives in the next house over. Though he is a man who has seen his share of deranged behaviors at the sanitorium, what might he know of the tribulations of marriage? He remained unwed, thus I am reluctant to seek out his opinion on this matter. Who is left, dear sister?

****

Beatrice lowered her pen momentarily as she pondered on this quandary in its entirety, because suddenly something came to her head, something she did not like. Her gut gurgled and boiled much like the thin stew had done earlier in the pot on the wood stove with this recent revelation that had entered her mind and took hold so strongly, she could hardly breathe. Could Charles have something to do with the infant's death? It could not be true, but was that because she did not want it to be or because it was not possible? His words from earlier rang back into her ears. *I will do what I must.* She'd assumed that meant one thing, but now she wondered if it had a differing meaning entirely.

She dipped her pen back into the ink and finished her letter, making these thoughts more clear on the page so they no longer jumbled her mind, but with such accusations now plain on the page, she knew she must hide the bundle of letters away so they would not be seen by anyone. These were not things that one wanted announced. They were simply too full of evil and not at all what Beatrice wanted to believe, especially not now, just as she was ready to bring a child into such a home. It could not possibly be true. It was more likely that she herself was experiencing some kind of hysterics that the women from the auxiliary made mention of as a possible causation of pregnancy. Perhaps her mind was simply playing tricks with her.

Chapter Twenty-Six

2022

The next day, Maddy was fixing herself some lunch when Tim came in the back door with his suitcase. "Hey! You're home! I thought you weren't going to be back until late."

Tim set his luggage down and kissed her. "Caught an earlier flight. I missed you."

"I missed you, too!" She grabbed his hand and pulled him into the living room. "Come and check out the place. It looks so different with all of our stuff in it."

She gave him a tour of their new/old house fully furnished with their old furniture. "We are definitely going to have to get a few more pieces," she said. "This place is a lot bigger than our one-bedroom apartment in Portland."

"Yeah, but it looks great. I'm sorry I stuck you with all the work."

"It wasn't that bad. Oh! And guess what? Ellie is coming for a quick visit on Wednesday on her way back to Portland."

"Yeah? Our first visitor."

"I still have so much to do to get the place looking good and finish setting up the guest room before she comes though."

"You've got a few days."

"Yeah. I guess," Maddy said.

"Well, I really need a shower and then I need to take a nap. I worked my butt off this week, and I'm spent."

"Okay," she said. "Go ahead."

Tim headed up the stairs. Normally, it might have bothered her a tiny bit that he'd been gone for an entire week, and he didn't really express that he missed her much beyond just saying so, but she knew that was his way. He didn't usually lavish her with gifts or niceties. She'd gotten used to it over the course of their relationship. While he was an overall loyal and even-keeled partner, romance wasn't really his thing. It wasn't really Maddy's thing either, so it worked both ways. She was happy to have him home, even though she'd actually enjoyed her week alone, at least in hindsight.

That night, with Tim once again snoring in the bed next to her, and with Maddy now finished reading for book club, she picked up the bundle of letters, excited to dive back into them where she left off. She remembered what she and Frankie had talked about at the café, about how he would sometimes find things in old newspapers to use in plots for his stories. And she had almost told him about the letters when Ellie called and then she'd forgotten all about it.

Paging through them now, she knew there was a story here. The letters left so much to be interpreted, but they were also full of intrigue. Maddy couldn't stop thinking about them. She wondered if she could find out more about Beatrice somehow. Frankie had mentioned the microfiche, and she was sure that given Kirsten's interest in history, she would have the resources and knowledge to help her find out more.

Could she do it? Actually write a book based on Beatrice's letters? The idea was definitely compelling. If she thought it was interesting, maybe others would too. Just not Tim. That was something she needed to accept and not let it stop her from trying. Yes. She could do this—or at the very least, she needed to try.

One small problem, as she carefully searched through them one more time. The letters had no last names anywhere.

****

The next morning Maddy told Tim about Stillwater, so per Kirsten's suggestion, thinking it might be a fun thing they could do together to unwind a bit, they spent the morning being dorky tourists in the town touted as the birthplace of Minnesota. The weather was beautiful, and the town was exactly as Kirsten had described—charming and historic and full of cute shops and restaurants. They walked along the St. Croix River in a beautiful park, which was named after the owner of the historic inn a few blocks from the waterfront. They learned all about that on the trolley tour they took where they also saw old mansions built in the late nineteenth and early parts of the twentieth centuries by the lumber barons who brought wealth to the town.

After that, they ate lunch at a restaurant that had once been a freight depot where trains loaded and unloaded timber or goods from other major cities at the time including Chicago and St. Louis. The building had been converted into a restaurant with patio seating that had a magnificent view of the river too, just like most of the other spots in the town. The tour of the houses had appealed to Tim's interests, and Maddy enjoyed the lunch and shopping, and really just spending time doing something that felt normal again away from their own house. It was exactly what she needed to reset, and while they were eating it finally gave her a chance to tell Tim about the letters she'd found.

"Wow. That's crazy," he said.

"I know! Right? I'm thinking about basing my novel around them."

"Yeah? Wouldn't that be considered non-fiction then?"

"I mean, I'm not going to use the exact events. Besides that, I'm only gleaning bits and pieces of this woman's life from the letters. It's not the whole picture. And there's no murder obviously, but it's a start. I've been struggling all week trying to figure out a launching off point and now I think I've found one. It's sort of all thanks to Frankie because of a conversation we had in the café one day."

Tim nodded. "Sounds great," he said, and then he changed the subject and started talking about things he did and the friends and family he had visited while back home.

She wasn't the least bit surprised that Tim wasn't very interested in her book idea because he wasn't into books in general, but she was a bit shocked that he hadn't been more taken by the letters. Wasn't it the exact kind of thing one would hope to have happen when purchasing a Victorian era home? Was the fascination with the architectural aspects of the home not intertwined with the historical events that connected the two? Maybe not. Maddy wasn't all that interested in the building features per se, but the idea that a person had lived in the home and had walked the same halls as her was beyond fascinating to her. To be able to put real people into history had always been more interesting to her than to simply ingest statistics. It made it less abstract and more emotionally tangible. All she had to do was inject some heart into the story and maybe Tim would see that history could have all the things they loved about their new house.

Regardless of his non-interest in reading, Maddy still wished Tim would express a little more support for her writing. All she wanted was for him to at least ask to see something she had written without her needing to beg him to look at it. She had always asked about his work, even if she didn't understand it or care about it. She cared because Tim cared. Wasn't that how a relationship worked? She had no idea why this small thing bothered her so much, but it did.

Maybe it was because writing was such a solitary activity. She didn't think she was asking for a lot from her husband, she just wanted someone to bounce thoughts off of, someone who seemed a tiny bit interested. Maybe she was simply barking up the wrong tree. Maybe it was time to accept that Tim wasn't the person for her to involve with her writing, so maybe if she could find someone else to share these ideas with it wouldn't sting so much. Of course, now that she was thinking about it, she realized she did have someone else that was taking an interest, someone who was also another writer, someone who had already expressed a desire to see her work. Frankie. It was so obvious, she couldn't believe she hadn't thought of it until now. Maybe she'd ask Frankie if he wanted to be her critique partner. She was probably jumping the gun a bit given she hadn't actually written anything yet, but the idea motivated her. She looked over at Tim and she considered telling him about it, but she didn't need to tell her husband everything; in fact, hadn't she just resolved to stop telling him about her writing altogether? Having someone else to talk about writing with might even be key for her to not be so desperate for her husband's approval.

Chapter Twenty-Seven

1912

At the table, while they sat breaking their fast, Beatrice stole glances at the mortician, wondering if she actually knew the man with whom she'd been sharing a marital bed. If his appearance this morning was to be of any determining factor, he was most certainly deranged. His shirt was wrinkled, and what little hair he did possess was not properly smoothed over as was always the case. When he spoke this time, it startled her for *she* had been deep in thought.

His voice was raspy as though he hadn't slept well. "Have you an announcement for me to look at this morning ready to be sent to the printer?"

"I…do not. I'm afraid I was unable to produce one after much effort."

"You must go back up at once and try again," he barked.

"What if I cannot?"

"Then we both shall have failed," he said, sourly.

"Charles, I do not believe—"

"Please, Beatrice—" he begged, his tone so fraught she feared he might actually weep. "—for the sake of our family, just go up and write."

With that, she gave a terse nod, got up from her seat, and went back to her writing desk. She wasn't expecting to accomplish anything but was simply happy to be out of her husband's presence. But when she sat with her pen, she did as he'd asked. She produced an announcement well suited for the death of an orphaned, infant girl. She wasn't sure if fear or sadness had spurred her on, but either way, it was done.

In two days' time, the parlor would be transformed as it had been many times before. The gaslights would glow softly, the delicate fragrances of newly bloomed flowers would waft throughout the parlor, and Beatrice would play melancholy piano pieces while townsfolk entered to pay their respects to an orphaned child.

But the night before all of that happened, Beatrice was up late into the night, unable to sleep. It was well past midnight, and she sat at her writing table giving in to the hysterics that were trying to ruin her. She had attempted to pour it all into her pen and paper in an effort to quiet the madness that had taken hold inside of her, but it was to no avail. Questions were eating away at her, questions that had answers if she so chose to seek them out.

So, she took up a candle and placed it in its holder, and she quietly made her way down the stairs. She entered the parlor which was completely darkened except for the flicker of her light. Upon a pedestal in the front of the room draped in a fine red cloth sat a simple pine box. It was so small, it made her midsection ache. She rubbed her bulging belly as to calm it.

Beatrice, in her crazed state, came up with the notion that the only way to resolve the conflict stirring within her, within this entire space, was to lay her eyes upon the infant who took up residence now in the box before her. Why she believed this would give her peace, she did not know, though a strange inkling of a thread continued to weave itself around her head and while she could not catch hold of it long enough to make sense of it, it was telling her this was the way to sanity, to salvation.

The child, for whom she had named Estelle in her fraudulent death notice, she knew nothing about except that she was an orphaned babe left stripped bare in a ditch, unloved. She had become ill and because of her terrible misfortune, Beatrice's own family would be saved. It was a cruel tradeoff for which Beatrice felt she must acknowledge in order to resume a quiet and peaceful mind for the sake of her own babe. She thought to perhaps place a token of her gratitude within the dark confines of the small casket as an offering. And so, in her trembling hand, opposite her candle, she held the small photograph of her mother and sister. Perhaps, she thought, introducing the child to them would bring her soul peace and comfort in her crossing over. Perhaps she would find the spirits of her family on the other side waiting to greet her. This was the dream that Beatrice held herself, the belief that when her own time came, they would be there waiting, and the thought had always comforted her.

And so, she placed the candelabra down on the pedestal, mindful of her quickening breaths, and she peeled back the adorning cloth on the coffin's edge. Slowly, she then lifted the corner of the box. As it rose, her body shook with fear, for though she had been in the business of death for some time now, she had not witnessed a still babe, at least not one this young and certainly not alone in the dead of the night with her hysterical condition being as it was. Because of this, she did not know what might lay before her and in her terrified state, her eyes remained tightly shut.

Beatrice reached her hand inside to place the photograph, and it was then that she could tell something was amiss. She forced herself to pry her eyes open, but in the pitch blackness of the room, she was still unable to make out what was within, so she picked up the candle and shone it toward the box and it was then that she knew the secret her husband had been keeping from her.

She gasped and dropped the photograph inside the box in order to stifle her scream. The lid came down fast with a deep bang, but Beatrice somehow managed to keep from dropping the candle. She turned and exited the room quickly so as not to call the attention of Francis who she knew to be sleeping in the mortician's intake room just down the hall.

To her relief, all remained quiet in the house, and Beatrice took to her bed, slipping in as softly as she could without waking Charles. She had become rather adept at maneuvering her belly and the mortician did not stir once as she covered herself with the blanket. Her breathing settled, but that was all that did so.

Rattled yet by fear and confusion, she remained awake for a long time trying to make sense of the charade she had witnessed below. All she could fathom was that her husband was not the baby-killer she had perhaps thought but was instead a man of weak resolve who would knowingly prey upon the good people of Pine Grove in an even more ugly and deceitful manner than she'd originally believed.

She suddenly did not know which was worse.

Chapter Twenty-Eight

2022

Maddy spent most of Sunday getting the house and spare bedroom ready for Ellie's arrival mid-week. While she did that, Tim set up his office. Later, when she peeked in on him, it looked like he was already at his drafting table working, so she left him be. She took a bath and then flopped into bed.

After Tim joined her, she said, "I had this great idea. What if I invited Frankie to come for dinner when Ellie's visiting?"

"Who?" he asked.

"Frankie. The guy from The Pine Cone Café."

"The guy who works behind the counter?"

"Yeah."

"Hmmm," Tim said.

"What?"

"No. I just…is that who you want to set your best friend up with?"

"Sure. Why not?"

"I dunno. She's got a Ph.D. now and he's…a café worker."

"Remember I told you that he's also a writer?"

"Yeah. I remember," he said.

Irritated, she said, "He's actually incredibly intelligent. I've had a few more conversations with him since you met him. He's in the book club. He's also quite personable."

"Okay," Tim said, sounding unconvinced.

"I'm sure you'll like him too when you get to know him better."

"I dunno. He just doesn't sound like Ellie's type."

Maddy shrugged. "We'll see."

****

Monday, Tim went to work and Maddy continued reading through the bundle of letters. She was taking her time, not only because she didn't want them to end, but also because the ink had begun to fade in some spots making it difficult to discern words here and there. She had to literally and figuratively read between the lines. It was hard enough making heads or tails of some of the differences in various phrasing, so all of that made it a slog in some ways, but Maddy was also trying to really absorb the details and get a feel for the overall tone.

It was formal, but also soft and charming in a lot of ways. The quality and style was similar to that of the book club selection and also felt like the right tone for what Maddy wanted to write. She wasn't sure if she could pull it off yet, but she was anxious to try.

She decided to make a little spreadsheet on her computer in order to organize what she knew about Beatrice. To do that, she basically ended up starting over at the beginning of the letters before she had even reached the end of the bundle, but that was okay. The second time around, she was starting to formulate a much better picture of who Beatrice was. She was eager to take the information to Kirsten to see if she could find out even more.

So, before noon that day, she headed to the library, but when she walked in, she saw that Kirsten was not standing behind the desk like usual. It hadn't even occurred to Maddy that there could be two librarians in a place so small, but of course there had to be. Kirsten obviously didn't work every single day and she had to be able to take vacations and sick days. Disappointed, Maddy wasn't deterred. She didn't technically need Kirsten to help her find information, so she decided to see if she could come up with anything on her own.

She sat down at the one public computer the library had and she scoured the database for things she knew about Beatrice, but her keywords failed to find any concrete results. Beatrice. Mortician. 1912. Pine Grove. The results were all fairly obscure, and she spent a long time following a few promising leads down a rabbit hole. Ultimately, she came away empty-handed and frustrated. Was this the life of an author? She didn't even have the detective skills to solve a real-life mystery, let alone come up with one out of thin air.

She packed up and left the library set to come back on a day when Kirsten was there. Since she was close, she went to the coffee shop to work some more on her spreadsheet. This time, Frankie was seated in his usual spot, writing away with no hesitation, at least it appeared so to Maddy. She smiled at him as she took a seat at what was now becoming her usual table.

Frankie's hands stopped typing and they started up a lengthy conversation about writing. This time, it wasn't anything specific, just some straight ahead waxing on the general philosophies of what constituted good works from bad. Maddy soaked it all in. It was exactly what she needed, what she'd been longing for and missing.

After a bit she said, "Oh, hey, I was wondering if you're free at all on Wednesday night? Short notice, but if you'd be interested…well, remember how I mentioned that my best friend is coming into town? I just thought it would be nice to have a little dinner party type-thing, nothing fancy. It would just be the four of us, because, well, we don't really know anybody here, yet, but, if you'd like to come, we'd love having you."

"That sounds great! I'd love to come."

"Great. Yay! I'm excited. I'll just write down our address for you." She pulled her notebook out of her bag and jotted it down, handing it across the aisle to Frankie.

He glanced at the paper before folding it in half and sticking it in his pants' pocket. He didn't say anything more after that and went back to his work. Maddy understood. She'd taken up too much of his precious little time this morning before he had to start his lunch shift, and he probably just wanted to get back to his writing.

Maddy got home just before Tim. He looked beat, so they found an Asian takeout place within the delivery zone and ordered dinner. When the food came, Tim hardly touched his.

"Is everything okay?" she asked him.

He sighed. "Just tired. It's a lot being the new guy, trying to prove myself. I want to do a good job, but it's pretty stressful. I'm not sure that Dave, my supervisor, really likes me."

This came as a shock. Maddy had never heard Tim express a lick of self-doubt before. "What? Everybody likes you. You're very likable."

"I dunno, maybe at parties. This is different. I feel like I'm trying hard, but the guy is so hard to read. He's kind of a cold fish."

"I'm sure it will take some time, but he'll come around," she said.

"I hope so, if not, maybe all your efforts on this place will be for naught."

"What do you mean?"

"Maybe I'll get fired and we'll have to go back to Portland with our tails between our legs."

"That's not going to happen."

"I thought you'd be excited at the prospect of going home."

"Not for that reason. Besides, I'm starting to warm up to the place. At least a little. I mean, look, the house hasn't caused any bodily harm to me lately, so, maybe it's warming up to me somewhat too," she said with a light laugh.

Tim gave a brief smile. "Well, it's a mutual understanding then."

"Yeah, something like that."
****

Maddy was so excited to see Ellie and to host her very first dinner party at their new house that she had gone all out. By the time Ellie arrived at the front door, Maddy was exhausted, but so excited to see her best friend. Ellie looked the same for the most part, except possibly a tad more European than the last time she'd seen her. She was wearing a black and white striped T-shirt under a linen romper. Her hair was longer, but still full of thick curls, and amazing looking. Ellie had always had a carefree look that somehow still managed to be hip and arty.

"I'm so glad you're here!" Maddy said, squeezing Ellie tightly before she showed her inside.

"Wow, Mad, this place is crazy!"

"Yeah, well, we still have so much work to do on it, but it's coming along."

"It's creepy chic," Ellie said. "I mean that in the best possible way."

"No, yeah. You're exactly right."

She gave Ellie a tour of the house and then she let her shower and get settled in while she got the rest of dinner ready. Frankie arrived before Tim got home from work and while Ellie was still in the guest bedroom getting changed.

Frankie hadn't dressed up for the occasion, but that didn't bother Maddy. He wore his usual casual board shorts and T-shirt with some Vans shoes.

"Welcome," she said when she opened the door.

"So, I am in the right place," he said. "I didn't know you lived in this old house."

"Yeah. This is us."

"I almost thought maybe you'd written the address down wrong."

"Nope. Welcome to Twelve Pine Street. Please, come on in."

She got him a drink, and a few minutes later, Ellie came down. She left them to chat while she finished dinner. Shortly after that Tim arrived, and they sat down to eat. Maddy had prepared a whole chicken, which she'd never done before. She wasn't really sure what possessed her to do it considering she could have purchased a rotisserie chicken already cooked for less than ten bucks, but she wanted it to be special. Her first real meal in their new home with her best friend there

181

visiting—it was so grown up.

To go with the chicken she also roasted some fingerling potatoes and organic purple carrots in the oven and because that was all pretty healthy, she bought a loaf of sourdough bread for good measure. And for dessert, she decided to bake something from scratch. A lemon tart. This was slightly over ambitious, she realized too late, because she hadn't really thought out the fact that she would need all of the room in the oven for the bird and the veg, so the tart went in late.

In fact, they'd eaten dinner and it had gone well up till that point, but now they sat drinking wine waiting for the tart to bake and the conversation had gone a bit stale. Tim wanted to keep babbling about architecture because he'd given Frankie the tour and he and Ellie had done a good job at feigning interest while he went on ad nauseam about obscure details that Tim had taken for sincerity, but Maddy could tell it wasn't. Ellie wanted to talk about England which was fine until that talk started to bleed into her babbling about her relationship and how it came to a crashing halt when Jasper, her ex-boyfriend, had told her that he wasn't ready for a serious commitment. And the more wine Ellie drank, the more she came back around to that awkward topic.

Frankie, who had been nothing but polite, was a lot quieter than Maddy had expected him to be. He'd been pretty easy-going and unencumbered in her previous interactions with him, but tonight he seemed uncomfortable, out-of-place, possibly distracted, or maybe all three. And that got Maddy wondering if maybe Frankie knew something about the house. He'd been weird the minute she opened the door.

When the tart was finally ready and she served it, in an effort to try to rein the conversation back in, Maddy decided to tell them all about the letters. And it did seem to perk up at least Frankie. "They were in a secret built-in drawer?"

"Yeah. And from what I've gathered, the writer, Beatrice, was a mortician's wife, which would mean that a mortician lived here."

"Whoa. How creepy," Ellie said.

"I thought so at first," Maddy said. "Honestly, when we first moved in, I seriously thought the place was haunted, but as I read the letters, I dunno. I'm starting to feel like this woman was going through some stuff."

"Like what?" Frankie asked.

"Her tone had sort of a desperation, like she was almost begging her sister to come and save her or something, but her sister and her father both seemed like they didn't really care about her at all. Oh, and then something strange happened. A boy died in some kind of accident, and I can't really figure it out because it doesn't sound like it was her child. Now, I'm beginning to wonder if the kid haunts this place."

"Holy shit, Maddy!" Ellie said.

"I know, right?" Maddy concurred. "Anyway, it's been interesting to read the letters, and they've inspired me to write something based on them. It's coming along okay even."

"Really?" Frankie said in a soft tone. "That's awesome. Like I said before, I'd love to read what you have some time."

"Nobody is haunting this place," Tim interjected abruptly. "She only got that idea because some kids told

183

her someone died here."

"No…they didn't say somebody *died*," Maddy said. "They said someone was *murdered* here."

"Oh my God," Ellie said. "Seriously?"

"It was just kids being kids," Tim said. "It's because the house is old and gothic. That's all."

Maddy glanced over at Frankie to see his reaction, but he didn't offer any further input to the conversation. In fact, he didn't say much else at all, and then shortly after finishing dessert, he stood up and said that he had a great time, but he should probably be heading out. It was only just after 9:30 at that point and Maddy felt bad because he definitely did not seem to have a great time or even a good time.

She didn't know if it was because he hadn't clicked with Ellie, or if it was because they were generally duller people than who he typically hung out with. She hoped that it was actually something less dramatic than that, like he just had an early shift at the café the next morning or maybe he wasn't really a night person.

Ellie was tired from her travels, Tim was worn out from work, and Maddy was exhausted from all of the cleaning and cooking she'd done, so they all went to bed shortly after doing some light clearing of the dishes. Maddy lay in bed and thought a bit more about Beatrice before she fell asleep. Had she hidden the letters because she was scared? Like Maddy had stated at the dinner table, the tone of the letters certainly seemed to take on a desperate tone. What had gone on here? Was Beatrice in trouble? Because Maddy hadn't been kidding around. She really did get a bad vibe initially, with all of the strange things happening in her wake, but now she wondered if the ghost in this house was not actually a child, but Beatrice herself. And maybe she wasn't trying to haunt Maddy but get her to uncover the mysteries she'd locked away in the hidden drawer after all this time. Because no matter how many times Tim told her that there hadn't been a murder in this house, she wasn't convinced. Even while in bed, with a sheet covering her in the middle of a warm summer, a chill ran the length of her body.

Chapter Twenty-Nine

1912

Beatrice stayed in bed all day and did not go down to attend the service being held that eve in the room directly below her. Though she could tell from the noise that her announcement had been effective in bringing a goodly amount of folks to the Westmoreland Funeral Parlor, she couldn't undo her part in such a horrid lie. The turmoil in her knowing of it continued to make the child within her own self unhappy as it kicked and fought with her insides.

Charles made an awkward attempt to comfort her later that evening when he came to bed. It was at that point that she knew she could no longer hold it inside. She had to expel it in order to appease the baby, and so she lashed out, "I know of the trickery you've played!" she screeched. "The coffin was empty! I know there was no child, that it was a ruse in order to gain funds for the business. That is it, is it not? Am I correct in my assertions?"

Flat on his back, Charles lay next to her with his head on the pillow. With his specs now off, and in full bedclothes, he looked frail and as dour as one possibly could.

"Why?" she asked in a whisper.

He turned to her, his brow furrowed tightly. "I had

no other choice. Believe me, Beatrice, I have felt sick over it myself, but…" He trailed off and did not continue.

She waited, thinking this was just him taking his time with his words. When none came, she grew more upset. "But what, Charles? I am your wife. You must share your thoughts with me if we are to be a family."

But he did not give her a proper answer. "Do not fret over this. It will be okay," was all he managed to say with little confidence accompanying the words. He turned and drank down a glass of milk sitting on the table beside him before blowing out his candle.

Beatrice spent another night with a sour tummy, and she worried if things continued like this the baby would suffer from her discontent. So, she decided to get out of the house to cleanse her spirit by attending an auxiliary meeting one evening and it was a very good thing she had.

****

My beloved sister,

The ladies of the auxiliary informed this writer that the traveling carnival is due to arrive in Pine Grove soon! I can't believe it to be true. I had somehow neglected to see the notices posted about town. I could barely speak for the rest of the meeting after the announcement was made. My thoughts veered from the talk of charity work, as my only focus was with regards to speaking to you again, Sister. The excitement of that being forthcoming is so great, I can barely contain myself. Not only does a carnival sound joyous, but the potential of hearing you sing again would nourish my soul a good deal.

This news had made it bearable for me to keep

from becoming overwhelmed otherwise. I have much to tell you upon your arrival to town. I am awaiting the days until I am able to bask in your presence again.

For now,
Beatrice

****

Even as the autumn days were getting shorter and shorter and the air had a bite to it as the dusk set in, the circus arrived on a lovely evening. Beatrice strolled over to the carnival grounds with several of the ladies from the auxiliary. The festivities had been set up on the very outskirts of town on the Gold's farmstead which had already harvested crops for the season.

Charles had not requested to come along; Beatrice had not tried to convince him otherwise, knowing he would not find the festival's offering to be well-suited for his character. Being asked to suspend disbelief was not an easy task for a man like him, but Beatrice could accept that these things were not for everyone.

Upon entering the carnival gates, Beatrice was transfixed by the sights and sounds and smells. It was thrilling, unlike anything she'd ever experienced. Children and adults alike projected the kind of youthful energy that filled the cool air with radiant excitement. Sugared candies were doled out by a vendor and barking men called to people to see the wonders and curiosities behind the curtains. The ladies from *Our Lady of Hope* had a booth set up to sell their pies, cakes, and handiwork, but Bea set off on her own immediately upon entering as she was overly anxious to find Jane.

With a click to her step, she circled the path trying to assess which tent or booth might contain her prize.

With so much to take in, she strode by games for young ones and food vendors aplenty, peep shows which she did indeed peep into just to see if her sister might be within the draped curtains, but alas—no. She saw rare animals and oddities of all sorts, trapeze, magicians, and clowns, but she did not find her sister.

As it got on in the evening, Beatrice was losing hope, but on a second round of searching, she stopped in front of a tent she had not yet ventured. She was almost too scared to enter, not because of what it was, but because she was terrified of being let down, but she knew she must do so now. It was time.

The painted wooden placard on the tent flap was written in a fancy cursive:

Madame Rose
Medium. Seer. Tarot.
Fortunes Told Here

Beatrice had never had her fortune told, but that was not the point of her stop. She would buy a ticket if she must, if only to be allowed to ask Madame Rose if she knew Jane. She stepped inside and queued up in the first small room. The space was tight and had a mystical quality that held Beatrice's mind aflutter while she waited. Chimes and trinkets dangled from the tent top creating a high-pitched cacophony of sounds. A rainbow-colored bird in a cage squawked along as if it knew the tune, whilst a black cat sat on the table directly below the cage as if on guard. A soft glow from dozens of candles spread around the room was calming in comparison to the rest of the whimsical chaos swirling.

When it was Beatrice's turn, the ticket taker held the curtain open for her and she stepped in. This room, she found, was in stark contrast to the antechamber being utterly devoid of anything except two mismatched chairs and a single candle burning on a thinly spindled table. A small, hunched woman sat in one of the chairs. Without a glance up, she beckoned Beatrice to take the other. Liver spots covered much of her face and her mouth puckered as an indication that she lacked teeth within. Her eyes were coated in a milky, white haze and a silk scarf covered her head. She was perhaps the oldest person Beatrice had ever laid eyes upon.

"I am Madame Rose."

"I am Beatrice and I—"

"Hush, child. I do not like too much information clouding my head."

"My apologies."

"Now. I will tell your future."

"If you don't mind, I've come to…I was hoping for some information about—"

"Hush, now. My mind is busy seeing."

Beatrice did as she was told for the clairvoyant woman frightened her a good bit. What this old woman might be seeing did tantalize Bea. She was not opposed to her future being laid out before her, she realized all at once. In fact, she was positively curious. Perhaps the old woman would offer her a quick glimpse ahead with regards to her child, her marriage, and perhaps the funeral parlor, in addition to her getting news of Jane. The sign said she was capable of both skills.

While Beatrice waited in anticipation, the old seer had actually closed her eyes and began humming softly while swaying in her chair. When she opened them again, she said, "I see a family…"

"Yes, I am—"

"Silence, child!"

Beatrice jerked in terror as the woman's words cut sharply. She closed her eyes again and hummed for what felt like too long. Beatrice was restless now and had a strong desire to leave there, as she had grown warm and weary from all of the walking and searching she'd done. The old woman's humming only added to the lulling effects forming in her bones.

Suddenly, Madame Rose spoke again and this time it was with a bold declarative nature. Her eyes fluttered open. "They will betray you."

"Oh, good heavens," Beatrice said as dread crept into her skin. "In what manner?"

"In the most evil of manners." The woman's eyes began to close.

"My sister," Beatrice said, hoping to keep the old medium with her for longer, "she—"

"Yes. Your sister. That's who will betray you."

"But—"

"That is all I can see," the old woman said. She reached out and touched Beatrice's hand gently. "Take care now and go forward with much caution, my child."

Beatrice was dizzy with the revelation thrust upon her in such a crass manner. She got up and was shown out through the back flap of the tent by the ticket takers so abruptly that once out into the fresh night air, she felt turned around and confused. She stumbled through the gates, exiting the carnival altogether. Consumed by the seer's words as she began her journey home, she gained clarity on the meaning of the fortune in its entirety.

Her family *had* betrayed her. It was simple and true. Not only her father, but now a fresh upset over the absence of her sister took hold. It was a piercing heartbreak that made it so Bea could barely breathe. Where was her sister, now, when she needed her guidance and support more than ever? In her maturity, Beatrice was beginning to see that Jane was just as selfish as her father. She'd abandoned her without thought or concern, much like Jakob had done. Why did her own flesh and blood not return her affection? What was so difficult about it? Was something wrong with her?

Beatrice didn't know how she might begin to take caution, as the old woman had advised. It seemed far too late for such a warning as the two people who should have been her life-long companions had all but deserted her long ago. There was no more reason to be heading off the evil before it arrived, as her father and sister had already managed to rip her heart out, thereby doing all the damage they could.

She wondered only momentarily if the fortune teller was not to be believed. Could the old woman really have such abilities to see beyond the concrete? Whether she did or not, Beatrice was definitely now in a state. The words rang so true it was hard not to take them at face value. That she had been invigorated only hours ago, but now walked home alone in the bitter darkness left her drained of spirit.

When she returned, she did not speak with Charles regarding the events knowing full well that he would discount the entire thing. But the words of Madame Rose, Beatrice had decided, were anything but wrong and she was depleted from them, yet she felt a compulsion to get the emotions all out before resting—for the sake of good health for the baby. And so she sat down to write:

To my sister,

I do not understand why I did not find you this night where I believed you to be and I cannot lie—my heart is forsaken by it. Do you mean to hurt me? Are you much like Father and less like the woman I always thought you to be? Has this writer done something wrong to warrant such disrespect?

How shall I rectify such treatment? Is the only way to cast you aside entirely? Who have I to turn to if not my sister?

I will stop here as I am worn through, and I must sleep now. Tomorrow is another day, and I shall put this behind me and think of only good things that are to come for the sake of my child. I will not let the ugliness seep into my own blood as I do not wish to impart it onto my own offspring.

Beatrice

Chapter Thirty

2022

The next day, Maddy woke up with a slight headache and would have liked nothing more than to stay in bed all day, absorbing the rest of the letters, but she had to get up and entertain Ellie before she flew back to Portland. Already she could hear Ellie rattling things around downstairs in the kitchen.

Reluctantly, she got out of bed, got dressed, and halfway down the stairs, she heard Ellie let out a high-pitched wail. Maddy flew down the rest of the steps and ran into the kitchen only to see a black cat standing near the back door. "Jesus, El! You scared me. I thought someone was trying to murder you."

"Are you seeing this? It's a black cat! Your house is *so* haunted."

"No," Maddy said, calmly approaching the cat and reaching her hand out. "This is Boots. He belongs to the neighbor next door."

"How do you know?"

"Because I met him when I met the neighbor. He must have slipped in the door when Tim left for work this morning." Maddy opened the back door and Boots immediately and happily scampered off.

Ellie shook her head. "I don't think I like this place much, especially after everything you said last night."

"Well, lucky for you, you get to leave today for Portland."

Maddy saw that Tim had left them half a pot of coffee. She poured two cups and carried them over to the living room, where they sat on the couch to drink them.

"Are you hating it here? For real?" Ellie said.

"I *am* homesick, but I'm not actually hating it here. I've joined a book club, and I've started writing something that I think might end up being halfway decent, which I'm excited about, so I'll be fine."

"Yeah, but, like why did you guys buy such a ginormous, old house?"

"For one thing, I think Tim was shocked by how cheap it was and that we could actually afford it. This house would have been over a million dollars in Portland, but here it was within our budget. And he also really wants to have a buttload of kids to fill it up."

"He's still pretty set on that, then, huh? Even after everything you guys went through with your sister?"

"Yep."

"What about you? How do you feel about it?"

"I don't know. I mean, I always wanted kids, and I still think maybe I will sometime in the future, but I'm not gonna sit here and say I'm not terrified by what happened."

"Yeah. Well, there's always adoption," Ellie said.

Maddy nodded. "Hey, sorry about Frankie last night. I'm not sure why he was acting so weird. I've had a few really decent conversations with him before, but he seemed really different here. I'm not sure what that was all about."

"I was wondering," Ellie said. "But it's okay. I'm

still not over Jasper."

Maddy laughed. "That's obvious. I was hoping Frankie would change that, and you two would fall madly in love, you'd want to stay in Pine Grove with me forever and ever, and our kids would grow up together just like we did. They'd be besties and we'd all live happily ever after."

"That's a sweet little fairytale," Ellie said, "but I thought you were trying to write a murder mystery."

Maddy frowned. "Probably more realistic, I suppose."

"God, I hope you don't actually get murder in this place when I leave. Though, I'm really not too sure." Ellie cackled like a witch.

Maddy gave her a playful shove. "Oh, the neighbor, John. He's a retired homicide detective; he'll protect me."

"For real?"

"Yeah. And, if I can get something written, I'm going to ask him to read it…you know…for validity."

"Perfect," Ellie said. "I get to read it too, right?"

"Definitely."

"I can't wait!"

"Well, you're going to have to wait because it's not done yet," Maddy said.

"I kinda wonder though," Ellie said. "I think the reason Frankie was acting weird is because he has the hots for you."

"What? No way! I was with Tim at the café the day we met him. He knew I was married from day one."

"That doesn't stop guys from pining."

Maddy shook her head. "No." But the more she mulled it over, the more she started to question it.

"I dunno, Mad. I think it's possible."

"I don't think so. I *am* curious why he was acting so strange. I have a feeling there's a really simple explanation."

"You're going to ask him?"

"Sure. Why not?"

"Why not? Because I don't think you're going to like the answer," Ellie said with a smirk.

****

After sending Ellie off in a rideshare car to the airport, Maddy decided to try again at the library and hoped this time Kirsten would be there to help her research the house and Beatrice. But when she got there, she was immediately let down. The other, older librarian stood in Kirsten's place. Why Maddy was reluctant to ask this woman for help, she didn't know, and she was losing patience, but she really thought for some reason that it would be best to wait for Kirsten to return. Maddy asked when she would be back. She informed her that Kirsten was at a Midwest librarian conference but would be back tomorrow.

"Oh, were you here to pick up the book club book?" the librarian asked. She held up a copy of *The Life We Bought*.

"Yeah. Actually, I do need a copy." Maddy dug around in her bag and found her library token. Instinctively, she handed it to the woman.

"You don't need to give it to me. You can just take the book and walk out."

"Oh, right. I forgot. Thank you."

Not wanting to go home quite yet, Maddy headed for The Pine Cone to get some more writing done. When she walked in, the friendly, middle-aged lady with the round face who reminded Maddy of her mom was behind the counter. Maddy ordered an iced tea, and while the woman poured it, she held a huge grin on her face. It wasn't that strange, given how friendly she was, but Maddy couldn't help but feel there was more to it. And soon enough, she realized she was right.

When she handed Maddy her glass, and said, "You aren't Maddy by chance, are you?"

"I am. How did you—"

"I don't mean to pry. It's just that I've been hearing so much about you. I thought it might be you."

"Uh…" Maddy wasn't sure how to respond to that. "Hearing about me?"

Nodding her head, she said, "From Frankie."

"Oh." Uh oh. Was Ellie right? Was Frankie telling his co-workers about her? She felt her face warm over.

"He said you're a great writer."

"He told you that?"

"Yeah. Some people may think it's a little weird that my son tells me everything, but it's really just because we're always together," she said. "At home. Here."

"You're his mom?"

"Yep. I'm Ginny! I own this place. Anyway, it's so nice to meet you, Maddy. I won't keep you. I know you've got lots of important stuff to write."

Maddy stepped away from the counter and found an empty seat. Her mind was trying to compute this new information, because when she met Frankie, he told her he'd recently moved here, but that was obviously not true. He'd also never mentioned anything about living and working with his mom, though Maddy recalled thinking he was the owner of the café the first time she and Tim came in, so that checked out.

Something still didn't add up. Why had he lied to her? Why the secrets? What was Frankie hiding? And why had he told his mother about Maddy? He had no idea if she was a great writer. She didn't even know yet if she was a good writer. She hadn't written anything worth showing to Frankie yet, but now she wasn't so sure she wanted to if and when she did. She hoped to God that Ellie was wrong, but she was starting to think otherwise.

She fired up her computer, but her mind was too distracted, and she wasn't successful in getting any new words on the page, so she took out the new book club book the old librarian had given her and tried to read that for a while, but when she failed at that too, she took the bundle of letters from her bag. She'd brought them along hoping to show them to Kirsten, but instead she got back to reading and cataloging the information in her spreadsheet. Since she was unsure of the exact order of the letters because they had no dates on them, she tried to create a timeline where she could plunk some of the facts in and have it all make sense.

As she read, she got to the part where Beatrice wrote to her sister that she was expecting a baby and Maddy audibly gasped in the middle of the café. Luckily no one seemed to notice. She was shocked at how attached she'd become to this woman over the course of the letters. The pregnancy news automatically filled her with a new sense of dread and foreboding for Beatrice.

She did not like where this story was going. Not at all.

Chapter Thirty-One

1912

The next day Beatrice woke with a strong sense she must make peace with the occurrences of the prior evening, thus she thrusted all of her untethered energy into preparing an elegant sup of Cornish game hen, new boiled potatoes, steamed carrots, and freshly baked sourdough. For dessert, she tried her hand at something special. A newfangled recipe that was on trend. It was called Orange Fool and was a delicious fruit-flavored custard pie with a whipped topping.

Charles, seemingly baffled by the overabundance of food at the table, gave her a peculiar look. When she sat down across from him, Charles cleared his throat. "Did you have a nice visit with your sister last evening at the fair?"

She saw not the eyes of a madman when she looked across the table at him, but a husband concerned for his wife. She could not lie to him. How could she hold in her own secrets when she had told him nights previous that if they were to be a family, he had to relinquish his deepest, darkest thoughts to her? It was time for her to do the same.

"Oh, Charles. You will think I'm hysterical if I tell you this. I'm afraid you will have me committed to the women's asylum, yet I must share it with you. I went to the festivities to speak with my sister…only I did not tell you the whole of it. Instead of speaking with Jane, I talked with one who communicates with the dead, for you see…my beloved sister…is gone."

"Gone?"

"Yes. For quite some time now." She paused to pull her words together. "The thing is…there have been times when…well, I had a strong bond with my sister even when she wasn't exactly with me. It afforded me great comfort and strength in the past. But she vanished rather suddenly one day. I don't know why she left. Perhaps it was because I became older, more sensible. I've often thought she might return one day, but alas, she has not. I had hoped the old fortune teller would be able to reconnect us. Instead, she told me some rather disturbing news. It was something I believe I knew all along but chose not to see." Bea lifted her glass of water and swallowed it all down for she was suddenly rather parched.

She went on. "I thought on it all afternoon as I cooked. I considered bringing the matter to Dr. Boyle to see if there was a remedy for such things, but I think I've settled it myself. I think I am ready to move on from it all and put it behind me."

She watched Charles ponder this new information in the same way he took in all of his news. "I see," he finally said.

"You must think me mad." She took out her hankie and wiped away tears, for she had never told anyone about this secret. It was a blessing to relinquish it.

"I do not think you to be mad."

Sniffling, she said, "I'm so relieved. I have only told you because I think it best for us to share all of our truths. You must be able to do the same with me."

He nodded and looked down toward the table and thought for a long spell. Then he said meekly, "I hate to speak poorly of my own flesh and blood."

She pondered the meaning of these words before she put them all together. "Francis? The false funeral was his doing?"

He gave a quick glance behind him toward the intake room and nodded and continued in hushed tones. "He is my brother, and I care for him, but he will be my demise, I'm afraid."

She shifted her body and forced the mortician to look at her. She took his hands in hers. "You must assert yourself. This is your business. Why do you let him control you so?"

"He saved my life…from the fire that claimed our parents. If not for his strength and courage, I would not be here."

"Nonsense," Beatrice said. "If not for you, he'd still just be a simple lumberyard laborer. You are wiser and older than he. You must tell him you won't do as he says any longer. Can you not ask him to leave?"

"It's not so simple as all that. Who would take the midnight shifts? Who would drive the carriage? Dig the graves? Besides, he provided me with capital to get things off the ground. I knew I was taking a risk by asking. He holds it over me. He holds everything over me. I never should have trusted him. He's not a good person. I should have tried to make my own way, but I wasn't able. I have failed myself," he said, in anguish. "I have failed you. I apologize."

Beatrice looked into the mortician's tearful eyes and saw the man she knew, a good and kind man. "You haven't failed me. You must speak to him. Tell him you no longer wish to go along with his deceit."

"What if we lose everything?"

"So be it. We don't need to have a large brood. A few children will do just as well. We can sell this magnificent house and find something cozier, more reasonable, to cut expenses if we must. We don't need all of this," she said, smiling at her husband.

"Are you sure?"

"Yes."

As Charles nodded, she saw relief fall over him. She too was relieved to have everything between them out in the open. After the meal, she excused herself early, explaining to him that she would clean up the dishes in the morrow. In truth, she suddenly succumbed to the wariness, knowing she would finally be able to get some rest because the child inside of her had settled. She got into her bed that evening and fell asleep with a smile upon her lips.

Chapter Thirty-Two

2022

On her walk home, Maddy saw John sitting on a rocker on his front porch. A book in his hand, a cozy blanket sat on his lap with Boots curled up sleeping soundly in its folds. She smiled to herself recalling the notion that she'd once thought of John as an old, cranky recluse.

"Hi," she said, stopping on the sidewalk in front of him. "Are you reading *The Life We Bought*?"

He looked up at her and nodded. "Have you started it yet?"

"I tried. I'm struggling with it."

"That makes two of us," he said, lowering the book.

They both laughed.

"This is definitely going to be a DNF for me," John said.

"DNF?"

"Did not finish."

"You can do that?"

"Of course you can. It's not school, Maddy. Kirsten isn't handing out gold stickers to the best readers."

"Right. I just—"

"Just don't tell Pam," he said. "I'll probably fake it

during the meeting."

"No problem. I wish I could do that, but I'm no good at lying, so I'll try to power through," she said.

"Hey, I didn't say anything about lying," John said, but he was giving her a sly grin.

She smiled back. The subject of lying reminded her of something. "I have a question for you…"

"Shoot."

"You've been in the book club for a long time, right?"

"Too long," he said.

"How long has Frankie been part of it, would you say roughly?"

"Oh, a couple of years now…maybe four? Why?"

"I was just curious."

"Oh, but he was gone for a while there."

"Really? Gone where?"

"Don't know. I try to make it my business to not know other people's business. Unless they committed murder that is," John said.

"Right. Okay. Well, I guess that means Frankie hasn't killed anyone that we know of, so that's good. Thanks, John. I'll see you later."

"See ya, Maddy."

When she got inside, she started doing the dishes that had stacked up from Ellie's visit when she heard a noise. At first, her mind went straight to attributing it to Boots, except she just saw the cat on John's lap—unless he had slipped in behind her again. She walked into the living room and heard the sound a second time. She hadn't imagined it. Stopping at the top of the stairs, she heard the sound more clearly now as it carried down the staircase. It was definitely coming from upstairs, and it didn't sound like a cat.

It sounded like scratching or scraping.

Her heart raced. She considered going back out to talk to John, but she felt too silly. She pulled her phone from her pocket and was about to dial up Tim on her phone when she saw a missed text from him on her locked screen.

—*I'm home. Where R U?*—

Breathing a sigh, she climbed the stairs and found Tim at his drafting table. "Hey," she said. "What are you doing here?"

He turned in his chair to face her. "What do you mean? I live here."

"I know, but…"

"It's almost six," he said with a bite to his tone.

She looked at her phone again to check the time. "Oh, I didn't realize it was so late. I lost track of time at the café."

"Was Frankie there?" he asked, turning back to his drafting table.

"No."

"What was up with that guy, by the way?"

Maddy set her laptop bag down on the floor and put her hand on her hip. "What was up with him?"

"I wasn't wrong about him. He was a dud."

"That's not very nice," she said.

Tim's volume increased ever so slightly. "Why do you keep defending him?"

"I agree that he was acting a little weird, but he's not a dud."

"He definitely is," Tim said. "Did Ellie like him?"

"No."

"See?"

"That's no reason to be rude," Maddy said.

"I'm not being rude, just saying the guy seemed boring. That's all."

"Well, I don't know. He's been pretty nice to me at the café. Maybe he was just having an off night or something."

"He's been nice to you, huh?"

"Yeah."

"How nice?"

Now Maddy's voice raised up. "What?"

Tim wheeled his chair around to face her. His back was rigid and his face was equally stiff. "Come on, Maddy!" He shifted uncomfortably in his chair, and when he spoke again it was clear he was irritated with her. "Is there something going on with you two?"

She was confused. This came out of left field. "Going on? Are you serious right now? Why would I be trying to fix him up with my best friend if I liked him?"

"I have no idea." Tim paused. "All I know is that you've been acting weird lately."

Baffled, she asked, "I have? How so?"

"I dunno…just different. The only reason I can think why that might be the case is that you have the hots for that guy."

Now she was equally irritated. "That's ridiculous, Tim!"

"Is it?"

"Yes!"

Maddy stormed off into her own office and slammed the door shut hard behind her. She slumped onto her window seat and looked down at the garden in the backyard. She'd completely neglected it so far this summer, and now it was terribly overgrown. But from this vantage point, she could see all sorts of gorgeous flowers shooting up through the weeds and undergrowth. The beauty breaking free from the ugliness calmed her mind, and for a second she wondered if Beatrice herself had been the one to initially plant the annuals. Or were they perennials? She could never remember which was which, but she would add it to the list of things to figure out.

Now that she was a tad calmer, she reflected on what had just transpired with Tim. She wasn't even sure why she was defending Frankie. It seemed fairly clear that Tim was right about the guy. She didn't think he was a dud, but it did seem that maybe he wasn't such a great guy after all, though it wasn't because of the dinner party. It was because he obviously wasn't being truthful about something.

She had no idea why she was mad at Tim except that the accusation came so out of left field, she was shocked and hurt by it. Had she been acting differently? Maybe. But that didn't give Tim the right to make strange allegations that weren't true.

Not wanting to go back out and face her husband yet, she took out Beatrice's letters and she stayed sitting on the window bench until she finished reading them all. No more savoring; she was ready to find out what happened to Beatrice and her family. She devoured the rest of the notes one after the other. When she was finished, she set the stack down carefully and reflected.

While she was sad that she had no more to read, she was also disappointed. There seemed to be little resolve. Maddy shuffled through the letters again quickly to see if she had missed any, but it appeared this was it. It was heartbreaking that Beatrice clearly had never heard from her sister, or if she had, and there was nothing to indicate she had, no return letters, or anything other mention of her coming for a visit.

What had happened to Jane? Maddy had no way of knowing if Beatrice had seen her when she attended the carnival or not. She wanted to believe she had, but she couldn't be sure.

And there was no obvious conclusion to Beatrice's life contained within the set of letters either. What ultimately had happened to her? What about the baby? What about the funeral parlor?

Toward the end, the letters took on a darker tone. Had something tragic occurred like she'd speculated earlier on? Maybe she was being overly dramatic. Maybe she was reading into things because that was how her pessimistic mind worked. Maybe Beatrice had gone on to have a happy life. Maybe. Though Maddy just couldn't stop thinking there had to be more to the story.

Chapter Thirty-Three

1912

The short but necessary conversation with her husband renewed Bea's spirit and gave her new confidence in her marriage going forward. The timing could not have been better as they had reached a milestone. Charles came to her one day as she sat resting on the davenport in the sitting room adjacent to the parlor with her quilting held firmly in her lap. He handed her a bouquet of flowers, which she found amusing considering the room was already overflowing with arrangements almost identical to the one he'd given her.

"Happy anniversary," he said sweetly.

"Thank you. They are lovely. Has it been a whole year already?" she asked, though she knew that it had been.

Sniffing the flowers, she thought back on how their marriage had come to be. Charles had written to Bea's father at the lumber company to inquire about the cost of pine for caskets. After some back and forth with their correspondence, he arrived in Stillwater to negotiate with her father. She felt as though she knew him from his words on the page and he must have felt the same as he spoke to her kindly. In that first year of his business, he returned regularly gathering supplies and always with a tip of the hat to her at the table where she sat handling other letters for her father.

She didn't think her father would ever let her marry, nor did she think any bachelor would want a woman nearing twenty-nine years. As fate would have it, Charles had neglected taking a wife while he focused on growing his funeral business from nothing, and by the time he was ready to do so, he spoke with Beatrice's father about her prospects. And now, here they were, in a place Beatrice never thought she might be.

She set the floral bundle beside her. In return, she shuffled her heavy body and patted the seat next to her, asking him to join her. She produced a wrapped gift of her own and handed it to her husband. He smiled sheepishly at her as he opened the new ledger, the thing she knew would make him the most happy.

"It's wonderful," he said, reaching his hand for hers. He gave it a gentle squeeze. Then, unexpectedly, Charles pulled his hand away and he produced a small, wrapped package from his inner-breast pocket and placed it in her hand.

"What is this?"

"A small token."

She unwrapped the gift while he sat beside her watching shyly. Inside the box was an elegant pen. It was much fancier than the one she currently used to write with and looked to be rather expensive. "Oh, Charles. This is too much."

"Nothing is too much for you," he said with a smile that made him blush from cheek to cheek.

Beatrice placed a kiss upon his lips and told him for the first time that she loved him. Shortly thereafter, as she sat in the garden, she overheard Charles talking with Francis in the receiving room. She didn't want to pry, but she did notice some weeds nearer to the open door that needed attending, so she busied herself with the task and just happened to also be able to listen in on the conversation taking place inside.

"There will be no more false charity," Charles said. 'I will run an honest funeral home."

"You will lose it all," Francis replied.

"I will work harder to gain more business from the outer reaches of town, I will keep searching for cheaper supplies," he paused. "I may need to relieve you of your duties."

"You wouldn't."

"If that's what I must do to provide for my family, I will."

"I am your family, too," Francis said with a bite to his raised voice.

"I'm sorry," Charles said, holding firm.

"You will regret this, brother!"

Beatrice tucked herself behind the closed door and soon Francis came bolting out of it rushing off down the path, just as she suspected he might do. When he was gone, she smiled, proud of her husband for standing on his own feet.

****

The beginning days of December brought not only cooler weather but also a few customers to the Westmoreland Funeral Parlor. Once again, the house buzzed with activity. Beatrice made haste. She worked herself to the bone to make sure all went smoothly. And now that her marriage was as strong as ever, things began to get back to being somewhat normal and talk of money troubles fell by the wayside.

Things between Charles and his brother seemed to resolve back into their usual work demeanor; all was seemingly well. In fact, Beatrice noted Elizabeth coming around the house more so than previously. Beatrice assumed this was because she was keeping a close eye on her now that the pregnancy was advancing.

One afternoon, Elizabeth asked Beatrice if she would like to take a carriage ride. Fresh snow had fallen; Elizabeth assured her it would be a peaceful adventure. Francis drove the carriage while Elizabeth was attentive to Beatrice's every move.

"Are you quite comfortable?" she asked as she tucked a woolen blanket around Beatrice's lap.

"Quite. Thank you. The scenery is beautiful."

"Stunning," Elizabeth said. "You've been feeling well, have you not? No cramping or aches?"

"Perhaps a few minor aches."

"In what region?"

"All over," Beatrice said with a giggle.

"You must remember to not overdo things now," Elizabeth warned. "Let Charles handle it all."

"I'm fine. Really."

"I've brought along some nice tea for you," Elizabeth said, producing a jug. "This should help relax you and will take care of the aches and pains, too."

"That's very kind of you, but you're doing too much for me. There's no need to fret over me."

"We're sisters," Elizabeth said. "I'm happy to fret over you." She reached over and touched Beatrice's belly. "Besides, I must keep you and the little one healthy. That's my job."

And fret she did. For the next few, she popped in and out often checking in on Beatrice. It was wonderful to have a real companion. Elizabeth often brought small cakes and warm elixirs along. The two sat whenever there was a spare moment and chatted about the baby, which seemed to please them both.

Preparations for the arrival of the child were now well underway as the time was getting nearer and Beatrice had never been so happy in all her life. She was relaxed and much calmer than she expected she would be, but she didn't slow down as her sister by marriage continued to advise her. But as the services continued steadily, Beatrice wanted to make sure everything got done, including decorating the home for the upcoming holiday festivities.

Here and there, she floated about the place. In and out of Charles's office, cooking in the kitchen, and tidying up the parlor and sitting room, Beatrice found that on several occasions Francis appeared to be lingering about in spaces she rarely saw him—in places she had duties to do. Additionally, she found that his eyes would hold too long on her midsection.

"Pardon me," he would say if she caught him in the act and he would move on, but later the same scene would play out in another part of the home.

She did not think much about it as she suspected her dear sister by marriage had instructed him to keep a close watch. It was only out of character in that until now he had hardly seemed to pay Beatrice mind at all, or rather, he certainly had not gone out of his way to be pleasant to her. She found it a good bit strange considering how amiable his wife could be.

And perhaps it was for good reason, because one afternoon, with snow falling wildly outside the large windows of the parlor, Beatrice stood hanging pine boughs up along the top frames in anticipation of Christmastime when in the midst of tying a strand of red ribbon into a bow, she felt a sensation stir within her that was more powerful than any she'd felt before. As it grabbed on tightly and wound itself around her mid-region like a snake, she let out a sound that equaled the intensity of the pain.

Her knees buckled and she found herself doubled over on the floor of the parlor. In a moments' time, Francis was at her side. "Come," he said, lifting her. "We must get you to Elizabeth."

She wanted to stay aware, but things were fuzzy as Francis took her under his broad shoulders and helped her through the garden path toward the carriage house. "What about Charles?" she recalled saying.

"There's no time."

Just before the blackness hit her, she cried out as another intense wave of pain coursed through her with a force she never thought possible.

It was followed closely by an immense tear she had not felt before until that very moment.

Chapter Thirty-Four

2022

After Maddy had finished reading the letters, she was in a strange headspace, and wasn't ready to talk about things with Tim since their argument over Frankie. She took a bath and tried to distract herself with the book club read which continued to be weird and confusing, but it did help her forget about her own struggles for a short time, so she took that as a win.

It was late by the time she went to bed, and Tim was already sprawled out on his side of the bed dead asleep. It seemed like a new trend since he'd started his job, and she still wasn't used to it. She understood that he had a lot of new responsibilities, but she also wondered if this was going to be their life now. It was such a stark contrast to their old life. Or at least the life they had just after they got married and before Tim got this job.

He was the one always wanting to go out to bars and movies and hang out with friends until impossible hours, and Maddy was the one who had preferred the solace of home, staying in and simply hanging out with Tim. The nights they stayed in were her favorite. Often they snuggled up in bed together and read until late. Well, Tim usually leafed through an architecture magazine, and Maddy read for her writing program, but to her those were the parts of the marriage she preferred.

The honeymoon phase was clearly over. She lay awake for a long time thinking about her life and comparing it to what she knew about Beatrice's life. It was crazy to think that the things described in the letters had taken place right here. She had possibly gone to sleep right in this very room with her husband, the mortician, over a hundred years before now. She felt an odd connection to this woman she'd never met. Had she raised her children here? Would Maddy do the same? She fell asleep wondering about the past and future of Twelve Pine Street.

Tim was already gone from bed when Maddy got up the next morning, which was fine with her because she knew things would still be weird between them. She wasn't ready to deal with the lingering awkward tension and wished they'd resolved things before going to bed. Instead, she'd gotten a restless night's sleep interspersed with vivid nightmares.

When she finally got out of bed, it was late morning. Her plan was to grab a coffee and do some writing at the café so she could get to the library as soon as it opened at ten, but she was also nervous about seeing Frankie. Why were all of her interactions so confusing lately? She just wanted things to be normal so she could focus on her book instead of people and their drama. She decided to go anyway because she couldn't avoid the café forever and maybe he wouldn't even be there today.

One step inside the doors had her stomach tightening.

"Morning," Frankie said from behind the counter.

"Hi." She ordered a coffee as if she were just a regular customer because that was what she was.

He got her drink and handed it to her without any pleasantries, and she figured this was all for the best, especially knowing that her husband thought she had feelings for him or vice-versa, and for all she knew, the latter could be true. The thing that bummed her out was that it meant she was losing a writing buddy.

After sitting down, checking emails, and reading the internet for a while, she found herself staring out the window of the café. Besides being lonely, she also just felt stuck. And it took everything in her to not break down into her coffee. This was not how she'd envisioned things going at all. She'd really hoped that she would be here, happily working away on a book by now, but instead she was stressed, distracted, and wallowing in her own self-doubt.

She glanced up and saw Frankie coming toward her. "Hey," he said. "Do you mind if I sit down?"

She nodded toward the chair across from her and closed up her laptop.

"I wanted to apologize for how weird I was the other night at your house."

"Okay," she said. She felt a bit warm and nervous about what he might say next.

"The thing is," he began, "I haven't been completely honest, and I want to explain." He paused. "I've lived in Pine Grove my entire life, but I've been fighting to get out for most of that time. This place has a way of pulling me back in. I hate it. My dream was always to go to New York and make it as a writer, and I did go. That part was true. I was living there for almost a year, but it was so damn expensive, and my job at the lit mag didn't pay enough. And then my dad died suddenly of a heart attack, and my mom needed me to come back here to help run this place, and it made perfect sense to do so, no matter how much I didn't want to. But I feel dumb telling people that I'm thirty years old, and I live with my mom in the same small town I've lived my whole life and I work as a busboy. So, I didn't lie to you necessarily. I sort of stretched the truth. I told you I came here for a woman. It just so happens that the woman I was referring to is my mom. I'm really sorry."

Maddy looked at him. "I'm glad you told me. Why do you hate it here so much?"

"I don't know. Just my own weird issues, I guess. I just feel very stuck. My family is so entrenched here."

"Wait," she said. "That still doesn't explain why you were acting strangely at my house."

"Right. That. It's because that house, your house, is the home of my great-great grandfather."

"The mortician?"

"Maddy—" He spoke softly. "—your house wasn't just a house. It was…a funeral parlor."

"What?"

He nodded. "Back in the day, they called them funeral parlors or funeral homes because they were both. They were peoples' homes; they held the funerals in their parlors. And that was why I was uncomfortable that night. I didn't think it was going to be a big deal, but I've lived here thirty years, and I've never been inside before, and I couldn't tell you because I didn't want to freak you out."

"Freak me out? How?"

"Besides the fact that you mentioned thinking the

house was haunted and that you clearly had no idea it had been a funeral parlor…" He trailed off, obviously unsure if he should continue.

"Go on," Maddy urged.

Frankie sighed. "There's a lore that my great-great uncle murdered his wife in that house. I don't know if it's true, but it's hung over the family for all these generations like a black smog, following us around wherever we go."

Maddy sat up straight. "Was her name Beatrice, do you know?"

"Uh, I'm not sure. My mom would know. She was super into my dad's family history. I'm guessing if she was the mortician's wife, then that was probably her."

"Why would the mortician have wanted to kill his wife?"

"I have no idea," he said. "The whole thing is depressing either way."

"It really is. I feel almost like I know her from reading the letters." They sat for a minute each with their own thoughts, and then Maddy said, "I'm sorry about your dad. Your mom is so sweet. She reminds me of my own mom. I can see why you came back."

"Yeah. She's a good one."

"And I understand about you hating it here, but it's not so bad…from an outsider's point of view."

"It could be worse," he admitted with a shrug. "It's just that five generations of Westmorelands and not a single one ever spread their wings. It's frustrating sometimes…"

"Wait. What did you just say? Your last name is Westmoreland?"

"Yeah."

"So you're Francis Westmoreland the fifth, huh?"

"How'd you know my full name was Francis?"

"Beatrice mentioned him in the letters."

"Really? She talks about Francis?"

"She does. So, that means…Beatrice's last name was also Westmoreland."

"Probably, yeah."

That was the one missing piece of information that Maddy needed in order to dig deeper into Beatrice's life story. Well, besides the fact that she now knew how it ended: tragically. But she still felt like there must be more to uncover.

After Frankie went back to work, Maddy packed up her things and headed straight for the library. This time Kirsten was there behind the counter with a mug of coffee, and Maddy was so excited, she practically threw the bundle of letters at her.

"Hey, Maddy! Whatcha got for me?"

Maddy launched into the story and had printed out her condensed chart and timeline for Kirsten to look at since she knew she wouldn't have time to read all of the letters. After she finished filling Kirsten in, and Kirsten had skimmed the printout, Kirsten's eyes practically beamed with matched enthusiasm. "This is so cool! I've heard about the Westmoreland Funeral Parlor, but I didn't know you actually lived there!"

"You've heard of it?"

"Yeah. That house is legendary, at least from the rumors and gossip. I actually haven't ever done any research myself, but this is a great reason to do it."

"So, can you help me?"

"I can try. What do you want to find out exactly?"

"Mostly, I would like to know what happened to

221

her. If the rumors are true, it sounds like her husband killed her. I would like to verify it if that's possible somehow?"

Kirsten nodded. "Unlike now, old obituaries almost always gave the cause of death. In fact, that was the main thing they indicated, almost to a gruesome degree, though I'm not totally sure about murder cases. Let's see what we can find anyway." She started typing into her computer. She clicked around a bit and then she wrote a number down on a slip of paper for Maddy. "Okay. This is the microfiche that contains her obit from the Pine Grove Gazette. It might have your answer."

Maddy took the slip of paper. "Wow. Okay. Thanks."

"Good luck."

Maddy walked to the shelf housing the catalog of reels and hunted for the one with the corresponding number. When she found it, she took it back to the machine and started searching. It took a while to figure out the right touch in order to scroll through the images and there were more than she had anticipated, so it was slow going, but finally, it came into view. She sat and stared at Beatrice's obituary for a long time.

Westmoreland (nee Weber), Mrs. Beatrice E. of Pine Grove, Minnesota. Born January 27, 1889; died Dec. 6, 1912, age 23 y. 11m. 6 d. Departed from trauma. Preceded in death by a still son. Interment at the Pine Grove Central Cemetery.

It hit her with a force she wasn't expecting, and she tried to hold in tears that had begun to well up. That she was so emotional from reading an obituary for someone she had never known came as a bit of shock, but she

222

couldn't help it. She hadn't been expecting that. Or had she? She'd had a strange inkling it wasn't going to be the happy ending she was hoping for, and in retrospect, it made sense. The letters had ended abruptly, and for a good reason. No, actually for a bad one. Maddy figured as much, she just hadn't expected it to be for *this* reason.

She put the reel back on the shelf and returned to Kirsten who was waiting with wide eyes. "So? What did you find out."

Using her phone, Maddy had taken a photo of the obit. She handed it to Kirsten to read. She was afraid that if she attempted to read it out loud, she would not be able to stop herself from an embarrassing emotional outburst.

"Oh, no," Kirsten said. "Oh, God. That's so sad."

"Trauma? That seems like murder to me."

"It does," Kirsten said. "Though the preceded in death by a still son is throwing me off a bit."

"How so?"

"It could mean that she died during childbirth."

Maddy put her hand over her mouth. "Oh, God."

"What?"

"Well, she was pregnant. And the last letter in the bunch was just before she probably would have given birth according to the timeline I made."

"That was a very common way for women to die back then, unfortunately."

"Yeah." And then Maddy did the thing she had been trying really hard not to do. She cried. The kind of cry that shook her entire body with violent spasms, but she couldn't stop them once they began. Embarrassed, Maddy put her hands over her face. She felt so stupid crying in front of Kirsten.

Kirsten handed her a tissue, but she didn't react beyond that.

"I'm sorry," Maddy said, unable to look Kirsten in the eye. "I must seem like a lunatic crying about a person who lived a hundred years ago, but...I lost my sister last year. She died in childbirth, too. This feels a little too close, you know?"

"Oh, Maddy. I'm so sorry."

"Yeah. It was a...well, anyway, you don't have time for this. I'll let you get back to work."

"What? Look around this place. Do you see anybody else here? I absolutely have time for this. Don't be silly. Come on, let's go sit down. I mean, only if you want to talk about it. I'm a good listener. Do you want some coffee? I have a thermos."

Maddy nodded and they sat down at a table near the center of the room. After a few sips from her mug, Maddy told her about Jess. "She was the perfect big sister. She was protective and kind and uber talented at everything. Everybody loved her. The only mistake she made was accidentally getting pregnant with a guy she hadn't known very well. He wanted her to get an abortion, but she decided she wanted to keep the baby and raise it by herself. And once she'd decided that, she was so, so excited. It was all she could think about and all she ever talked about for those seven months."

Maddy laughed and then blew her nose before she went on. "Everything was going well. We were planning a baby shower and she'd started to decorate a baby room, but toward the beginning of the sixth month of the pregnancy her blood pressure started to elevate and the next thing we knew, she was on bedrest. She told me she was scared and that if anything should happen to her…well, she asked if I'd raise the baby. Of course, initially, I thought she was being dramatic, but she wouldn't stop, so to make her feel better, I said I would. Tim and I were already married at that point, so it made some sense. She was so serious about it, in fact, she had legal documents written up and the father signed away his rights and everything.

"And then she was diagnosed with preeclampsia and they admitted her to the hospital and hooked her up to all sorts of machines. I naively still assumed it would all work out because I had never heard of anybody dying in childbirth in this century. As it turned out, I was the idiot. It all happened so fast.

"And though they couldn't save Jess, they did save the baby. It was a girl. And suddenly, I had no big sister, and I was a mom. But the baby was perfect and tiny and way too early and she only lived for three days before she went to be with her real mom."

"Oh, honey." Kirsten reached out and touched Maddy's hand. "That's so, so awful. I can't even imagine going through something like that."

Maddy wiped her eyes. "It was hard. And though I wasn't ready to be a mom, when I held her little hand through the incubator, I instantly fell in love. And now I don't know if I want to have my own kids because I don't know if I could go through all of that again."

"I can see why. That's super scary."

"I just…I can't believe when we bought the house, I made a joke to Tim about it being filled with little Victorian ghost kids. It turns out I wasn't that far off."

"You couldn't have known."

"No. I guess not." They sat for a short time and

finished their coffee before she stood up. "Anyway, thanks for listening. I should probably get going."

"Of course. Do you mind if I held onto the letters for a bit? I'd love to read them."

"Be my guest," Maddy said. "And if you're able to use your librarian superpowers to find anything else out about the whole thing, please let me know."

"I definitely will. Thanks for sharing…well, all of it, with me."

When they got up, they hugged and Maddy thanked Kirsten again before leaving the library.

Chapter Thirty-Five

2022

When Tim came home from work that evening, Maddy was on the sofa trying to read.

"Hi," he said, tentatively. "Can we talk?"

She glanced up at him and he sat down next to her with a big, beautiful bouquet of red roses in his hand. "I got these for you." He held them out to her.

She took them and smelled them. "Thanks. They're beautiful, but, Tim, I—"

"You were right," Tim said, interrupting. "I've been acting like a complete ass. I'm sorry. Can you forgive me?"

"It's not your fault."

"No. Everything you said last night was true. I'm an idiot. The thing is…it's true. I am jealous of Frankie. I've been feeling like you've been pulling away and you couldn't stop talking about that guy, so, I put two-and-two together."

"I shouldn't have been talking about him so much. I can see now why it might have bothered you, but I don't have any feelings for him. I was excited to have someone I could talk to about my writing, someone who had the same passion for it as I do. That's all."

"And I get that, but…well, the thing that really bothered me, that I didn't like at all…it was that he asked if he could read your book."

She turned to face him. "What? Why did that bother you?"

"Because Mads. I want to be the first person to read your book."

"You do?"

"Yeah. Of course. I'm your husband."

"Why didn't you ever say so?"

"Because I've been trying to give you space. I didn't think it was a good idea to put tons of pressure on you."

And then Maddy lost it. She set the flowers down on the couch beside her and she bent down, covering her face with her hands, and broke down in tears for a second time that day.

"Hey," Tim said, patting her back. "It's okay. What's wrong?"

"This is it, Tim," she said into her hands as she sniffled. "The third bad thing I was waiting to have happen. It turns out, I didn't need to wait for it because it's already happening."

"What's happening?"

She came up for air and wiped her nose. "I'm failing at writing. That's why I've been acting so weird. I can't do it. I'm no good. I have nothing. And I was afraid to tell you because I figured you'd say you told me so, that being a writer is a ridiculous pipe dream that I should stop chasing and instead I should start focusing on the thing we'd agreed on before we got married. And you were right, it's just that I'm still too scared to do that too, so I don't know what to do with myself. I'm useless." She looked at him, ashamed. She'd so wanted to prove to him that she could succeed at this, but it crushed her knowing it wasn't going to happen now.

"Mads, slow down." He wiped away the tears from her cheeks. "What are you talking about? What thing are you talking about? What did we agree on before we got married?"

"To have a bunch of kids. That I wouldn't work, but instead stay here and raise the kids."

"God, Mads. No way. I'd never tell you to give up on your dreams. And I don't think you have to choose between writing and being a mom. I wouldn't want to pick between being a dad and having a career, so why would I expect that of you?"

"I don't know. I just…"

"I told you that I believe in you; I still do."

"You also said you thought I was setting myself up for failure, and you were right about that."

"I wasn't saying you were going to fail, I was trying to temper your expectations because I know you. You expect to do stuff perfectly immediately on the first try, probably because you usually do, but writing is hard, Mads. I knew that. I just wanted you to slow down and not…well, do what you're doing now— putting too much pressure on yourself. I thought maybe if I didn't ask about it or check over your shoulder, maybe it would be fine, but I guess I was wrong. That doesn't mean I'm not supportive. I think you're just being too hard on yourself."

"Really? God. I've misconstrued everything," Maddy said. "I'm clearly the idiot here, not you."

"I think we are both equally stupid," Tim said, wrapping her in a tight embrace and squeezing. "And, you know…I was thinking about it, and I think we should get a dog."

"Really?" Maddy said.

"Yes. Definitely. Oh, and I'm gonna start getting stuff done around here too, like I promised. In fact, I've got something else for you." He handed her a large manilla folder.

"What is it?"

"So, I was able to get these from a few of my new connections from work. It's the original blueprints of the house. It will help us with the remodel, but also has some cool information about the history of the house."

Maddy opened the folder and looked through the diagrams of the various rooms. "Wow."

"And check it out," Tim said. "Here's the part I wanted to show you. This page is the original specs of this room—your office. It's listed as a sewing room."

"Really?" Maddy said, thinking about how she'd sewn the seat cushion there.

"And look at this right here," Tim said, pointing to the diagram. "This was originally a fireplace, just as we suspected. I wonder if it's not still behind the piece of sheet rock."

"Oh, do you think we can look?"

"Definitely! This weekend I'll bring some tools up and see if I can reveal it."

"Cool," Maddy said.

"Am I forgiven?"

"You are. What about me?"

"Only if you agree that I can be the first one to read your book."

"But…what if there's no book to read?"

"There will be. I'm sure of it," Tim said.

He pulled her in for a passionate kiss, their first real kiss since they'd moved into the house at Twelve

Pine Street, and Maddy knew then that it wouldn't be their last. "Now…have you considered, instead of going to the café to write, sitting down in your creepy writing room? I bet you'll have no problem coming up with some terrible, awful ideas in there."

Maddy looked at him, shocked that she hadn't actually attempted to write in her new office yet. "You know what? You're right again. I haven't tried that yet, which is really stupid, because I worked so hard to get that space set up just right for it."

Tim smiled. "Well, there you have it. I can't wait to read the book when it's finished."

After Tim left to start tackling his chore list finally, Maddy went upstairs and sat down at her desk and opened a new blank document. She didn't do what she'd done all of the previous times she'd tried to make headway. This time, she simply let go. Maddy had never been good at doing that, but she was trying to turn a page, so she set her fingers down on the keys and she didn't overthink it, instead she just went for it. She typed out a title at the top of the page as if she were on autopilot.

The Mortician's Wife
by Maddy Barton

Suddenly, it was like the story just unfolded before her in her head, at least a good portion of it. She knew it was going to be up to her to try to make sense of what had actually happened to Beatrice, but she also started to think maybe she didn't need to know everything about the real story. It was fiction, after all. She was starting to put some of the puzzle pieces together though, and because she felt like she practically knew Beatrice, she wanted to do her justice. She wanted to tell the story as she saw it. All sorts of thoughts swirled in her head. Had she actually been killed by the mortician? Or had she died in childbirth? It was definitely more complicated than that.

She opened a new blank spreadsheet and plugged in a few plot points. With each new one she jotted down, another idea came to her, and she added that one too. Maddy dug in and it was like something was guiding her fingers on the keyboard. Maybe it wasn't something but someone. Maybe it was her sister, or maybe it was Beatrice. They had both been so strong and had forged their own paths. Maddy wished to be like them. She wanted to overcome her feelings of inadequacy. She wanted to write a book and have people respect her talents. As it turned out, she didn't need to prove anything to her husband. She just needed to believe in herself. And she felt so strongly that Beatrice's story was worth telling. Maybe it was exactly why she had been shown the letters in the first place.

Chapter Thirty-Six

2022

Maddy began taking long walks through the neighborhood to think and ponder plot points as she continued working on the book. She found walking to be incredibly helpful, not only for generating ideas, but also to get out the energy of the new puppy they'd gotten. He was a husky-mix they named Snowy. He was a white ball of fluff, and he brought a new energy to the house that was so fun and exciting if a bit exhausting. Still, Tim was getting up early with Snowy and Maddy was getting a glimpse of what he might be like as a dad, which was pretty cute. The fact that they had been handling the stress well was also pretty reassuring to Maddy if and when they did decide to have kids.

Today's walk wasn't just their usual aimless puppy walk though. Today, Maddy knew exactly where they were headed. She and Snowy strolled through the town center until they arrived at the Pine Grove Central Cemetery. Weaving their way through the various plots, they stopped when Maddy found the one she was seeking. She stood in front of Beatrice's modest headstone. Before leaving home, she'd cut a bunch of flowers from the garden in the backyard, so now she got on her knees, wiped the dirt and grime from the placard, and placed the flowers down on the ground next to it. She looked at the grave for a long time just ruminating on the poor woman's life, making parallels that may or may not have existed to her own life.

She didn't speak out loud to Beatrice because she would have felt foolish, but also because she didn't think it worked that way. But she did ask in her head for Beatrice to help guide her along, to help direct her to the lost bits of her story, so that she could be put to rest. Because that was how Maddy saw it, how she felt it. Now more than ever, she was convinced there was a presence in the house, all around her, that sought peace. And something told her that it was Beatrice. And if Maddy could help be the one to bring peace to her, she would. She had to try.

She decided she wouldn't tell Tim about this specific sense she had. He obviously hadn't believed her when she proclaimed that the house was haunted. She knew he would think she was being overdramatic or that she was creating things that didn't exist because of her pessimism, but Beatrice had existed. Sure, Maddy's accounts, what she was writing in her book, were maybe just a fictionalized version, but Maddy felt certain it was so much more than that. In many ways, the book had taken on a life of its own, or better yet, a life of a dead person. Ghost, spirit, a soul whatever people wanted to call it, Maddy hadn't really thought much about the whole concept of an afterlife until she lost her sister. Now, she wondered about it constantly. Much in the same way she believed that Jess had guided her to her YouTube Channel a while back, she had a strong sense that Beatrice was trying to lead her to something. She had no idea why, but she had an inclination that she was close to figuring it all out too, to unraveling the mystery of the house and that of the mortician and his wife. Something sinister happened there, but exactly what it was, she wasn't entirely sure yet, but with any luck, or maybe some help, she would figure it out and document it.

She got up and she and the puppy exited the cemetery.

Later that same day, Matty walked over to the library, eager to see Kirsten. "Hey, have you finished reading the letters yet by chance?"

"Are you kidding? Twice over. Oh my God, Maddy! They are so interesting."

"Right? Oh, I found out a little bit more from Frankie," Maddy said.

"Ah, he confessed that he is one of the descendants of the Westmoreland clan, did he?"

"It took some coaxing," Maddy admitted. "But eventually, yes, he told me."

"Yeah. The poor guy seems tortured by it for some weird reason."

"Is it weird, do you think?" Maddy asked, and she had no idea why the words came out of her mouth, only she had remembered the strange thought she'd had over the weekend, and since then it kept popping back into her head like an alarm she'd set on her phone, nagging her, making sure she didn't let it go.

"What do you mean?"

"I don't know. It just seems odd to be trying to hide from something that took place over a hundred years earlier."

"Things die slowly in small towns. I went to school with Frankie. Kids were still talking about the," Kirsten made air quotes, "haunted funeral home and the murdering mortician. And everybody knew that it was his family, so…"

"Ah," Maddy said. "Anyway, did you have any new thoughts from reading the letters? Because I started to think that if Charles did kill his wife, wouldn't there be some story in that gazette about it? The one that ran the obits? Or even his obit. How did he die? Could you see if you can find those reels for me?"

Kirsten nodded. "Yeah. You know, I had the same thoughts, so I already checked, but I found nothing on either of those counts."

"Huh. That's odd," Maddy said.

"It is."

"Could you check one more thing for me?" she asked Kirsten.

"Absolutely."

"Well, I was thinking how strange it was that there weren't any letters from Beatrice's sister in the pile. Don't you think she would have written to her at least once? I went through the rest of the bookcase looking for more secret drawers and everything, but I didn't find a single letter from Jane."

"Wow. How sad. Why wouldn't her sister write to her, I wonder."

"The only thing I could figure was that she was no longer living, and Beatrice didn't know it, because she mentioned in one of the early letters that she worried for Jane's safety, which makes sense. The life of a carnival worker probably was pretty dangerous. And if she had been killed in an accident or something, maybe Beatrice wouldn't have been informed."

"True," Kirsten said. "Back then, unless someone

else got word to her, she would have no way of knowing if her relative who lived even a state away had passed on. That was why so many people got away with murder. It reminds me of H.H. Holmes, the Chicago serial killer from the later part of the 1800s. When the police questioned him about the disappearance of several of his victims, including two of his former wives, he simply told the investigators that they had decided to move away, and nobody thought it odd or had any good way to follow up with the claims, so they just took him on his word, which we now know was not good."

"Wow. That's crazy."

"Pretty terrible, really."

Maddy nodded. "So…could you search for an obit for Jane?"

"Hmm…except we don't know her last name. Westmoreland was Beatrice's married name. We don't know if Jane ever married, do we?"

"No," Maddy said. "But if she didn't, she would have kept Beatrice's surname, right? That was in her obit. Hold on. Let me find it on my phone again." She pulled it out and found the photo she'd snapped. "Okay. Here it is. It says Beatrice Westmoreland nee Weber."

"Great," Kirsten said. She started typing into her computer, but after a few minutes, she said, "Huh. I'm not seeing anything for a Jane Weber."

"That's strange," Maddy said.

"It is."

"Bummer. I was really hoping this might explain something. I'm not sure what, but…"

"I guess the mystery continues," Kirsten said.

When Maddy got home, she opened up her

document and though she was discouraged that she hadn't figured out anything new from Kirsten, it hadn't entirely drained her ambition, so she dug deep to continue her efforts to write. This went on for a few solid weeks and eventually she'd laid the groundwork and had what she felt were some pretty solid early chapters of the book. It was all coming together so well, even Maddy was in disbelief. As her excitement grew, she picked up the pace and was writing several thousand words a day.

Before she knew it, Maddy neared the point in the story where Beatrice's real life was beginning to converge with what Maddy did not know to be factual, but rather, what she imagined had taken place. She knew she was going to need some more time to do soul searching before she continued on with the story, so she edited and revised what she had this far, and printed the pages. Then, with a little trepidation, she gave it to Tim to read.

Chapter Thirty-Seven

1912

When Beatrice came to, she was in a small room that appeared to be clinical. Based on the fact that her feet practically hung off the edge of the tiny bed, she gathered she was in the infirmary at the orphanage. She recalled from the tour Elizabeth had given her that they had a few rooms for cases that required children to be quarantined from the others. There were no windows in the room, only a rolling cart with medical supplies and a chair positioned next to the bed in which Beatrice now lay.

Still groggy and sore, her hand went instinctively to her belly, and immediately she could tell the baby was no longer inside of her. She looked around, but no one else was there. "Charles?" she called out. When nobody appeared, she grew sleepy again. Her eyes fluttered closed. Moments or perhaps hours later the door to the room opened and Beatrice saw Elizabeth come through it.

"Beatrice," she said with a soft tone. "How are you feeling?" She dipped a cloth into a wash basin nearby to wet it. She wrung it out, then placed it upon Bea's forehead.

"Where's Charles? The baby?" Beatrice asked her sister by marriage.

"Shhh. You rest now."

She tried to sit up, desperate to know what had become of her child, but Elizabeth produced a hypodermic needle from her pocket and thrust it into Beatrice's arm. It felt almost vengeful to Bea and she tried to understand why that could be, but she had limited time to do so because soon the room began to swirl and her vision faded. She dreamed feverishly of things that made no worldly sense though the visions came with a soundtrack to that of an infant's cries. The sounds were so familiar to Beatrice it was as if she could interpret their meaning. A language only a mother could understand.

When she woke again, the room was dark. No light came through the small glass pane at the top of the closed door. She didn't dare call out this time as she had no desire to be put back under, yet she had a strong urge to get up and find her child. Slowly and with much concentration, she pulled her body into a sitting position, then she tried to swing her legs around to the side of the bed, but they felt as if they were barely attached to the rest of her body. Everything was in soft focus as if she had been reborn on a cloud. Where was her husband, the mortician? Why was he not by her side?

Depleted of energy, Beatrice collapsed back down onto the pillow and wept. Her chest expanded and contracted as it arched and ached for her baby. The absence of the spirit bound to her for nearly nine months was a torment she had not felt in all her days. It hurt worse than the loss of her mother, and she had not yet set eyes upon the being. Surely her child was close? She sensed it. Her bosom quivered for it. Her mournful cries amplified the hollowed space and bounced off the wall like a cacophony of choir singers in the church chapel.

This was all her fault. She should have heeded Elizabeth's cautions. She should have been taking things slower. Had she done too much? Had she consumed something she should not have? Had she not been giving the child what it needed? Had she brought harm to it? These unrelenting, nasty thoughts consumed poor Beatrice and she could not control her sorrowful outbursts.

Likely attracted by the noise, a young woman in a nursing gown who was not Beatrice's sister by marriage entered the room. Her expression was that of pity, but also concern. She offered Beatrice some water from a pitcher on the cart, which she accepted. "There, there. Now," she said.

"Do you know where my child is?" Beatrice asked her.

"I'm sorry. No." She shook her head. "I'm just the new night nurse. I was told not to bother you."

"Please, can you go and find out," she pleaded desperately. "I delivered a child. I would like to see it."

"I will go and see," the young nurse said.

"Oh, thank you. Thank you. God bless you."

While she was gone, Beatrice fought with herself to remain awake and upright, but it felt as though the woman had been gone for hours. In the darkness, and after expelling her emotions so forcefully, she'd exhausted herself and closed her eyes again.

When she opened them back up, the room was still and quiet, but a light now shown from the glass in the door from the hallway. Had the nurse returned and left again when she found Beatrice asleep? Surely the young woman had not forgotten her promise? Beatrice lay there praying for her return, praying that when she did a swaddled babe would be resting in her arms. But her prayers went unanswered because the next person to step into the room was not the young nurse, or even Elizabeth, but the mortician himself. His color was ashen. He looked as though he'd just see a ghost.

"Charles," she said. "Where's the child? Is it well?"

"I'm sorry to say that it is not."

"Are you certain?"

"Elizabeth has just explained to me that he was born still and without breath." He choked on his words as he spoke them.

"He? A boy?"

Charles nodded.

Beatrice cried silently into a handkerchief Charles handed her.

There was nothing left to say and so they did not say a thing. And the next day, Elizabeth helped dress Beatrice in a fresh gown, and she handed her a small glass bottle of laudanum to ease the pain before sending her and Charles on their way. When they arrived home, everything was more or less the same as before, yet to Beatrice nothing would ever be so.

Chapter Thirty-Eight

2022

The warm summer days trickled to an end, but Maddy barely noticed because she spent most of her time now working in her office, clicking away at the keys. And as she completed each new chapter, she printed it out for Tim, who read it in bed alongside her. Now that things had calmed down for him at work and he found his work/life balance, Maddy found her own work/life balance, too. With the dog sleeping curled up on the bed between them, Tim read her manuscript, and Maddy read for the next book club meeting.

Sometimes after Tim finished with a chapter, he'd turn to her, and they'd discuss it. Tonight was one of those nights. He paused, set the stack of papers down flat on his lap, looked at her, and said, "It's really sounding like the mortician is guilty at this point."

"Why do you think so?"

"I mean, for one thing, the husband is usually the killer."

"Why is that exactly?"

"Money and love can make a man kill."

"True, but that does not make for a very interesting or original mystery novel," Maddy said.

"I suppose," Tim said. "What else then? If not money or love?"

"That's a great question. Anyway, I'm fairly convinced Charles didn't do it."

"Oh? Why is that?"

"Well, for one thing, that was all just town lore, that the mortician killed his wife."

"Didn't Frankie tell you that? Because to me, that sounds more like family lore. That's a whole different animal from town lore," Tim said.

"How so?"

"Family lore is usually embedded with some truth, I think."

Maddy pondered this before she said, "I dunno. I just didn't get that tone from the letters. I think Beatrice's husband loved her. Though it did sound like he was stressed out from the business failing. He was probably worried because he knew he had a baby coming."

"See…money could have been the motive then," Tim said.

"If he was feeling pressure because he wanted to provide for his family, then killing them doesn't make any sense."

"Why not?" Tim asked.

"Think about it. You only feel pressure to do right by your family when you love them. If you don't care about them, you wouldn't be that concerned over the whole matter. No. I think money may have been a catalyst to their troubles early on, but I don't think that was what ultimately led to Bea's murder."

"What did then?"

"I don't know exactly." Maddy frowned. "I'm still working it out."

"Well work faster, Detective Barton," he said. "I

can't wait to see how it all ends."

She smiled, reminded of exactly why she loved Tim and why she married him in the first place.

****

On a day when Maddy was struggling to come up with any new words at home, she packed up her laptop and walked over to the café, hoping the change of scenery would spark something. Frankie was behind the counter.

As Maddy waited for her drink, she said, "I forgot to tell you, there's a possibility the mortician's wife may not have been murdered after all."

"Oh, yeah? What makes you think so?"

"Kirsten and I speculated she died in childbirth." Maddy pulled out her phone and showed him the obit. "I assumed trauma was an old-timey way of saying she died in childbirth since they say the son died, too."

"Preceded usually means the person died before them though," he said.

"Okay. Sure, but the baby may have died just before her. I've been doing some research and the most common way for the mother to die during childbirth is from hemorrhaging and that usually happens a short time after the baby is delivered."

"But the baby would have died from what then?" he asked. "Because the mother hemorrhaging wouldn't have killed the baby, right?"

"Right," Maddy said. "The obit mentioned it was a still son; so, the baby wasn't alive when it was delivered."

"So, it was a coincidental double tragedy?" Frankie said, skepticism in his voice.

"It can happen," Maddy said. "It happened to my

sister last year in fact."

"Really? I'm so sorry. I didn't know."

"Anyway, I thought you'd be interested to know that maybe the lore is just that."

"No. Yeah. I am. Thanks for telling me."

But after Frankie handed Maddy her drink and she sat down to write, she couldn't stop thinking about what they'd discussed. She knew it was obviously very possible for two terrible things to go wrong, but had that been the case here as it had for her sister? She still didn't believe that the mortician had murdered his wife, but maybe it wasn't a complete accident either. What if it was made to look like an accident?

What was the motive though? Tim was right, love and money were the most obvious choices, only in Beatrice's case, she had something else to offer, something precious she had been carrying around with her for nine months.

Lost in a make-believe haze, Maddy realized she was staring at the table next to her where a mom and her young daughter of maybe three or four years sat eating lunch. The little girl was opening packets of salty crackers and plopping them into a bowl of soup. The ratio of crackers eventually practically outweighed the soup. The mom looked over and told the little girl that she had enough crackers and she should just eat the soup.

The girl tilted her head, giggled, and held up one tiny finger. "Just one more, please, Mommy?"

The mother nodded and the little girl opened another packet. Maddy assumed she was going to put the crackers into her bowl, but instead she took one out of the plastic and held it out to her mom, like a peace offering. She scrunched up her sweet little nose and waited until the mom finally smiled at her and took the cracker from her daughter. It wasn't anything special, but something about the scene that played out in front of Maddy had melted her heart in a way she hadn't expected.

Chapter Thirty-Nine

1912

After Beatrice took to her bed and refused food and drink, Charles came in often to check on her. He brought in a vase of fresh flowers, placed them on the table before her, and pulled the heavy window coverings to the side, pinning them back to let in the light of the day.

These attempts did nothing to replenish Bea's spirit. When he finally retreated back down the staircase, she took a drop of the laudanum onto her tongue and drifted off into an opiate dream-state, but even that didn't help matters anymore. When she woke, she still felt as though someone had torn her heart from her chest.

On the third day, Beatrice woke. She reached for the glass vial of medication and found it was not there. She called for Charles. When he arrived at the threshold, he told her she'd had enough. He replaced the vase with fresh flowers which she tore from the vessel and threw at him. He sat with her for a spell rubbing her arm until she calmed.

"I've sent for Dr. Boyle to come and sit with you," he said. "Perhaps he can help."

And soon the doctor appeared beside her. She had no words for the old man. He'd never lost a child. What did he know of it? The doctor spoke, but Beatrice closed her eyes and her ears to it, tossing a pillow over her face, hearing nothing but a muffled tone. When it grew thin and wary, Dr. Boyle finally quieted altogether and vanished from the room.

Later that afternoon, Elizabeth entered the room. She bathed and dressed Beatrice and put her hair up. "You shall feel a good bit better after it's all over," she said. She walked her down the stairs where a small service was about to begin for the child. When Beatrice saw the small pine box, she ran to it and threw her body over the top of it. After a moment, she began to try to peel the corner of the coffin away, as she'd done another time, but the box had been nailed shut. She whipped around and shrieked, unconcerned about the people sitting quietly in the chairs set about the parlor. "I want to see him. I want to see my baby!"

Charles came toward her. "My darling…please, come sit down."

"No! I do not believe he is in there! I want to see it with my own eyes."

As Charles placed a hand on her arm to guide her to a chair, hoping no doubt to calm her, she pulled away. "I don't trust you! This is just more of your trickery!" Now Charles reached for her waist, and she kicked and thrashed as he lifted her and carried her out of the room as she screamed and wailed, "Where is my baby? I want my child!"

Back in the bedroom, Charles had no choice but to administer another drop of laudanum to his wife's tongue. After she quieted, he blackened the room once more with the curtains and exited.

Chapter Forty

2022

As autumn set in hard and fast, the leaves dropped like rain and Maddy, Tim, and Snowy spent a few full weekends raking and tending to the yard with their newly acquired tools, including snow shovels that would likely be needed soon enough. They also had contractors coming in and out on a regular basis now, measuring and starting on some light demo work for the new kitchen that Tim had designed with Maddy's input. But between the house projects, and training the puppy, Maddy continued to write.

When she was stuck or just needed a break, she and the dog walked to the cemetery to visit with Beatrice. Even as the cooler days whipped in, she found a sense of peace in the space inside of the cemetery gates. Something about being there seemed to help her think. She continued to talk things out with Beatrice as well.

Sometimes, she talked to Jess while she was at it. Why not? She couldn't be near her sister's grave, so this was the next best thing. Her mind had, in some strange ways, begun to bleed Beatrice and Jess's lives together.

It was always so serenely quiet there, except for the howling wind that came with the fall weather. Some people might think she was crazy to find such comfort in a cemetery and maybe she was. She had never seen another soul there—though she definitely felt some. The people who had been buried there died so long ago they may not have anyone left to visit them. Most of the stones were now cracking and weeds grew up alongside many of them. Forgotten. There was something so sad, yet strangely beautiful, about it.

She sat on a bench nearby Beatrice's plot, and let her mind go. This newly conceived technique did wonders. The strangeness of plotting at a plot wasn't lost on her. The place had secret powers, she was convinced, that allowed her to get inside the story. She took in the briskness of the day, while Snowy chewed on sticks or chased blowing leaves. Maddy also did a fair bit of listening in the eerie quiet of the cemetery. Sometimes she imagined the whipping wind to be Beatrice's voice trying to reveal her secrets through the air. The story practically wrote itself in that way and Maddy feverishly jotted things down in her notebook so she wouldn't forget them before she got home to transcribe them all out. She stayed until her fingers got too cold to keep writing.

On her walk home, she stopped at John's house and knocked on his door. They'd gotten oddly close at this point, attending book clubs together, or Maddy might bring him over a meal or two occasionally, fibbing that they'd had too many leftovers. During the day, if she ever needed anything or got spooked by the house, which she still did on occasion, even with the dog around, she wandered over and she and John would always end up having coffee and discussing books. Today she had a different topic to ask John about, so she put Snowy in the house, because while Maddy and

John got along great, their animals did not.

They sat together at the kitchen table with coffee. Maddy warmed her numbing hands around the mug.

"You may want to invest in some gloves," John said. "I'd recommend some thick ones. You're gonna need them soon. You aren't in Portland anymore."

"I know. It's on my list."

"How's the book coming?" he asked.

"Getting there," she said. "What do you know about opium?"

John raised his brow.

"It's research. For the book."

He gave a knowing nod, and told her everything he knew about the drug, and then he went on tangent, talking about various cases he'd solved throughout his career, which Maddy gobbled up. After listening to several stories, Maddy asked him her own long list of follow up questions, which were often just based on her general curiosity, though one was more specific in nature.

"How far back do the Pine Grove crime investigation records go? Do they still keep files from 1912?"

"Ah…so you've been filled in about the history of your place, huh?" he asked.

Maddy nodded. "No thanks to you."

"I didn't want to spook you," he said, coyly.

"Do you believe the rumors?"

John shook his head. "That the mortician killed his wife? Nah."

"Why not?"

"Murder wasn't that commonplace back then. People died easily enough from so many other things, there was no sense bothering to kill one another. All they had to do was wait it out; it was just a matter of time before nature took care of it for you."

"Sure, but there were some," Maddy said.

John nodded. "Of course. There will always be the good, the bad, the ugly in people."

"You're quoting a Western, aren't you?"

"You know it," John said with a smile.

Maddy wasn't ready to give in, so she pushed further. "Accidental deaths were obviously very common, so how hard would it have been back then for people to make it look like a murder was an accident?"

"Oh, I suspect it was incredibly easy. They had very few methods for solving cases, no technology, no databases, hardly any of the forensics we have now. And even now, some people still get away with things. So yeah. I'm sure it happened."

"Right," Maddy said, her wheels turning.

"More coffee?"

"No, thanks. I gotta get back to my writing."

"Let me know if I can help with anything else."

"I will," Maddy said. "See you later." She gave Boots a few good head scratches and went back to her office to work. She knew John had a lot of knowledge about crimes, but she was still inclined to go with what her gut, or the walls, or the wind was telling her about Beatrice's ending.

A few days later, when she stepped out her front door to head to the cemetery, a brand-new pair of thick, wool mittens rested on her front porch. No ribbon, no card, but Maddy knew where they'd come from. It didn't take a detective to figure that out. Maddy smiled to herself as she slipped them on her hands, and she and the dog headed out to try to solve a much more difficult case.

That night, Maddy turned to Tim in bed and said to him, "I want to have kids."

Tim turned quickly to face her. "What?"

"I think I'm ready."

"Really?" His blue eyes lit up. "Are you sure?"

She nodded slowly. "Yeah."

"What made you change your mind?"

"I don't know. Nothing in particular. I've always wanted to have kids. I just had to get over my fear." She paused. "Remember when we were dating and went to that swanky sushi place downtown near the waterfront and you asked me how many kids I wanted to have? You didn't ask me *if* I wanted kids, just how many."

"Yeah. I remember. You laughed at me."

"It just struck me as so funny, because all the other guys I knew were terrified of the idea of having children, but not you."

"I dunno." Tim shrugged. "I'm an only child. I just always thought it would be fun to have a bunch of kids, form our own baseball team, maybe start a family band."

Maddy laughed. "I know. And I loved that about you." She leaned over the fur ball between them in bed and kissed him.

****

Tim kept his promises, and one Saturday afternoon—armed with a crowbar and a hammer—Maddy followed him into her office to see the unveiling of the fireplace. It was perfect timing as the room had started to get drafty as the cooler weather rolled in. And while the radiator spit out a little heat, the clanking and hissing mostly just added to the house's incessant chatter.

"Are you sure you want me to do this?" he asked before he began the demo.

"Yeah. Why wouldn't I be?"

Tim shrugged. "I mean, it's possible the fireplace is long gone and there's just an ugly hole there now."

"Okay, so what do we do then?"

"I guess we can patch it back up."

"That's fine. It doesn't have the matching wallpaper on it anyway, so I was hoping for at least exposed brick, but now I'd also really love if there was a fireplace too."

"Right. Okay. Here goes then." As Tim began prying chunks of drywall off, Maddy stared at the dark blotches on the wallpaper near the floor just next to where Tim was working. She remembered thinking how it could be blood when she first saw it.

And as a thought continued to evolve in her brain, Tim yelled, "Eureka!" and pulled the front panel off to reveal a black firebox.

"Oh," Maddy said, disappointed.

"What? I thought this was what you wanted?"

"Yeah. It's just…it's not ornate or anything. It's just an ugly black box. Is it even functional?"

"Probably not. We'll have to have an inspector come out, but we could always replace the insert with something nicer and have a mantelpiece mounted over it. It adds something to the room though."

"True," Maddy said.

"It gives it a real writerly feel now," Tim said.

"Yeah. Maybe," she said, biting her lip.

"What?"

"No. It's just…I don't know, something about it is…depressing."

"It's period. That's for sure," Tim said, as he started to clean up the mess from the demolition.

And as she stood staring at the fireplace, she wasn't sure why she was so upset by the black box. It was like a dark cloud had entered the room. It was so dreary, so empty, and hollow. What had she been expecting? She shouldn't have expected anything.

Up until five minutes ago, she had no idea the fireplace existed, but now, there was something about it, something cold and sinister that did not feel right. Seeing the dark spots on the wallpaper only reinforced this feeling. Suddenly, Maddy saw in her head, almost like a vision what Beatrice's final moments may have been.

Chapter Forty-One

1912

Beatrice woke to find her bottle of medication had been refilled. As she reached for it, a soft knock came. She lowered herself back down. Dr. Boyle entered the room and took a seat next to her bed. And like the last time, he spoke to her, but this time she did not actively fight against his advice. She was too tired to do anything but let the old doctor's words settle around her.

He told her she was strong and full of fire. He'd seen many women in his day, but none like her. She would persist. She could have more children. They would go on to do great things. She mustn't be defeated, not by the tragedy that occurred or by the handling of it.

When the doctor left, Beatrice sat up in bed, wondering whether or not to trust the old doctor's wisdom. Maybe he hadn't walked in her shoes, but one thing was for sure, he was not mad, not like so many had said.

She thrust herself up, grabbing the laudanum, and she crossed the hall and entered into her sitting chamber for the first time in weeks. Beatrice sat for the last time at her writing table as she finished composing her final work. It weaved her skills as a writer together and she was proud of this accomplishment. When she finished the note, as always, she folded it, and she crossed the room and stood in front of the fireplace. It was cold in the room, though a smoldering fire lingered in the box. Soon it would be just remnants of ash and soot, which felt worthy of an ending.

With her note in one hand, she reached for the mantel and lifted the bottle of laudanum. She put it to her mouth, fighting the urge to drink down the entire contents of the jar. Instead she took only one small final dose and tossed the glass into the firebox and with a poof, the flames exploded. The vial shattered into fragments as the fire popped and hissed. It took longer for the effects to hit her now, as she'd grown accustomed to the poison, but soon, a softness filled her vision.

She heard a noise behind her. Twisting, she assumed it was Dr. Boyle returning, and as she did the note escaped her fingers, floating into the ether. A stark and hard realization hit her. The fortune teller had warned her, but she hadn't understood that the sister to be cautious of was the one who was living. And then something else hit her.

Chapter Forty-Two

2022

Eventually, it got too cold to visit the cemetery. Not for the Husky pup who was born for this kind of weather, but for Maddy, it was another story entirely. Everyone had warned her about how bad a Minnesota winter could be, and she figured out quickly that they hadn't been joking around with her. She hadn't fathomed so much snow could fall in such a short period of time and stick around. It was quite pretty though, and since she didn't have to drive in it much, she was okay with it so far. She liked that there were days that were still bright, even if they were colder than she'd ever imagined, though she was slowly acclimating. On clear days, she would have Tim drop her at the library so she could run her thoughts about the book by Kirsten, but they also texted and emailed regularly too, like real friends.

And one day, as they discussed a plot point that involved a bit more research than Kirsten could provide from the library computer system, they decided to take a trip to Stillwater to peruse the Washington County Courthouse historical records. Kirsten offered to drive, knowing Maddy hadn't mastered wintery Minnesota road conditions yet.

It wasn't a long or particularly treacherous drive. In

fact, it was only about ten minutes, and the scenery was breathtaking as the powdery white snow from the last storm had coated nearly everything along the route. They took mostly back roads from Pine Grove to Stillwater. The streets weren't too slick, and Kirsten was a good driver, so Maddy was a little surprised to find herself feeling somewhat queasy on the way. She chalked it up to being a little tense. Once they arrived in Stillwater, she was too distracted by finding the information she needed to notice how unsettled her tummy was.

They did some digging for records pertaining to the Elmwood Orphanage and they also searched more birth and death records of people with the surname of Westmoreland and Weber. That's when they stumbled across an obituary that made them pause.

Clara Jane Weber (nee Baxter) and unborn child, female of Stillwater, Minnesota. Born September 27, 1867; died May 19, 1893. Age 26 y. 8m. 8 d.

"Do you think this is Beatrice's sister?" Maddy asked Kirsten as they read it. "Maybe they referred to her by her middle name?"

"The dates don't work though. This woman died in 1893, so Beatrice would have only been what? Four years old at the time." Kirsten paused. "I think this may have been Beatrice's mother."

"That would make the unborn child…"

"Beatrice's sister."

"Oh my God. That would make sense why there was no obit for Jane Weber."

"Or a birth record," Kirsten said.

"So…that means…Beatrice was writing letters to her dead baby sister."

Kirsten nodded slowly. "I think so."

"Which is why she never mailed them and kept them hidden away in a secret drawer."

"Yeah. They likely never named the unborn child, so Beatrice must have just gone with Jane—her mother's middle name."

"Wow," said Maddy, completely gutted by this revelation.

On the drive home, Maddy sat in the passenger seat unable to concentrate on anything except that single piece of information.

"I wonder why she did it...created this whole narrative in her letters around her sister being alive and traveling with the circus."

"I'm guessing she did it as a means to cope with the loss," Kirsten said.

"Yeah," Maddy said. "If she had been living today, I bet she would be a fiction writer."

"Probably."

"Instead, she had to resort to writing letters."

"At least it explains why her sister never replied to them."

"I can't decide if that makes it better...or worse," Maddy said.

Kirsten nodded. "I know, right?"

****

A few days later, Maddy was feeling mildly nauseated again. This time she couldn't blame it on a car ride. She decided to take a pregnancy test and that was how she discovered she was with child. She was still a little scared, but she was also excited. Something inside of her told her she was being watched over and protected and it put her mind more at ease. It sounded weird, but in her brain, it made total sense even if she was suddenly hurling into a trash bin in her office between typing out the last chapters of her first novel.

There was a short reprieve in the cold and snowy temps in mid-November and Maddy took the opportunity to get out of the house. She put on the new puffy jacket she bought and slipped her hands into her new wool mittens from John, and she walked to the café. When she arrived, Frankie's mom greeted her and got her a hot beverage and a muffin.

"Ginny," she said. "Can I ask you something?"

"Anything, dear."

"What all do you know about the Westmoreland family lore?"

Ginny's perpetual grin didn't fade, but her eyes got wider. "You're referring to the mortician and his wife?"

"I am."

"From what I've gathered, the mortician was a very odd man, as you might assume, him being a mortician and all. His wife was pregnant when he killed her. I believe maybe he didn't want the baby. Could have been money troubles too, at least those are some of the whisperings the family used to do back in the day."

"What happened to the mortician, do you know? Was he ever punished for the crime?"

Ginny leaned against the counter. "That's a good question. I'm not sure about that, but I know his brother moved into the home after the wife and child died."

"His brother? And that would have been your husband's great-grandfather?"

"Exactly. Fascinating, isn't it?" Ginny said.

"I'll say."

"Frankie told me you own the house now. I've

always thought it was a beautiful place myself, though he has a real aversion to it."

"I've noticed that. Do you know why exactly?"

She shrugged. "Who knows. I think he just got tired of all the gossip over the years. He's not a big fan of unwanted attention, or any attention really. He'd rather just sit in a dark room all day and write poetry. That's just who he is." Ginny chuckled. "Anyway, do you like the house?"

"It's definitely starting to grow on me," Maddy said.

"Well, I'm just glad to see a nice young couple like you and Tim fixing it up and bringing it back to life. I know some people are weirded out by the fact that it was a funeral parlor, but that makes it all the more interesting to me."

"You don't, by chance, happen to have any old pictures or other memorabilia, do you? I'd love to see what the house looked like back then."

"You know, I do have a few things in the attic that my husband saved. I'd be happy to show them to you."

"Really? I'd love that…if it's no trouble," Maddy said.

Ginny waved her off. "None at all. I haven't seen them in a long time and since Frankie isn't interested, I have nobody to show them to. I'll bring them in, and the next time you're here, we'll go through them."

"I can't wait."

****

Maddy still had questions about Frankie that lingered, things that didn't add up. She wasn't sure what the questions were exactly, but something nagged at her, something about him that, if she could figure it

263

out, would unlock some mysteries. At the next book club she sat across from him in the semi-circle of chairs as they discussed the Western John had forced them to read, and Maddy looked straight into Frankie's eyes trying to pry information out of him through some sort of osmosis.

She couldn't stop thinking about Francis Westmoreland the First. What did Francis Westmoreland the Fifth know about his great-grandfather? Did he know something that made him ashamed to come from the bloodline? To carry down the namesake? Something about his attitude on the subject and his "for better or worse" comments told her he knew a lot more on the matter than he was willing to admit. What was Frankie covering up? Maddy wondered. And if he wasn't willing to divulge it, maybe the answers were sitting in that box of old stuff in his mother's attic?

She couldn't wait any longer to find out, so Maddy headed to the café to see it with her own eyes as soon as she could. When she got to The Pine Cone, Ginny's face lit up and she asked a young girl to take over the counter for her while she went in the back room to get the box.

They sat down at a booth near the front window. Maddy was hopeful as Ginny began lifting the lid off the top of the box. A musty smell hit her nose and the hormones of the pregnancy made it all the more potent. She tried hard not to gag, but she coughed and covered her mouth.

Ginny paused, looking alarmed. "What's wrong?"

"No. Please. Go ahead and open it. I'm dying to see. I'm just sensitive to smells right now."

"Oh?"

"I'm pregnant."

Ginny looked exactly how Maddy's mom had looked when she told her over video earlier that week. "How wonderful," she said. "Congratulations." She set the lid on the floor. "Let me get you some water."

"No. Thank you." Maddy's wave of nausea passed and she removed her hand, waving it at Ginny. "I'm fine. Really."

"Okay. If you're sure." Ginny pulled a stack of items out of the box and set them between the two of them. "I hope it's not disappointing. It's been so long since I've looked through this now, I've forgotten what's even here."

They went through the items one by one. It was mostly photos of family members well after Beatrice and Charles's time period, but still much older than Ginny. She pointed out people she knew and said their names and how they were related to her husband.

There was one picture that was much more recent. It was one of Frank Sr. and Frankie Jr. when Frankie was maybe twelve or thirteen. They were sitting on lawn chairs, with plates of food on their laps, at a picnic or barbeque of some sort. "This was actually a Westmoreland family reunion," Ginny said.

To Maddy, the father and son looked to be polar opposites in almost every way. Frank Sr. was a stout man, with dark, mischievous eyes, though he was smiling widely, while Frankie—tall and lean—had a softer expression on his face. It wasn't one of joy, necessarily, because he wasn't smiling, but there was thought behind it. Still, Frankie looked uncomfortable, out of place, perhaps.

"Did Frankie not want to be there, in typical teenage fashion?" Maddy asked.

Ginny laughed. "I'm afraid, even then, he hated family gatherings, while Frank loved them."

"Did they have a good relationship...otherwise?" Maddy asked.

Ginny took the photo back and gave it a hard look for a minute before she sighed. "It was complicated."

"I'm sorry. I overstepped. I shouldn't have asked," Maddy said.

"No, no. It's fine," Ginny said, grinning at Maddy, though this time the smile held some sorrow in it. "Frank was a proud carpenter. He had his own business building custom cabinets, gazebos, and decks, what have you. He loved working with his hands, keeping busy, chopping, carving, that was his language, how he communicated, but Frankie was more sensitive, more introspective, even from a very young age he kept a journal and enjoyed writing little stories that he would type up on an old typewriter. He learned to communicate through stories, actual words.

"Frank just didn't get it. He would drag Frankie to help out at the construction sites or try to get him to build a birdhouse with him, that type of thing, but Frankie wasn't interested, and the two butted heads more often than not. Frank expected his only son to take over the business someday, but Frankie didn't want anything to do with it. So, yeah. It was a strained father/son relationship in many ways. They did love one another. They were just very different people."

"Ah. I see," Maddy said. "That makes sense."

Ginny nodded, looked down, and started going through the pile again. As the stack of items from the box got shorter and shorter, and none of the photos or documents pertained to the funeral home or Beatrice, Maddy's hope of discovering anything helpful began to dwindle too, but then Ginny pulled a square print from the pile that looked much older than the rest of the things.

"Oh, this is the one I was hoping to show you," she said, as she slid the old photograph across the table toward Maddy. "I think this is the mortician and his wife not long after they had wed."

Maddy examined the picture. It was a little blurry and a lot drab, but what more did she expect of two people in black and white standing in front of a funeral home? "Wow," Maddy said. The house was barely recognizable in the background in that it looked pristine and new. But Maddy quickly turned her attention to the foreground.

"So, that's what Beatrice looked like," she said more to herself than to Ginny.

Beatrice appeared in a long gown. It wasn't white, and it wasn't black, but given that the picture was in black and white, it was hard to know exactly what color it was, besides knowing it was a shade between the two, possibly a light plum color, Maddy speculated. Bea's hair was pinned up with a few soft curls hanging loose around her face, and she held a hat in her gloved hand. Charles wore a perfectly tailored suit, glasses, and a black top hat. While neither of them smiled, Beatrice had a slight twinkle in her eye, telling Maddy that she was not unhappy to be standing there with the mortician.

And Maddy keyed in on those eyes. Not because of the expressed delight in them, but because she'd seen them before. She knew those eyes. She'd stared into those eyes a few days prior in the semi-circle at the library. Frankie didn't look at all like Charles, who had smaller, darker eyes with a pensive look about them. No. Frankie looked like Beatrice, which made no sense, because technically Beatrice wasn't a Westmoreland, not by birth anyway.

"Hey, Ginny?" She pushed the picture back toward her. "Is it just me, or does Beatrice sort of remind you of someone?"

Ginny held the picture up and gave it a closer look. "Who?"

"You don't think she and Frankie have the same eyes?"

"I see what you mean, but...she wouldn't have been part of the bloodline."

Maddy nodded. "Right. That's what I thought."

After they finished going through the things, Maddy hugged Ginny and thanked her for letting her snoop. Ginny said she was happy someone was interested and thanked her for listening.

On the walk home, Maddy tried to work out how exactly Frankie may have come to possess the same eyes as the mortician's wife and then it came to her. There was really only one answer.

****

As her belly grew, Maddy began converting the guest room into a baby room. She had Tim paint the walls a soft yellow. She wasn't sure why she went with yellow, but it called to her when she was in the home improvement store looking at the color samples. It wasn't a bright lemon yellow like Tim preferred, but a soft, subtle hue that was calming and happy.

She lay in bed one night, exhausted from the work she'd done on the baby's room that day, while Tim lay next to her reading the next pages of her manuscript.

Maddy's eyes were so heavy, but she was anxious to hear his feedback. Just as she thought she couldn't hold out any longer, he set the papers down and turned to her. "Oh, God. So...Beatrice's sister-in-law took the baby?"

"Uh huh."

"Why? Oh, wait. I remember...Because she told her sister in one of the letters that she thought it peculiar that a woman who worked with children didn't have any of her own. And she thought that was weird, so she asked Elizabeth about it, and she'd said something about how they didn't have the tools for it, right?"

"Equipment. Yeah," Maddy said.

"Okay. And how did the mortician not know the baby wasn't in the coffin?"

"Because his brother delivered the casket sealed."

"Right. The nails," Tim said. "So what happened to Beatrice?"

"I'm still writing that part."

"Well, hurry up. I want to know how it ends!"

Maddy lay in bed working through the last part of the book. Just as she drifted off to sleep, she came up with the final piece.

It was exactly what she needed to finish the book.

Chapter Forty-Three

1912

Dearest Jane,
I'm sure you have received word by now of the conclusion of my condition. Stillbirth. I should have been prepared for such a thing, yet my heart wouldn't let me go to a place so horrible. Why did I not go along with my child in the way that Mother did? I wish with all my being that I had, for it feels impossible to remain here, to continue to exist in this earthly realm without my son to cradle in my arms. I can hear his cries. They haunt my waking dreams.

I am reliant upon the drug now, and it is a sick and twisted demon that I no longer wish to partake in. I see glances of you now too, dear sister, as I skirt the edges of the world beyond. I am comforted by the fact that you hold my child in the beyond, and so I will fight to remain here with my husband, who I have come to cherish and love. In fact, I have decided that I will speak with Elizabeth about the children at the orphanage. Perhaps there is one there that would like to come home with us.

The dear doctor from next door has been whispering these thoughts in my ear and I am inclined to listen for he is kind and intelligent. The townspeople were wrong about him. At first I didn't want to hear what he had to say, but why should I not? He has done nothing but offer wisdom and guidance. I have slowly come to realize he is correct. I can overcome these bumps in the road. I can still have a good life. I must be strong now.

This will be my final note to you as I must do everything to focus on this life. I will persist. I have people here who love me. I no longer need to tether myself with the dead.

I bid you one final goodbye,
Beatrice

Chapter Forty-Four

2022

As Christmas grew near, Maddy and Tim went to a tree farm and got a real pine to put up in the front windows of the parlor. Maddy went a little nutty with the decorations. She strung lights and garland throughout every inch of the house. She definitely had nesting urges, which was good because it was now too cold and snowy to go anywhere. Her parents were also scheduled to come for a visit soon. She was so excited, she could hardly contain herself. She put all of the nervous energy of the pregnancy and the upcoming visit into her book and before she knew it, she had a completed first draft.

Anxious to hear what Tim thought, she stared at him in bed as he took in the last few pages. She had no choice really, as she could no longer lie on her back or belly. She was forced to face the truth of her husband's opinion of the book.

Tim set a page down and turned to her. "Did Beatrice kill herself?"

Maddy stayed quiet.

He asked again. "Did she?"

"Maybe. Maybe not."

"So what happened to the mortician?"

"Keep reading!"

Tim picked the paper back up and continued to read. It was a particular kind of torture because Tim was not only a slow reader, but he also had a terrible habit of stopping every so often, setting the pages down to mull over the whole scene before turning to Maddy to discuss it.

She did enjoy the part where he seemed excited to talk it through, thought she tried as hard as she could to not give too much of the story away. Instead, she kept nagging him to keep going. It was equal parts frustrating and amusing for her.

Chapter Forty-Five

1912

"What are you doing here?" Beatrice asked of the shadowy figure stepping out from behind her. Though her vision was soft, she could see that the shadow did not belong to the person she believed it to be. "What do you want?"

"I've already got it," the person said.

As Beatrice's hand slipped from the mantel, a sharp pain spread through her.

Charles heard the echoed thwack of something hitting the floor above him. He rushed up the stairs to find his wife inside her sitting room, collapsed. A pool of blood surrounded her on the hardwood floor. He fell beside her and lifted Beatrice's head but found no life in her eyes. He lowered her body back down as he cried out. He was now coated in blood with his wife dead beside him where he sat.

Unsure of his next moves, he got up and searched her writing desk and everywhere around the area searching for answers but found nothing. He would have expected a note of some sort, her of the writing sort, for he could only surmise that she had been too far gone with the drug and had chosen to end things. But with no note, he surely would be cast under suspicion. What should he do now? He began to panic. If he called for help, it would appear as though he had caused such a chaotic and violent scene. How could he prove otherwise? There wasn't another soul around.

Half-delirious now with grief and fright, Charles could now only focus on getting away. He wanted to run from the atrocities he had done and borne witness to, so he went into his own sitting chamber and collected a bag with the few things he would need to get him by, including the last bit of savings he owned and had hidden in a floorboard there, and, though he thought clearly enough to remove his soiled clothing, in his state, he hadn't made any attempt at ridding them as he made the decision to flee from Twelve Pine Street. The house, the business, the wife, and everything he'd worked for was gone. He had failed. All he had wanted was to have a good life, but what he failed to see was that it had been there in front of him the entire time.

Chapter Forty-Six

2022

"Aha!" Tim exclaimed.

Maddy had nodded off, but she jolted a little beside him in bed.

"So, that explains why the town thought he killed her, huh?"

"Yeah," Maddy said with a tired smile.

"Makes sense. What about his brother? I suppose he took over the business then."

Maddy finagled her belly around before sitting up a little. "Huh. You know…I hadn't thought about that before, but I suppose he did. Now that I think of it, Ginny actually told me that Francis moved into the house after Beatrice died." She was quiet for a second pondering this new information.

"So, Francis was obviously the killer then?" Tim asked.

"Maybe," Maddy said with a smirk.

Tim grabbed up the paper again and started reading the final pages, the conclusion to the story.

Chapter Forty-Seven

1912

After Charles changed out of his soiled clothes and
packed a few of his belongings into a bag, he flung his
pack over his shoulder and stood at the top of the stairs
ready to flee when he felt the presence of someone
behind him.

In his state, he momentarily hoped it to be his love
back from the dead, but as he turned, he found someone
else there, someone unexpected. She stood before him
confident and tall, wearing a white nursing garment.

"Elizabeth? Is that you? What are you doing here?"
he asked.

"Going somewhere, Charles?"

"I…"

She laughed. It was not a polite laugh, but a
maniacal sort of sound.

"What do you want?" he asked, lacking any
patience, remembering his plan to get away.

"Always running from danger, aren't you?" she
said.

He noticed then that she held in her right hand an
orange-hot fire poker.

"What are you doing?" he asked again, though his
thoughts were beginning to come together.

"I had asked your brother to handle this

undignified work, but to my shock, for the first time, he refused me. Nevertheless, I knew that it wouldn't be so difficult to do on my own. This way, even your brother won't suspect what I've done. He's almost as simple as you."

"I don't understand. What are you saying?"

"You see, Charles, I knew that Beatrice was going to be the more difficult challenge. Frankly, she was stronger than you, more savvy. So, I kept her supplied with the drug until it drained her good senses in order to assist me in my mission."

"Your mission?" Charles began. His head spun as he processed what she was saying to him.

While this new information sunk in, Charles suddenly felt dizzy, which was the exact time Elizabeth took a step closer to him and shoved the mortician without hesitation. Charles, completely taken off guard, didn't have a moment to catch himself, and he tumbled down the steep staircase backside first. His satchel bounced down alongside him and offered a bit of cushion to his head when it hit the hardwood flooring at the base of the grand staircase.

When his body impacted on the landing, his right leg was badly hurt, but he remained breathing. As he lay there, he began putting a few of the pieces together. Elizabeth had been the mastermind behind the plans to have Francis destroy the business. And Francis went along with it. While he wasn't the most sincere brother, and almost succeeded in ruining him, in the end he had chosen not to inflict bodily harm on him, for which Charles was now grateful. He recalled Beatrice's poor attempts to convince Charles that he was stronger than Francis. Using that fuel now, it propelled him. He took a deep breath and got himself up as Elizabeth sauntered down the stairs already claiming victory. Soon, she was before him wielding the fire iron. It no longer glowed orange, but he nevertheless felt the heat emanating from it as she placed it to his chest.

He would fight, knowing what she had done to his Beatrice, even if the evil staring upon him at the other end of the weapon was a woman. As she thrust the iron toward him, he kicked out with his left leg like a horse. She lost her balance only momentarily and as soon as she recovered, she jabbed the poker into Charles's left side. He cried out from the intense pain of the burn and stumbled a few steps back. He was now up against the foyer wall, but he would not give up. Though he could not save his dear wife now, or even the business he'd worked so hard for, he would not let this woman take him along with everything else, not if he could help it. He would not give her the satisfaction.

She raised the hot piece of metal once again and held him against the wall.

"Why?" he whispered. His face was dampened by tears. "Pray tell. Whatever has possessed you to do something so sinister?"

She sneered. "What gives you the right to be so pious? To possess all of the happiness? While you sit high in the tower of this manor house, Francis and I make do in our small boarding rooms when we are not up at ghostly hours attending to infirmed or dead. We've toiled for too long, breaking our backs, only to witness you and yours be blessed with a child, while we…"

"No!" Charles argued. "That blessing was stolen from us."

"Yes," Elizabeth said, "Rightly so."

Charles, disgusted by the woman's jealous motives, made a fist with his right hand and swung out with all his might. His knuckle made contact with Elizabeth's left shoulder and knocked the poker from her hand. The look on her face was one of stunned shock. She was clearly not expecting such a fight from the man before her.

As she twisted and bent to retrieve the weapon, Charles kicked at the back of her shin with his good leg. While Elizabeth fell forward onto her knees, Charles buckled as his strength gave out from his broken leg, though he mustered one last attempt to reach the poker before Elizabeth. Both of them launched their bodies in the direction of the iron rod. Charles felt himself nearly on top of the woman clawing at anything and everything. While he could not see the weapon wrapped among the many folds of Elizabeth's dressing materials, he grabbed at the space he expected it to be in hopes of finding it with his fingers. And when he did, so too did Elizabeth, and they tugged and struggled against one another to seize control of the object for what felt like an eternity, clawing and scratching, until at last Charles had the weapon in his grip.

He scurried to his feet. Elizabeth remained on the hardwood floor in a fetal position, whimpering, resigned. They were both bruised, battered, and breathing heavily.

Charles used the poker to give his tired, beaten body some leverage. As he caught his breath, he stood over her and said, "It's over. I will not sink to the same level of darkness as you. It will not bring back my family. I took an oath as a mortician to assist people after their final breath, and so I will not be privy to harming another soul ever again. That was never my intent. I got lost for a short time, listening to snakes in the grass, which turned out to not be my brother as I'd long suspected, but you, Elizabeth, his partner. It was my beloved Beatrice who brought me back and reminded me of my true virtues. I only wish I could have been stronger in helping her defeat her demon, who, as I now know, turned out to also be you. If only I had realized it sooner…"

His words trailed off, but he knew he could live with himself if he simply walked away from the madness now. He would not have been able to do that had he chosen to harm the woman before him, no matter what she'd done. He felt some satisfaction in that, knowing he hadn't run from danger this time, but also that he kept his wits about him. He hoped Beatrice would be proud.

And so he dropped the weapon to the floor near the front door, picked up his travel bag, and limped out of the funeral home and away from Pine Grove and the horrors he'd been witness to, without even a glance back, never to return again.

Chapter Forty-Eight

2022

Tim set the final chapter down. "So it was Elizabeth! That makes perfect sense."

"Yeah? You think?"

"Of course! She wanted the baby. She knew she could make it look like Charles had killed his wife. She got rid of the evidence that said otherwise."

Maddy nodded. Relief flooded her.

"I love it!" Tim said.

"Really?"

"Yes! It's amazing!"

"Thanks. But do you think it's too dark?"

"Well, it is a Victorian murder mystery, so I was expecting it to be tragic and it was. It's sad that he never found out his son was still alive, but at least in the end, the mortician survived."

"Right!" Maddy said. "Anyway, it still needs loads of work, but…"

"Stop it! Would you for once just be proud of yourself," Tim said.

"Yeah. Okay. I am pretty proud of myself."

"I'm proud of you too." He snuggled up next to her and rubbed her baby bump. "Should we name her Beatrice?"

"Beatrice Barton the second?"

"Huh?" Tim said.

"Never mind. It was a dumb joke. In all seriousness, I was thinking about Jessica Bea. What do you think of that?"

"I think it's perfect."

****

While writing at the café one day, Frankie came in and sat down across from Maddy. "How's the book coming?"

She hadn't shared much with him about the book, and she knew that she might eventually have to, especially now that she had finished the first draft. She wasn't sure how it all might sit with him. Of course, she would have to change the names before moving forward too, but for now, she left them so she could keep it all straight as she worked out the edits. She desperately wanted to ask Frankie outright about the photo of Beatrice and whether or not he'd seen things in her that Maddy had seen, but she didn't. Not yet.

"I'm not actually working on the book today," she confessed.

"No?"

"No," she said. "I'm writing a letter."

"Oh," he said. "Well, I'll leave you to it."

As he was about to leave, Maddy said, "Hey, would you be interested in being critique partners at all?"

He smiled. "Absolutely."

"Great. I think I'll be ready to share my story with you soon."

"Okay. I'm looking forward to it."

After Frankie walked away, Maddy went back to her letter. What was on her screen was something she actually hoped she would never have to share with anyone, let alone Frankie. As she came along in the pregnancy, she wasn't as scared as she thought she might be given all she'd experienced with Jess, but she also wasn't going into it naïve to the risks involved.

She fully understood Jess's desire now to have a safety net of sorts in place, though Maddy wasn't going to be needing legal papers or even a will because if something happened to her during the delivery, she knew Tim would raise their child. No. What she wanted was to write down her thoughts and feelings to her daughter, something that Tim could give her when she was older to let her know what she meant to her. Words were the one thing Maddy felt confident about, especially now that she had written an entire book. This was her gift to pass on.

****

Tim surprised Maddy by scheduling to have the old fireplace in her office replaced with a new insert so it could be a functioning gas fireplace. It only took a few hours and when the crew was done, Maddy went in to look at it. Tim came in behind her after paying the workers downstairs and he handed her a slip of paper.

"What's this?"

"One of the guys found this when he pulled the old firebox out. I must have slipped behind it somehow."

"Between the box and the wall?"

He shrugged. "I suppose so." Tim left to finish up some other work he was doing on the house.

When he was gone and she was alone again in the room, she sat down at her desk and examined the paper. Unlike the other letters, this one was blackened around the edges by the soot, but also strangely preserved by the airtight space in the hollow of the firebox. Maddy unfolded it and read:

Beatrice Eleanor Westmoreland's Last Will and Testament:

Shall I pass during or after the birth of my first child, I would simply ask that this notice be printed in the gazette. Westmoreland, Mrs. Beatrice E. of Pine Grove, Minnesota, Jan. 27, 1889; died—

A plain woman who wished to experience a life filled with happiness and love. She wished to be a good wife, sister, daughter, and friend. Above all, she wished to be a mother and experience a love she had not known. She believed a good mother she would make. If she could not be those things, she was at least a writer, and this was her last note.

****

To my sweet baby Jessica Bea,

If you are reading this, it's because I am no longer here to tell you these things myself. I wanted to write a letter to you because, well, I'm a writer. It took me a long time to have the confidence to say that, but writing has always been something that comes easier to me than expressing myself out loud.

From a young age, perhaps the age you are now reading this, I would write. I had a journal, and when I was lonely or sad or if something really great happened to me, I would put it all down on the page. My wish for you is that you know that I wanted you very much. I was a bit hesitant at first, but that was only because I was scared. Once you started to wiggle around in my tummy, I wasn't afraid anymore. I was so excited and I knew then and there that I would do anything for you to keep you safe. And I hope you are safe now, but remember, if you ever feel sad or scared or alone, think about writing it all down. If you want to write to me like I'm writing to you now, I promise you it will help make it better. I know because writing this now has helped me immensely.

    Love you always and forever,
    Your mom—Madeline Barton.

A word about the author…

Jody is a life-long Twin Citian, a wife, and mother. She got the writing bug while reporting for her high school newspaper and received a degree in Communications from the University of Minnesota. While starting a family, she began writing fiction and has since been published in The Keepthings and Mystery Magazine Weekly.

Thank you for purchasing
this publication of The Wild Rose Press, Inc.

For questions or more information
contact us at
info@thewildrosepress.com.

The Wild Rose Press, Inc.
www.thewildrosepress.com

CPSIA information can be obtained
at www.ICGtesting.com
Printed in the USA
BVHW052158190623
666129BV00029B/904

9 781509 249626